The Godfather President
By
Bobby Legend

The Godfather President

Published through Legend Publishing Company

All rights reserved Copyright © 2014 Bobby Legend Book Design and Layout by Mickey Strange: ISBN 978-0-9909373-2-6

Introduction

A powerful New York Don of the Valoppi Crime Family, who had beaten the Federal Government three times in court, suddenly finds himself running for US President—as a joke. But the citizens of the US are disgruntled with professional politicians and the stalemate within government and are now looking for something different in the realm of politics. Now they have found what they were looking for in the person of Jack Cotti, alias Johnny Uptown.

Chapter 1

"**D**oes the jury have a verdict?" the judge asked the jury foreman.

"Yes, we do, your honor," the foreman replied.

"Will the defendant please stand," the judge ordered. He then turned to the foreman and asked, "And what is the verdict?"

"We find the defendant...Not Guilty!"

The attendees in the courtroom burst out in applause and shouted in happiness.

The judge became angry and pounded his gavel on his courtroom bench to quiet the crowd. Once he had gotten their attention, he dismissed the defendant.

"Jack Cotti, you have been found not guilty by a jury of your peers. You are free to go."

With that, gangster Jack Cotti, alias Johnny Uptown, left the courtroom. Once he was outside the courthouse, reporters flocked around him to get his opinion about his trial.

"Jack Cotti, are you satisfied with the verdict?" asked a male reporter.

"Well, let me see. The jury found me not guilty. What

do you think? Of course I am satisfied. You idiot!" he replied in his deep, coarse, and gravelly voice; a voice so hard and tough-sounding that you could tell he was a wiseguy, especially with his New York accent.

"Mr. Cotti. This is the third rap handed down by the federal government that you've beaten. Do you think they will come after you again?" asked a female reporter, shoving her microphone into his face.

"Why waste taxpayer money on frivolous lawsuits?" Cotti's lawyer, Sal DomAchelli answered. "Now, if you'll excuse my client and me, we need to eat dinner and celebrate."

Cotti and his lawyer headed towards their limousine.

Another female reporter asked Cotti a crazy question that stopped both men in their tracks. "Mr. Cotti, the people love you. With all the hatred the voters have towards our politicians in Congress, why don't you run for President? I'm sure the voters would love a change from career politicians to a true-blue American. A man's man. What do you think? Would you make a good President?"

Cotti thought for a good ten seconds and then answered, "Hell, yes! I would make a great President. I know how to get this country going again. And I'd make damn sure that no more jobs would be sent to China or anywhere else. And believe me, those career politicians in Congress would do what I told them...Or else—"

Cotti's attorney interrupted his client: "Okay, that's enough with the questions. We must be leaving now."

With that, the two men hopped into the limousine and drove away.

"Can you believe those reporters?" Cotti asked his attorney. "They think I should run for President."

"Jack, I think they were being facetious. They were pulling your leg," the attorney replied.

"I don't know, Dom. Voters hate career politicians. This might be the right time for a guy like me to get into politics. Who knows? I might win."

They pulled up to Cotti's favorite restaurant: Gabriele's Steak House. They got out of the limousine, to find about fifty members of the Valoppi Family and members of his own family waiting for Cotti. The crowd erupted in shouts of glee over his beating yet another rap brought on by the federal government.

As Cotti and his attorney walked towards the restaurant's front door, they were mobbed by both members of both Families.

During dinner, Cotti had a few things to say to his Family members about the reporters' questions.

"Do you think I'd make a good President of the United States?" Cotti asked his wife Maria and Johnny Napolie, the Underboss of the Valoppi Family.

"Of course, Jack," said Napolie, in his deep and rough tough-guy voice.

"Hell yes, honey," answered his wife. "You'd make a great President, Jack."

"Jack, don't tell me that you're thinking of running for

President?" exclaimed Napolie. "You know the *Family* doesn't need the publicity."

"Johnny, you're full of shit," snapped Cotti. "The Feds know everything about me…and you too."

"Jack, don't get upset," interjected DomAchelli. "We're here to celebrate your acquittal."

"You're right, Dom. We're here to celebrate. More Champagne!" shouted Cotti.

The rest of the night was filled with song, drink, and conversation. The hours passed like minutes. The group partied until closing time and then went home to get some much needed rest.

Cotti fell asleep thinking about the words from that one particular reporter: *Would you make a good President?* He dreamt of grandiose ideas: How could he, if President, change the world for the better? He figured he was already president of a multi-billion dollar enterprise that employed thousands of able-bodied men so he could do the same for the national economy if given the chance. He believed he could make a better world for all.

He awakened with a new outlook on life. He actually believed he could win if he ran for a political office, especially for US President.

But then he thought about one person—the head of another Family who had gone into politics for the Italian cause and ended up murdered in front of those that believed in him. Cotti didn't want to end up like that. He would have to silence his critics or dissenters by any means necessary if he decided to run for office.

Sitting at the breakfast table with his wife and kids, he wondered what they would think about him running for political office, preferably US President.

"Hey, hon, what do you really think about me running for a political office?" he asked Maria.

"Are you serious, Jack?" his wife replied. "I thought you were just joking about that last night."

"Yeah, I was. But the more I think about it, why not? If I can get enough signatures to put my name on the ballot, I might have a chance to win. The people love a guy like me."

"Honey, you can't be serious," she retorted. "You're a mobster, honey. No one is going to vote for you."

"So what if I'm a mobster?" answered Cotti. "The voters in Staten Island just elected that guy…um…Mike Grimm for Congressman and he was indicted on twenty felony counts. He just resigned his seat after pleading guilty to one count of fraud."

"Yeah, Jack. But remember what happened to Joe Colombo? He was killed for bringing too much attention to the Families. I'm afraid that might happen to you if you decide to run for a political office."

"Baby, no one would ever think of whacking me. They know what would happen to anyone involved."

"Jack, can we talk about this another time? I don't want this shit talked about in front of the kids. It's time to eat breakfast…and not talk about politics."

Cotti remained silent during breakfast but he daydreamed about his chances of becoming President. He saw himself as a man about town—a James Bond type: debonair, suave, sophisticated, and intelligent—and a great dresser. He was so enthralled in his daydream that his wife had to call him three times to get his attention.

"Jack. Jack! Jack!" she shouted, not getting any reaction from him.

He finally came out of his stupor. "I'm here, honey," he mumbled. "What? What do you want?"

"You had your tie in the coffee. I yelled your name three damn times, trying to get your attention. What the hell were you thinking about?"

"Nothing, honey. I was just trying to digest my food," he replied, then lit his cigar.

"Jack, go smoke that damn cigar in the den. You're stinking up the kitchen."

"Okay, honey. Whatever you say."

Cotti didn't have time to stay around the house. He had to get going to run his multi-billion dollar enterprise.

The doorbell rang. It was his Underboss, Johnny Napolie, arrived to pick up Cotti to drive him to their destination: The Dergin Hunt and Fish Club, where Cotti did all his business.

***

Cotti and Napolie entered the building to the sound of cat calls and clapping for Cotti's acquittal.

"Way to go, Jack," one wiseguy shouted out.

"Good job," another said.

Cotti walked through the crowd of wiseguys to get to his table in the back room. He sat down and began going over business with Napolie. They talked for hours before Cotti brought up running for President of the United States.

"You know, Johnny," Cotti said, "I'm really serious about running for US President. There's a little more than a year and a half before the election. That means, I've got six months to get my shit together and get everything we need in place to get me on the ballot. I want our soldiers to help in this endeavor. And we'll have to get the other families in all fifty states to pitch in. They'll have to use their soldiers or whomever to get me those signatures. But I want them. No excuses."

"Jack, the Commission won't allow it," Johnny responded. "I mean, Valoppi had Colombo whacked when he refused to give up politics; and the same will happen to you. But they'll have you whacked long before you even get the signatures."

"Johnny, they'll know better than to whack me," Cotti snapped, "'cause they know what'll happen to them and their whole damn bloodline if they cross me."

***

"Listen to Cotti. Is he serious? He won't even get enough signatures to get on the ballot," the FBI agent said.

The FBI had secretly set up bugs throughout the Club

building and could listen to Cotti's conversations, especially when Cotti was sitting at his table.

"He won't get that far," another agent exclaimed, laughing. "When the Commission learns of it, they'll whack him. Just like Napolie said."

"Cotti is a narcissist and egomaniac," guffawed a third. "Everything revolves around him. He thinks he's the sun and everyone else is the littlest of planets."

"If Cotti is really serious, this is gonna be fun to watch," cracked another. "It'll be like watching a good comedy: Cotti and Friends."

"Hey, we better listen in on this conversation. We're cracking jokes about Cotti and company and we might have missed some great information," said the supervisor. "Let's get back to work."

They all put on their headphones, turned the recorder on again, and listened intently for any pertinent information.

Cotti and Napolie sang like songbirds for the next few hours, but said nothing of importance to help the Feds with their case against the men. Cotti talked politics, mostly.

It seemed Cotti was adamant at going into the political arena.

***

"If I go ahead with this idea," Cotti said, "we'll need signs, buttons, banners and everything else that's used in the election process. And we'll need to get the backing and money from all five Families. They, in turn, will have to contact the Aldermen, Unions, and every shop and store owner in all five boroughs. Plus, we'll need to control all polling booths around the country, which means we'll have to get the company that makes the voting machines to rig them for us, like they did for Bush in 2000. And we'll have to get the reporters we have on our payroll to write favorable stories about me running for elected office and why it would be good for the country to elect Jack Cotti as President. Johnny, I'll let you handle that."

Napolie looked confused. "What Party would you run for?"

"Hell, I don't know," Cotti replied. "I haven't completely thought it through yet. But I will."

"You could run as a Democrat," Napolie told him.

"I could. Or I could run as a Republican."

"Are you kidding, Jack? Then you *will* get whacked. Every wiseguy in the country would get a bonus for bringing you down."

"You might be right about that. I could run as an Independent."

Cotti saw something from the underside of the table fall onto the floor near Napolie's feet. It looked like a piece of old gum that someone had stuck under the tabletop.

Napolie leaned to pick it up and throw it into the ashtray. He suddenly threw a warning glance at Cotti, motioning him to keep quiet and not speak. He placed the object on the table and they both checked it out. Sure enough, it was a bug—probably planted by the Feds. Napolie tossed it back onto the floor and smashed it into little pieces with the heel of his shoe.

***

The feds heard the crunch of their listening device and knew one had been destroyed. Worse yet, though, they knew that the mobsters were on to them.

"Now what are we gonna do?" an agent asked his supervisor.

"Well, we still have two others that are operating," the supervisor replied. "We'll keep listening to their conversations until they find the others. That's all we can do. Now, get back to work."

The agents returned once again to their listening and recording, hoping that Cotti would slip up and give them something useful to use against him. But the two Goombas had found the bug, so their conversation pretty much dried up—not because they quit talking, but because they had left the premises.

***

Cotti and Napolie needed to find and talk with Tommy Zerroni, a highly decorated detective in the NYPD with electronic surveillance experience. Zerroni was also on the Cotti Family payroll: They needed him to find any other bugs within the Dergin Hunt and Fish Club.

Napolie contacted Zerroni by telephone and told the

detective to meet them at a nearby bar: Goomba's Heaven. Cotti knew that even if the detective was up to his ears in a homicide investigation, he would drop what he was doing and leave for the bar as ordered.

Cotti and Napolie were sitting at their table in the back room of the bar when Zerroni confronted them.

"What's up?" the detective asked. He sat down to join them.

Napolie threw the remains of the Fed's bug on the table.

Zerroni poked it and looked at it. "Where did you find this?" he asked.

"It fell from underneath the table at the club," Napolie replied. "What do you think?"

"It's a bug, alright. It's not one of ours, so it's gotta be one that the Feds use. If you found one...then there are others."

"That's what we think," interjected Cotti.

"Where there's smoke, there's fire," added Napolie.

"I'll have to check out your club later tonight," said Zerroni, "when most or all of your patrons are gone." He added, "I hope you didn't say anything that the Feds can use against you."

"We didn't," Napolie said. "We talked politics."

"Politics? What the hell was so important that you had to talk politics?" asked Zerroni, looking at the two Goombas for an answer.

"Jack's thinking about running for political office," Napolie explained.

Zerroni snickered. "Are you kidding, Jack?"

Cotti gave him an angry and serious look that made Zerroni shudder.

"Guess what office he's thinking about running for?" Napolie asked Zerroni.

"I give up. What?"

"President!"

Zerroni laughed out loud this time. "Are you kidding me? President? Are you serious, Jack?"

Jack gave him a cold stare and remained silent for nearly a minute before answering. "Yeah, I'm serious, Tommy. And I expect you to do your part, when asked. You get me?"

"Sure, Jack. Sure. Whatever you want me to do, I'll do it. No problem," Zerroni replied, his tone more deferential. "I'll head out and get my bug-hunting gear. I'll call you tomorrow morning and let you know if I find anything." He stood up, turned, and left the premises, wiping his sweating brow as he went.

With the meeting over, Cotti and Napolie lit their fifty dollar illegal Cuban cigars and left the bar.

"Where to now?" Napolie asked, as they got into his car.

"Let's go to my mother's house. I want to tell her my plans, to see what she thinks."

"Jack, are you really going through with this idea of yours?" asked Napolie, as he pulled his car away from the curb.

12

"I haven't made up my mind. But I'm leaning towards it," Cotti replied, puffing away on his cigar.

"Just remember, if you do decide to run, you're gonna bring a lot of heat to the Family."

"Hey, just think. If I do get on the ballot, I'll have the FBI following me to protect me, not harass me."

"Yeah, hoping every minute that they can bust you and put your ass in jail," snapped Napolie, throwing the nub of his cigar out the window.

***

Ten minutes later, they were sitting in the living room at Jack's mother's house in Queens, New York.

Jack made small talk with his mother, Jackie, as Napolie looked on. Then Jack got right to the point. "Hey, Ma, what would you say if I told you I was thinking about running for the President of the United States?"

She seemed shocked by his words, as if she couldn't believe what he had just told her. Then she began laughing hysterically, to the point that she made Jack and Johnny laugh, too. But while they were laughing with her, she was laughing at Jack.

"That's funny, honey," she said, still laughing.

Cotti gave her an angry look.

"You were joking, weren't you, Jack?" she asked.

"No, Ma, I'm serious."

She shook her head in disbelief. "How in the hell did you come up with that idea? You hate politicians and yet you want to become one? And not just any politician. You want to be the President of the United States. You're crazy!"

"That's what I told him, Mrs. C," interjected Napolie.

"Listen to him, Jack. He's your Underboss for a reason."

"But Ma, I think people will vote for me if I can get on the ballot. They're looking for something different, instead of a life-long politician. Politicians are bigger crooks than we are. We steal in millions; they steal in billions."

"Jack, I still think you're crazy." She looked to Napolie. "Johnny, you should record our conversation and then play it back for him, to show how stupid his idea sounds." She stood up, grabbed some cups and the coffee pot from the stove, and poured them each a hot cup of Java, as if hoping it would bring her son to his senses. "Johnny, is he really serious about this?"

Johnny just shrugged his shoulders, gave Jackie a disgruntled look, and answered, "Yeah, I think he is."

Jack just smiled as his mother gave him a defeated look. She would no longer fight him on the subject. She just wanted the best for her son.

"Well, honey," she said, "if you're really serious about this, I'm all for it. I'll help you any way that I can. And we'll get all twelve of your brothers and sisters to help in this crazy idea of yours."

"Okay, Ma. I just wanted you to know what I had in mind." He kissed his mother goodbye and he and Napolie went on their way.

***

Ten minutes later, they were in the car and heading for their home away from home: the Dergin Hunt and Fish Club.

"Jack, I gotta be honest with you," growled Napolie. "This crazy idea you have isn't gonna fly. I know the Families won't like it one bit."

"Quit your whining. You're my Underboss, for Christ's sake. We're the strongest Family in the world. If they want a war over this, then fuck 'em. We'll give them what they want."

"But this will lead to trouble we don't need. And the publicity we'll get over this will be insane." Napolie shook his head in disgust.

"Yeah, that's what I'm counting on. Lots of publicity. Let's just see what the people think of one of their own running for President. Let's get everybody on our payroll that's in the media: radio, newspapers, the internet, and TV and have them ask that question and see what kind of response we get. If we see that everyone is against me running...so be it. I'll forget all about it. But...if, for some reason, the vote is overwhelmingly for me running, then I'll give it a shot. Are you with me?" Cotti looked tough and confident, puffing away on his fifty dollar cigar.

"Whatever you say, Jack. I still don't like it."

"You'll get over it," Cotti replied. "And when we get

back to the club, I want you to make some phone calls and contact all those people we bought who work for the media. Make a time and date for all of us to meet so I can discuss with them what it is that I want from them. So, call Angie Cantelli and have him hold his hotel conference room open for the time and day of the meeting. And let's get it done within the next couple of days. Okay, Johnny?"

"Sure, Jack. I'll get right on it."

A few minutes later, they were back at the club, sitting at their back room table discussing the matter at hand.

"Johnny, I want you to tell the Capos that they'll have to pay an extra five percent on every transaction so I can pay the bills that I'll incur in my run for President. And it's gonna cost plenty."

"You got that right, Jack," replied Napolie, matter-of-factly. "You're gonna have to find some big money backers and some savvy political geniuses to run your campaign. It's gonna take some great campaign speeches to even get you in the primaries, let alone winning them."

"Yeah, I think you're right about that. I'll use Family money to start with. Then, we'll have to call in some markers…on Trump and all the other bigshots in the casino and real estate business. We've been going easy on them for the last few years. Now's the time to turn the screws on them. I'll give them an offer they can't refuse. And I'll explain to them that it's them…or me."

"I don't think Trump and his business partners will like that. They could make some big waves and get us in a jam,"

Napolie said.

"Well, Johnny, we'll tell them how it is. If any of them make waves...we'll kill 'em." Cotti lit another cigar.

"But Jack, you know that half their security is run by ex-FBI Agents. We'll be sticking our noses where they don't belong."

"You know, we need to get our Consigliere in here and let him give his two cents on my idea. Why don't you give Benny the Brain a call and tell him to get his ass over here? That we got business to talk over."

"Will do right now, boss." Napolie left the table and went upstairs to use a neighbor's phone, confident that the Feds didn't have a wiretap on it and therefore weren't taping the conversation. Even if the conversation was about nothing, Napolie always played it safe and wasn't about to give the Feds something that they could use against him in a Court of Law.

Napolie made his phone call and returned to continue his conversation with Cotti.

"Everything go okay?" Cotti asked. "Did you get in touch with Benny?"

"Sure did, boss. He'll be here within thirty minutes."

Cotti nodded and shouted to his bartender/brother-in-law Carlo, "Hey, Carlo, bring us some cannolis and a bottle of Amaretto brandy."

Two minutes later, Carlo did as ordered, setting the brandy, cannolis, and two glasses on the table.

"Thank you, Carlo," said Cotti. Carlo nodded. "And

how are the wife and kids?" Cotti added, making small talk with his brother-in-law.

Carlo returned to his duties behind the bar. Jack and Johnny ate their cannolis, sipped their brandy, and dipped the end of their cigars into their glasses while making small talk.

A few minutes later, Benny, Cotti's number three guy, walked up to the table, pulled out a chair, and sat down. "What's up, guys?" he asked. He reached over and grabbed a cannoli.

Cotti told his Consiglieri that he'd had a new idea that would bring more power and money to the family. "And I want you to tell me what you think."

"Hey, Carlo!" yelled Benny. "Bring me a cup of coffee."

"Are you going to listen to me?" Cotti asked Benny, his voice gruff.

"I'm sorry, Jack," Benny replied. Carlo set a cappuccino in front of him. Benny gave Carlo a wink and a nod. "Thanks, Carlo."

"Now, are you ready to hear what I've got to say?" Cotti asked Benny.

"Sure, Jack. What's so important?" the Consiglieri asked, looking at Cotti and then giving a puzzled look to Napolie.

"You weren't sitting at my table last night at the restaurant, so you probably didn't hear my conversation I had with Johnny and my wife. I'll explain to you what I told them."

Cotti told Benny what he had in mind.

"You wanna do what? Are you serious? JACK!" Benny exclaimed, looking at Jack and then to Johnny in disbelief.

"Those were my exact sentiments," Napolie said.

"Don't get so upset, Benny," Cotti told him. "I pretty much got it planned out. I'm gonna do one step at a time, and I've already taken the first step."

"And what is that?" asked Benny.

"I just told you. I've decided to try my hand at politics. I'm gonna try and get on the ballot to run for the President of the United States," Cotti exclaimed, holding his head up high, showing his pride at being an American citizen.

"Oh, my god!" moaned Benny. He looked down and held his hand to his forehead, as if a thousand pounds of dynamite had just exploded inside his head.

"Fuck, Benny. You sound like a woman giving birth," quipped Cotti.

"I'm sorry, Jack," replied Benny, apologetically, "but this is just too much to take in. I mean, do you know what will happen if the other Families find out what you want to do? Don't you remember what happened to Colombo?"

"That's what I told him," Napolie said to Benny.

"Jack, have you really considered the consequences?" asked Benny, leaning forward in his chair.

"I'll tell you what I told Johnny," Cotti explained. "They're either with us or against us."

Benny shook his head in disbelief.

"Don't worry, Benny," Cotti said. "I'll have a sit-down with the other Families and tell them my plans. I know they won't give me any trouble. I'll make them an offer they can't refuse." He felt very confident in himself.

"Yeah, if you make it out of that meeting alive," joked Benny, but dead serious.

Johnny nodded in the affirmative. "If you ask me, there'll be a war soon after that meeting."

Benny agreed.

Cotti lashed out at the two wiseguys. "Listen, you *fucks*," he snapped, "you're getting ahead of yourselves. Let me run this Borgata, will you, for Christ's sake?"

"We do what you tell us, Jack," said Napolie, lighting a cigar.

"Listen…guys, I understand your concerns." Cotti gave sad eye looks to both his number two and number three guys, then added, "Okay. If you guys do turn out to be right about this thing…and I get whacked or disappear, I want everyone to know that Johnny will take over the Family. You hear me, Benny?"

"Sure, Jack. Let's hope everything goes as you plan."

Jack knew right then that he had just put a bull's-eye on his back for Napolie and his crew. If Napolie now wanted to take over the Family, all the man would have to do is wait until after the meeting, kill him, and blame it on one of the other Families. But Jack couldn't worry about that now. He was too engrossed in his plans for politics.

"Benny," said Cotti, "I want you to get with Johnny and

he'll tell you what he wants you to do to get my plan started."

"What do you want me to do, Johnny?" Benny asked him.

"We have to contact our people that work in media. Jack wants to have a meeting with them and talk over his ideas. I'll take newspaper, magazines, and internet, and you can take the radio and TV people."

They all agreed and left the club. Johnny dropped Jack off at his home and drove away. They would meet up again the following morning.

Chapter 2

Jack was finishing up his breakfast at around ten the next morning and getting ready to light a cigar when Johnny arrived. Johnny sat at the table and intervened, lighting the cigar with his lighter and then lighting his own. Cotti's wife set a cup of cappuccino on the table in front of him.

"What do you have planned for today, Jack?" he asked.

"I want you and Benny to get busy contacting those people in media," Cotti said, "and then get a hold of Cantelli for the conference room. I will contact the heads of the other Families and set up a meeting."

"You don't want me to take you to the club?" Napolie asked.

"No, I don't think so. I'll take Partelli with me. He can be my bodyguard for today."

"Okay, Jack. You're the boss."

"We'll see how it goes here in New York. And if it goes okay, then we'll contact the heads of the Families in the rest of the country and have them get their contacts in media to follow our example."

Johnny just shook his head in agreement.

22

What else could Johnny do? Cotti thought. He had told Johnny: "either you're with us or against us." And Napolie clearly wanted to stay alive and live for another day. To do that, he would have to do whatever Cotti told him to do.

They finished their coffee and went their separate ways: Johnny to get together with Benny and Jack to get together with the heads of the other Families. Neither did too well.

***

Johnny and Benny, the number two and three wiseguys for Cotti, didn't have much luck. They got rejected over and over, with one excuse or another, so they decided to change tactics. Instead of asking, they were now telling: come in, or else. Everyone had to be in the conference room at the Selsor Hotel by two on Saturday afternoon, two days away. Now those media people knew what was **on the line** if they didn't do as ordered. For all the media people knew, they were going there to get whacked, but they didn't know for what. They were never told the reason for the meeting, only that "they needed to be there." They would be told "why" at the meeting.

That day came and the meek and mild media members slowly flocked into the conference room, wondering what it was all about. They questioned each other, hoping one of them had an answer.

The meeting was about to begin when two guys came in—now about ten minutes late—laughing and joking around. This irked Cotti and Napolie; they let it slide at that time but the order was given to teach these two knuckleheads some respect. That was to be done after the media explosion on the Cotti question: Would Jack Cotti make a good President?

Napolie started the meeting. "Ok, you guys. Settle down and take a seat," he shouted. "We got some important business to attend to. Mr. Cotti has some important things to say to you and will be speaking with you in a minute. But first, I want to thank you guys for showing up—including the two idiots that came in late. For those of you who don't know me, I'm Johnny Napolie; Mr. Cotti's right hand man."

"So why are we here?" shouted a reporter for the New York Times.

"I'll let Mr. Cotti answer that," replied Napolie. He handed the microphone to Cotti and then left the stage.

Cotti thought for a few long seconds and then began to speak. "Well, first, let me introduce myself," he said in his gruff voice. "My name is Jack Cotti. And I'm here to ask you to help me in my endeavor."

"What endeavor is that?" yelled someone from the crowd.

"If you'd shut up, I'll tell you," Cotti snapped. "Now...I have a very important job that needs to get done and all twelve of you guys and gals are the right people to do it."

"What is it?" asked a cute female anchor for Fox News.

"Yeah, we're curious," shouted a DJ from Radio KGB.

"Alright, I'll tell you in a second!" Cotti snapped. He waited until everyone settled and quieted down, and continued, "I want all of you to ask your readers, listeners, and viewers this question: Knowing the political discord in Washington, DC, between the parties and their professional politicians, would you, the American citizen, vote for a tough, no-nonsense type of guy that had, at one time, a criminal record? Would you vote for Jack Cotti for United States President?"

Most of the media professionals were absolutely stunned by Cotti's statement. They were confused, flabbergasted, and downright in disbelief. They were hard-pressed not to laugh out loud. They didn't know if Cotti was serious or if he was joking around. Not one brave soul in the audience wanted to find out.

"Mr. Cotti, no offense, but are you serious?" asked a female host of a TV talk show.

Cotti answered, "Yes. Very serious."

"But you're a mobster; the head of the Commission and the boss of the Valoppi Family," said a news reporter for ABC News.

"That's alleged mobster, Mister," snarled Napolie, giving the reporter the evil eye.

"Listen, you mugs," said Cotti, "I know how this sounds. A wiseguy running for President. You gotta know that I'll be taking a lot of heat from...Ah, Ah, certain people...certain people. But that's not gonna stop me. This country is in a big mess and I think I can get it back on track." Cotti was confident with his words and in himself. But he didn't know how his audience felt.

"I'll have to get the editor's OK," said the Times reporter, as he stood to speak.

Another stood and said, "Yeah, I'll have to get the General Manager's approval for anything that goes over the air."

But Cotti had heard enough. He didn't want excuses. He wanted action; and told them so. "Hey, hey! That's enough! I don't pay you guys for excuses. I pay you to do as I tell you. Whatever you gotta do...DO!"

"OK, Mr. Cotti. We'll do what we can," said the news reporter for an ABC TV entertainment affiliate. "I just hope it comes out the way you anticipate. Politics is not a gentlemen's game."

"Neither is the life of a mobster," barked Napolie.

"Hey, that's enough, Johnny," whispered Cotti. "Let's not provoke them."

Before the meeting broke up, Napolie told them to get in touch with him when they got the OK from their bosses. "That way," he added, "we can coordinate the time and day the question will be asked through all our media contacts, so we can inundate the entire state and surrounding states—hell, maybe the whole country—to a Jack Cotti Presidency."

"Jack, do you have anything else to say to them?" asked Benny, pointing to the crowd.

Jack again spoke into the microphone. "Ok, you guys.

Let's get this thing going. Hell, who knows? We just might change the world."

***

The people stood and began to leave, and Jack dismissed his audience. "Class...Dismissed!"

The media people mumbled under their breaths and to each other about their concerns—with their bosses and with their extra-curricular boss, Jack Cotti.

"Is Cotti crazy?" the Times reporter asked a TV anchor.

"It sure sounds like it," the anchor replied. "We know how the people will vote. They're not gonna put a gangster in the White House."

"No shit."

Others had the same reaction.

"A gangster in the White House? No way. I don't even want to tell my boss about this meeting. He'll think I'm as crazy as Cotti," said the talk show host to another TV hopeful.

"I know what you mean. But if we don't ask our bosses for permission to ask our viewers Cotti's question, what will Cotti and Family do to us?" the TV hopeful retorted.

"I hate to think about that. What will Cotti do to us if our bosses refuse to allow us to ask it?" replied the talk show host.

"That's a rhetorical question, isn't it?" asked the TV hopeful.

They both laughed and continued on their way without

further discussion.

***

As soon as the room cleared, Benny told Cotti and Napolie about the discrepancy in the number of people at the meeting.

"Hey, you guys, I was counting the people at the meeting and I counted thirteen."

"Yeah, so? What's the problem?" Cotti asked.

"Jack, the problem is: there should have been only twelve people at this meeting, not thirteen," exclaimed Benny. "We gotta find out the name of the person that wasn't invited."

Cotti and Napolie nodded in agreement, but didn't think too much about it. Cotti was happy with the meeting. He thought it had gone well. Time would tell if he would be dabbling in the art of politics, instead of the art of crime. But then, he thought, both were intertwined and intermingled. He chuckled at that thought and Napolie heard it.

"What's so funny, Jack?" Napolie asked.

"Nothing in particular. I just had a funny thought."

They left the conference room and headed for home.

***

What Benny, Napolie, and Cotti didn't realize was that a Federal agent was smack dab in the middle of their meeting. And when that Agent returned to tell his fellow peers about the meeting, he was the life of the party.

"Hey, you guys, I just recorded the craziest meeting of all time. I mean, it's better than listening to the heads of the Five Families cuss each other out," Agent Greg Meadows told the group of agents within his work group.

"Yeah, so what was it about?" asked Agent Ken Lundy.

"Ok, here goes. Listen to this," Meadows said, as he turned on the tape recorder he had used to tape the conversation of the meeting.

The agents gathered around the table to listen to the recording. When it got to the part about Cotti wanting to run for President of the United States, the room filled with laughter. The agents couldn't believe what they were hearing. After about fifteen minutes, the recording ended and the agents gave their opinions on Cotti's run in politics.

"That's the craziest thing I've ever heard. Cotti's playing with fire. If he thinks the other Families will allow him to bring the mob into public view, he is very mistaken. They will whack him, like they whacked out Colombo. No doubt about it," said Agent Dennis Arms, the supervisor of the group.

"How do you know he'll even get the media outlets to relent and ask the question to the people?" asked Meadows. "The higher-ups might think it's not important enough for their venue."

"Are you kidding?" replied Arms. "A mobster? No, I take that back. A gangster that just beat the Federal government in court three times? To the people of New

York, he's a rock star. I mean, he's on the front cover of Newsweek and Time magazines for Gangster of the Year, for Christ's sake. No! Every one of the media outlets will run with this story. It'll be big news for a week or so, until they read the results and find out that nobody wants a killer in the White House. How arrogant can Cotti be? He's infamous and it's gone to his head. They put him on the cover of Time and now he thinks he should be President. Give me a fuckin' break!"

"What party is he gonna run for? Will he run as a Republican or Democrat?" asked a puzzled Agent Keith Brunson.

"He never said. I say, if he runs...he'll run as a Republican," surmised Meadows.

Agent Greg Delahant jumped into the conversation. "No way. He's a Union man. He'll run as a Democrat."

"Hell, maybe he'll run as an Independent," suggested Lundy.

"Wait, guys," barked Arms. "Aren't we getting ahead of ourselves? First, he has to get on the ballot. And we all know, that will never happen—"

"It could...if he rigged the vote, like they did in Florida for Bush," interjected Agent Keith Brunson. He was booed by his peers for that opinion.

Lundy asked a very important question. "Hey, did we find out when Cotti is having the sit-down with the other Families?"

"No," answered Meadows. "With the one bug we have

left at his club near the table where he sits, we were able to pick up some of the calls he made to the Underbosses of the Four Families. But it wasn't clear if they had picked the time or place for the meeting."

"We still have Agents in the field, don't we?" Lundy asked his supervisor.

"Yeah, they're following him as we speak. But most of the time he loses our tail. What we pick up on the bugs is what's important. If we know where the Commission is meeting, then we can hopefully bug the room." He looked at his watch, saw that it was near quitting time, and dismissed his agents.

The group of Federal agents left their surveillance room and went their separate ways, as the nightshift took over.

Chapter 3

Benny "the Brain" Bartolo and Johnny Napolie at first had trouble setting up the meeting with media personnel, until things finally worked out. Cotti had the same trouble putting a meeting together with the other Four Families. He was given one excuse after another for them not being able to make it at a certain time or on a certain day. When one decided on a time and day, one or two of the other Family heads couldn't make it. Cotti found that very frustrating. He was used to getting his way. He never had to ask someone to do something. He was used to telling them: It was his way or the highway. But this time was different. He had to be persuasive in a gentlemanly way. He couldn't threaten. He had to be diplomatic.

Finally, after a week of waiting, the meeting was on, for two pm that same afternoon in the same conference room where Cotti had held the media meeting. The mobsters figured that the Feds would never have had time to put a bug in that room, so it would be safe to speak freely. Cotti actually believed the Feds couldn't get a warrant for placing bugs in that room because it was in a hotel, not a house, and anyone could use that room. That was the thinking, anyway.

***

Oh, how wrong Cotti was. Unbeknown to him, the FBI, the day after the media meeting, had placed bugs all around the room, hoping Cotti would use that room again and again. And to their surprise, they were right. He did.

To further their secrecy, on the day of the meeting, the mobsters arrived at ten minute intervals and came in through a hidden passageway that took them to a back room that was never used. But secrecy was hard to keep when the Feds were watching and listening twenty-four hours a day, seven days a week. That's how the Feds knew about the meeting: from the bug on Jack Cotti's phone at his club. They could listen in on all his phone calls from nearly every phone Cotti owned.

They got the feeling Cotti never really cared if they were listening to his phone calls. He acted like he was just calling friends. He apparently figured that the Feds knew all about him anyway. He never said anything incriminating that could put his ass behind bars, and even if the Feds thought something he said *was* incriminating, it was just "talk" to him—"getting things off his chest." Clearly, the Feds could go "Fuck themselves," as far as Cotti was concerned.

But the Feds thought differently about Cotti. They thought about him daily. And they watched his every move. Well...not every move, but *nearly* every move. And they listened to his every word. Well, maybe eighty percent. He was "job security" to them—that is, until they could bust him and throw his butt into prison for life, without parole. In fact, they were discussing Cotti the day of the meeting of the "Five Families."

"Hey, Adam, are all the bugs working in the conference room?" asked Meadows to Agent Butler.

"Yep. All five…loud and clear," he exclaimed.

"Five bugs for five Dons," quipped Ben Daily, sarcastically; he was just three months from retirement.

Everyone laughed at his stupid joke.

"Well, let's hope that we get some good incriminating evidence against them…or at the very least, Cotti," said Agent Keith Brunson, as he took off his headphones.

"Yeah, on all Five Families," interjected Lundy.

"Ok, you guys," said Arms. "Knock it off and take your places. The players are coming into the room. It sounds like the Dons and their Underbosses were the only ones to be invited."

The Feds listened intently through their headphones. Cotti was thanking the five Dons for coming.

***

Cotti had the table set with flowers, wine, water, cheese and crackers, and fruit of every kind.

"Before we get started, I just want to thank you all for coming today. It means a lot to me. I won't forget it." He placed his hand over his heart to show his gratitude. "And help yourselves to the wine and food." As Cotti spoke, wine was poured into their glasses. All but one Don lit up expensive cigars, the other already had one burning. "First, let me tell you what I have in mind."

"Ah, Jack, we've heard. What were you thinking?" barked Don Angelo Parrissi, head of the Lucchese Crime Family. His deep gruff voice had a heavy Italian accent.

"What was I thinking? About what, Don Parrissi?" Cotti replied.

"You know, Jack," interjected Don Vito Farcano, head of the Colombo Family. "I heard...we heard...that you were thinking of getting into politics. Is that true, Jack?"

"Yes, Don Farcano," Cotti replied. "That is true."

Loud grumbling arose from the small crowd of top wiseguys.

Cotti didn't want the meeting to get out of hand so early, so he tried to calm things down. "Let me tell you why I think it will be a good idea," he continued.

But they tried to stifle his idea and didn't want any more discussion on the subject. Don Tommy Talluchi, head of the Genovese Family, spoke up first. "Jack, I'm not one to speak up on such a volatile subject...but you know...it isn't a good idea to get our Families involved in politics: local or otherwise. It brings too much heat," he exclaimed in a thuggish Sicilian voice, puffing on his cigar between sentences.

All the people around the table agreed with him.

Cotti did not. "But let me tell you what I have in mind,"

he pleaded. Cotti was not the type of man to beg and they knew it.

Don Albert Scarfino, the head of the Bonnano Family, stood up. "I've heard enough!" he snapped, slapping his hand on the table. He began walking towards the door.

Cotti, red-faced with anger at Scarfino, shouted, "Goddamn it! You're gonna come back here and sit down—and listen to what I have to say! Then, if you disapprove—if all of you disapprove—then I will think differently about getting into politics."

Don Scarfino was nearly eighty years old, and his Underboss was only a few years younger, so they didn't want to start any trouble. They decided to do as Cotti suggested.

***

While Cotti was trying to sell these wiseguys on his lost cause, the Feds were taking bets that Cotti would get turned down. Only one out of the seven agents bet that Cotti would get his way. The rest bet that the four Dons would turn him down cold.

***

"Like I was saying," Cotti continued, "I'm not sure I'll even run yet. I first want the public to answer one simple question."

"And what is that?" asked Don Parrissi, smoking his cigar.

Cotti took a deep breath before answering Parrissi's question. "I got all the Family media people together working on getting the word out, which is: 'Would you vote for Jack Cotti as President of the United States?' That's it. That's what I want to find out."

Laughter spread throughout the room. First, one Don and his Underboss, then two, then another and another until they were all laughing in unison, some, so hard that they began coughing.

"Are you serious, Jack?" barked Don Talluchi, head of the Genovese Family. "You want to see if the people will vote for Jack Cotti for President of the United States? It's so crazy, it's funny. They will laugh you right out of the city. You'll be the laughing stock of the country. Oh....this is too funny." He laughed so hard it made him grab his stomach in pain, which made him stop laughing.

Farcano spoke up to put his two cents into the discussion. "Don Cotti, what is this obsession that you have? You want to run for President of the United States? Have you lost your mind? What makes you think that people will vote for you? This is the most ridiculous thing I've ever heard."

The other Dons nodded their heads in total agreement with Don Farcano.

"Don Farcano is right," interjected Don Parrissi. "You might think, Don Cotti, that what you are trying to do is an honorable thing. But these people, the voters, aren't going to show you any respect. They'll piss all over you. And that piss will spray all over *us*. We don't want or deserve the repercussions that this will bring to all the Families."

Again, all but Cotti agreed with Farcano's words.

"Listen," snapped Cotti, "you guys might laugh today, but let's wait and see what the people say!"

"We know what they'll say. NO! Just like we're gonna say," bellowed Talluchi.

"But what if they vote YES?" Cotti exclaimed. "If they do, we might get the chance to run not only New York State, but the whole fucking country."

"We already run the country," interjected Parrissi.

The four Dons snickered in agreement.

Cotti tried hard to convince his peers. "But Don Parrissi, if I win the Presidency, all the Federal taxes will be ours. We'll own the bank. We'll own it all. We'll run the military. We'll run the Justice Department, which means no more harassment from the Feds."

"Yeah, we heard the same shit when we gave Kennedy the election," Talluchi replied sarcastically, in broken English.

"Not only that," said Farcano, "but you'll be fodder for every wiseguy in the country. You'll bring heat to everyone in this thing of ours. All eyes will be on La Cosa Nostra."

Cotti shook his head. "I disagree, Don Farcano. All eyes will be on me...and away from you. I'll be the one taking all the heat. Just like I am now."

"Not true, Don Cotti," Farcano said. "All eyes will be on all Five Families, not just yours. You know this. Every time your name comes up, they'll mention 'Mafia,' in the same breath. No. I'm sorry, Don Cotti, but I'm against this...this thing of yours."

"Don Vito, I wish you would reconsider," begged Cotti. "Let's just see what happens with the media people. If they can get my question to the voters, then I'll set up another meeting for us to plan the next steps. 'Cause if the voters here in New York and the surrounding states say that they would vote for me as President, then I'll want each of you to back my play...in the run for President of the United States."

"How much money are we talking about?" Parrissi asked.

Cotti was taken aback by the question. All meeting long, the four Dons had been against his political run. Now, all of a sudden, Don Parrissi was asking how much money they'd be asked to kick in.

"Don Angelo," Cotti replied, "it's too early to say, but I would guess, to get started, I would need a few million from each Family. But if I win the primaries and get selected at the convention, each Family should contribute around five to ten million each. But I'll get that back for you—and much more—with the contributions that come in from all over the country."

"That's a lot of money you're talking about, Jack," exclaimed Talluchi.

"Yeah, but what each Family puts up, you'll get back a hundred times over. Remember, to run a campaign for

President will cost nearly a billion dollars. Imagine how much money we can reap from politics. Hell, that's the most corrupt business going. We steal in millions. Politicians steal in the billions. Every politician in Congress runs their crew like we do. They have an Underboss, advisor, and soldiers to do the grunt work."

"I don't know, Jack," said Farcano. "This is a bit much to swallow in one day. You know, when I heard a rumor of what you had in mind, I thought it was just bullshit. I didn't think anyone in the *life* would be crazy enough to get into politics. Especially a Don, for Christ's sake."

"Hell, Jack," asked Parrissi. "What party are you gonna run on? Democrat or Republican?"

"I'm not sure," Cotti replied, "but most likely I'll run on an Independent ticket. But I'll speak with all the political parties and then decide which one best fits me."

"Well, you better have it figured out before the question goes out," Talluchi said. "If…it goes out. I'm sure, because of who you are, many of the radio and TV personalities will be wanting to interview you, and I'm sure they'll ask you that question."

"And don't forget the newspaper reporters," said Parrissi. "They'll jump onto the bandwagon too."

"Jack, you're putting all of us here…all of our Families, this thing of ours, in jeopardy," Talluchi added.

"I know how you feel," Cotti said. "If I wasn't certain that this wouldn't work out for the better, I wouldn't do it. I wouldn't even think of doing it. But I've got a feeling that this will work out even better than expected."

"I, for one, think you're just downright foolish," exclaimed Scarfino. "And I don't think I can vote for this 'thing of yours.' I don't want to be seen agreeing with you on this stupid idea of yours. One of my soldiers just might think I'm getting too old and put me out of my misery."

"Don Scarfino, let's not be too hasty," said Talluchi. "We promised Don Cotti to listen to what he had to say. If he's finished, then maybe he and Napolie will leave us so we can talk among ourselves and decide which way we are going to go on this crazy idea of his."

"I guess we know which way Scarfino is voting," said Parrissi.

A few of the old wiseguys snickered at Parrissi's comment.

Cotti agreed with Talluchi, so he and Napolie went to the hotel's bar and had a few dry martinis.

***

All the Dons were in their mid-seventies, except Scarfino, so they didn't want any trouble from the much younger and crazier Jack Cotti and his Family—not today, anyway. They decided to do something that was against their better judgment.

Three minutes after Cotti and Napolie left the room, the Dons and their Underbosses gathered round the table to hash out their differences over this headache Cotti had given them.

Don Parrissi was the first to say what was on his mind. "Cotti's becoming a thorn in our sides. If we allow him to do what he wants, he will fail. I have no doubt."

Talluchi took over the meeting. "You heard what that arrogant prick said: 'If I get to the primaries'." He snickered, then remarked, "Shit, he won't make it a week once the question is on the air; if it gets that far. Five to one, the Media Moguls won't allow it. Every one of them will think it's a joke. They won't believe Cotti is serious and they'll have to ignore the request to ask his stupid question to their patrons."

Farcano nodded. "I agree with Don Talluchi. Cotti won't get anywhere with this...this thing that he wants to do."

***

The Feds were listening in intently on the conversations between the four senior Dons—not for any incriminating evidence, but to see how they would vote. They had a heavy bet going and nobody wanted to lose.

***

"We have to be diplomatic about how we handle Cotti," said Talluchi. "He's adamant about going through with this. So we can't start anything now. Let's do it his way, for the time being. We'll decide later how we want to handle him. Let's just hope he doesn't get his question on the air. Then we can let it rest. But he'll be a dead man, if this thing of his brings heat and publicity to all of us sitting here at this table."

They all nodded in agreement and began their voting.

Talluchi looked around the room and began pointing his finger at each Don. First was Parrissi, who gave a thumbs up. Farcano, too, gave a thumbs up. Talluchi nodded and then he pointed to Don Scarfino, who had stated to everyone that he was against Cotti's run in politics...in any shape or form. All the Dons were anxious to see how he would vote. If he voted against—all would vote thumbs down. This had to be a unanimous decision.

"Remember, Don Scarfino, we don't want a war with Cotti, not yet, anyway," Talluchi reminded him. "Let's just see what happens in the next week or so,"

All eyes were on Scarfino, who finally relented and gave a thumbs up. "Now we act as one," Scarfino exclaimed.

"Ok, it's settled," Talluchi acknowledged, slapping his hand on the table. "Cotti gets his way...for now. But in one week, I will contact all of you in this room for another meeting, and this time, without Cotti. We will decide, once and for all, if Cotti lives...or *dies*."

***

As they waited for Cotti to return and hear the news, the Feds were angry and dumbfounded by the Dons' acceptance of Cotti's political ambitions. Six of the seven agents involved in the betting were in disbelief over the fact they'd lost money to one of their peers.

"I can't believe the meeting turned out like it did," exclaimed Agent Meadows. "Man, I lost a hundred bucks on that bet."

"As did I," added Brunson.

"Me, too," said Lundy.

"And look who's got a smile on his face," said Arms, looking at Bailey.

"What can I say? I picked right." Bailey smiled.

***

Cotti and Napolie walked into the conference room to confront their peers.

"So, what did you guys decide?" Cotti asked them, looking to Scarfino for an answer.

"Don't look at me, Jack. Talluchi will answer for me," Scarfino answered.

Cotti looked to Talluchi. "Well, Don Talluchi, what do you say?"

"Jack," he answered, "we have decided that what you want to do hopefully won't reflect on the rest of us. So you have our permission to act on your idea—to a point. Just remember: if your publicity shines a bright light upon our Families, some at this table will feel disrespected and will have the Commission's approval to set things right. *Capisce,* Don Cotti?"

"Forget about it," Cotti replied, with happiness. "I will not let any of you down." He looked at all the Dons when he made that promise. "If I do, I know what to expect. Cosa Nostra Forever!"

"Hear, hear," said the four Dons in unison, as they raised their glasses in celebration.

The meeting broke up. After shaking hands and kissing cheeks, the Commission's heads went their separate ways. Cotti went away very happy at the outcome.

Napolie wasn't so sure; and told his boss as much in the car as they drove to the club. "Jack," he said, "something just doesn't sit right with me on this. Why would they allow you to do this thing when they were so against it? It just doesn't make sense. I'm worried."

"Johnny, forget about it. Everything's fine. We got the ok to go forward with my plan. Now we gotta get ahold of the media people to see how they're doing with their bosses."

***

The Feds, after overhearing the meeting with the Commission, decided to take preemptive action concerning the meeting that was coming up with the four Dons over Cotti's actions.

Supervisor Arms called his crew together and talked about his concerns. "Ok, guys, we gotta put tails on every one of these wiseguys on the Commission, twenty-four/seven, to find out where and when their meeting will be taking place. I wanna know exactly what's going down. If they're gonna whack Cotti, I want to know."

"For what?" Meadows replied. "Let them kill each other. That's one killer less in the world."

The other agents agreed with Meadows.

Arms did not. "Hey, if they're gonna clip Cotti and we know about it, we have to, by law, tell Cotti about it." The other agents gave him a disturbing look. "I'm sorry to disappoint you. But that's just the way it is," he added.

The Feds began planning their surveillance tactics to find out where the next meeting of the Commission would be held.

***

Cotti began contacting his media personnel to see how they were doing with their bosses. Only one of the twelve had gotten the "okay" to air Cotti's question.

However, Cotti did find out who that thirteenth person was at the meeting, from a detective working with the Feds. He was told it was an FBI agent who had infiltrated the meeting. Even though Cotti was told that the Feds knew everything that was said at the meeting, Cotti wasn't that concerned. It was only about him running for political office. Nothing else of importance was discussed. So Cotti ignored the words from the detective but thanked him anyway.

Chapter 4

While Cotti was busy finding out why his news correspondents were being denied his airtime, the Media Moguls were having a meeting of their own concerning the Cotti matter, in a conference room at the New York Times building. The group agreed to refuse to run the story. All but one member, that is.

"Mr. Murdoch," said Al Green, the news producer for ABC's New York affiliate, "what do you say?"

Murdoch remained silent for a good two minutes before giving his reply, as everyone in the room looked at him for his answer. "I'm afraid that I cannot, in good conscience, agree with you gentlemen and ladies. We are going to run the story and see what happens. Hell, you people know Cotti is a household name here in New York and around the country. He was on the covers of magazines for being the number one gangster in the United States. Now he wants to run for President. And that's news, my friends. I predict our ratings will go through the roof."

Rumbling and whispers resounded throughout the room over Murdoch's comments.

The producer for NBC news, New York affiliate, stood up and introduced himself. "I'm Danny Diehl, the producer for NBC news here in New York City. And I'd like to give you my opinion on this problem that's been created."

"Go ahead, son. We're listening," said Bob Bennet, general manager of the New York Herald.

"Well now, we can't agree with you, Mr. Murdoch. Cotti is not a news story. If he doesn't get the attention of the media, then his story dies quickly."

"Ok," Murdoch replied. "You people do as you please, but Fox News and our other news outlets will be running the story." With that, Murdoch and his associates left the room.

There was a lot of grumbling amongst the Moguls; they were not sure they had made the right choice. The majority agreed with Murdoch's outlook on the subject—about Cotti being a story. But to them, it just wasn't serious news. Who in their right mind would vote to put a mobster in the White House? Especially a guy like Cotti. So the story was moot in their eyes. Their morality button was showing. They'd rather Murdoch test the waters; and if he sank with the story, so be it. Then they could say: *We told you so.*

The Moguls put the story on hold for the time being, to see what Murdoch would do and what kind of response Fox News would get when that ridiculous question was asked of their viewers.

***

A few days later, Murdoch gave the ok to air the story. Bob Campbell, the anchor, was the first to ask the question.

He sat behind his Fox News anchor desk, told his viewers the story and past of Jack Cotti, and then he asked, "Would you vote for mobster Jack Cotti for President of the United States?" He added, "For those of you who are interested in voting, the number to call is on the screen as we speak. Press one to vote 'yes'; two for 'no.' And use Twitter to leave a comment or text us directly." With that, he went on to other news.

Nobody at Fox believed anyone would be interested in a Cotti Presidency. But just seconds after the story broke, the switchboard was flooded with phone calls from viewers. It was a response the news crew wasn't ready for, or expecting. The producer had to call in extra people to answer the calls and tally the outcome. And the phone calls and votes continued for a good two hours after the story broke, and thousands had twittered their opinions and comments. By the end of the night, over forty-six thousand votes were tallied, with eighty percent voting for a Cotti Presidency, and over six thousand comments were received, with most being *for* the mobster.

***

When Fox News put out Cotti's story, the Moguls from the meeting were all in front of their TVs, anxious to see Fox make a fool out of their news program. But that night, when the results were given, the Moguls were flabbergasted by the reactions of Fox's viewers.

Bob Campbell sat at his desk and thanked his viewing

audience for their incredible response to the Cotti question. "We had over forty-six thousand votes and over six thousand comments and opinions on Twitter. The response was amazing. We never believed that Jack Cotti had such a following. For more than two hours, our switchboard was inundated with phone calls: the majority voting 'YES' for a Cotti Presidency: Nearly eighty percent. Twelve percent 'against' and eight percent 'not sure.' And the comments were more than eighty-five percent for and fifteen percent against or with negative comments.

"Some of the more positive comments were summed up like this: one male viewer wrote, *May be a wiseguy, but he's also tough, and we need a tough President to run this country.* Another male viewer wrote, *Cotti comes from a poor family and became the leader of over three thousand Goombas. He'd knock some sense into those professional politicians and get things done...or else!* Others gave Cotti some political sayings if he does decide to run: one wrote, *Vote for Cotti. He's a Hottie.* Another texted, *Get down with Johnny Uptown.* Evidently, the viewers are tired of career politicians and want a change. The negative comments went like this: *He's a gangster and a criminal. We don't want him as President.* Another texted, *Are you kidding? Johnny Uptown is a clown.* A third wrote, *He's nothing but a criminal. How could people vote for a person like that for President of the United States?* These are just a few of the positive and negative comments to the question we asked."

"We will continue with this story in days ahead and will keep you abreast of any new news on Jack Cotti. Fox News has sent out an invitation to Mr. Cotti for an interview on today's findings. Hopefully, we'll have that for you in the next couple of days. And now to other news..."

While Fox went to other news, many of the Media Moguls were calling their affiliates to okay the same voting process for Jack Cotti that Fox News had used.

Danny Diehl, NBC's news producer, called his General Manager, Bob Greenfield, and told him to "get the Cotti question out on the air and to our viewers as soon as possible."

"Will do, Mr. Diehl. We'll get it out on the six-thirty news tomorrow night. In the meantime, I'll extend an invitation to Jack Cotti for an interview."

"Good," Diehl answered. "I just can't believe the response from Fox's viewers. Who in the hell wants a mobster as President? Let's just see how *our* viewers react. We have a more intelligent viewing audience than does Fox."

"I'll get on it as soon as I hang up," Greenfield promised. With that, the conversation ended.

The other Moguls who had gone to the meeting were also busy calling their underlings to get the Jack Cotti question out on the air.

All the different news organizations in New York were now going at full speed to be the next affiliate to get the jump on their competitors. Murdoch showed them that this *was* a news story and an interesting one. It was one that got their viewers thinking seriously about their career politicians and hoping to shake things up.

Cotti, if he did decide to run, would have to first make it through the primaries, then to get on the ballots, and then find funding to make his push for the Presidency. Nobody believed this would happen, except for one person: Jack Cotti.

***

The Moguls couldn't believe the outcome and neither could the Feds who were investigating Cotti and the Commission. They were just as flabbergasted as the Moguls.

"What the hell just happened?" asked Agent Arms. "Can you believe this shit? What the hell is happening to this country?"

"I'm glad we didn't bet on the outcome," interjected Baily. "We all would have lost."

"Now what do we do, Dennis?" Lundy asked Arms.

"What we do now is: Listen to the Commission's phone calls and find out where their meeting is being held. I know they're just as dumbfounded as we are at the outcome of the voting."

***

Arms was right. After the voting results, Don Talluchi was on the phone, contacting every Underboss in the Four

Families, including his own.

"Angie," said Talluchi to Angie Denneli, his Underboss, "we gotta set up a meeting with the other Families to discuss the Cotti matter. Let's hold it at the same place as before, in the conference room at the Selsor Hotel. I'll contact the other bosses and let you know when it will be. You just make sure that the place is well-stocked with wine, food, and cigars. We've got an important decision to make." He hung up his phone, lit a fifty dollar cigar, and then began making more phone calls. The first was to Don Angelo Parrissi.

"Can I speak to Don Parrissi? Tell him Talluchi is calling about an important matter," he said to the female on the other end of the line.

A few minutes later, Parrissi answered. "Yes, this is Parrissi."

"Don Angelo, this is Talluchi. We need to discuss a very important matter as soon as possible. It is urgent."

"Is this what we were talking about at the meeting last week?" Parrissi asked.

"It is. This Cotti problem has not ended as we expected. The people actually like this guy for President. Can you believe that? Cotti for President. What a joke!" exclaimed Talluchi.

"So, where's the meeting gonna be held?"

"Same place and same time as before. We just need to set up a day. When are you available, Don Parrissi?"

"I'm available any time you want. This is more

important than any other Family business."

"Good. I'll make calls to the other Families and find out what is convenient for them. Then I'll get back to you and let you know. Forget about it!"

"I'll be waiting for your call, Don Talluchi."

Talluchi made the other calls to the Families involved and set up a time, place, and day—in two days, at two pm.

***

Whether the wiseguys knew or didn't know that the Feds were listening in on every word of their conversations to each other, it didn't matter to them. They were gangsters and prison was part of doing business. And surely the Feds didn't care because it was their job to put these guys behind bars, hopefully forever.

The Feds were delighted with Talluchi's pick for the meeting. Hell, they already had the bugs in place and were ready whenever the Goombas were to listen in on that important conversation, especially when it was about whacking one of their own, and a Don, for Christ's sake. The Feds had two days to get prepared.

***

The days went by quicker than anticipated. Cotti was now the news of the day. He was even getting global attention. From Europe to Asia, every news organization was saying that the mobster, Jack Cotti, could become the next President of the United States. Even within the United

States, news correspondents were giving the Cotti story more attention than their regular news stories: plane crashes, ferry boat fires, or suicide bombings killing hundreds of people were now not as important as the Cotti matter. The story took off like a "bat out of hell" or a raging forest fire that keeps spreading until it's out of control. This is what was happening to the Cotti story. Everyone was talking about Jack Cotti for President.

Even other affiliates of the different news organizations, including newspapers in the surrounding states, began asking their viewers, listeners, and readers the same question as Fox had: Would you vote for mobster Jack Cotti for President of the United States? The reaction was incredible. Cotti's popularity had soared to more than ninety percent of those responding giving a favorable thumbs-up. Every news organization had the same outcome. No other person running for President was as popular as Cotti was now.

The Moguls didn't know what to think. Was it a fluke or were people serious? This story grew legs, like octopus tentacles, in nearly every state in the Union. They didn't like to admit it, but Murdoch, this old, old man, had made fools of them.

To the Media Moguls, Murdoch was the "man." He had known immediately that the Jack Cotti story had legs. He had been right on every aspect of it. He was the one that could say to all his disbelievers, "See, I told you so." But Murdoch wasn't like that. He had a nose for news and used it. Whether the others had it or not, they hadn't used it. So now, Fox News would be the first to interview Jack Cotti, if he would agree to it.

Murdoch made the call to Cotti, personally. "Mr. Cotti, Mr. Jack Cotti?" said Murdoch, as a man with a gruff voice answered on the other end.

"Yeah, this is Cotti. Who wants to know?"

"Mr. Cotti, this is Rupert Murdoch. I own Fox News. I'm sure you've seen the results of a Jack Cotti Presidency?"

"Yeah. So?" Cotti replied.

"Well, we would like to interview you at the station about your plans to run for President. That is, if it's okay with you?"

"Mr. Murdoch, is it? Well, *forget about it!* I'm not ready to be interviewed. When did you want to do this?"

"Any time you say, Mr. Cotti. You're very big news. You know, Fox was the only one to run your story. All the other media owners refused. They thought your story would die if they didn't run with it. And they would have probably been right, had I not smelled a big story."

"So what? Now you think I owe you to do this interview?" snapped Cotti.

"No, not at all. I think we can help each other. Like I said, I have a nose for news. And already, you've helped Fox in the ratings game. I think we can help each other. Who knows, Fox just might be the reason you get into the White House."

"Well, I gotta tell you, Mr. Murdoch, you're not the first to call for an interview. In fact, you are the fourth. Why should I give you first crack at trying to put me down and ruin my chances?"

"Mr. Cotti. That is not what I want. I know I should have contacted you sooner, but remember: Fox News stood up for you when nobody else would. I won't say you owe me because I know you won't turn me down. But Mr. Cotti, we are a lot alike. We are both tough negotiators when it comes down to business. You have your way of doing things, to get people on your side, and I have mine. And we both run multi-billion dollar enterprises that do illegal things at times. You do this for me and I'll help you find some big donors for your run at the White House," Murdoch promised.

"Forget about it!" Cotti said. But then, thinking about it more, he added. "Well, I'll do it, but on two conditions."

"And what are they?"

"First, you give me the questions at least eight hours in advance so I can go over them. Second, you don't ask me which Party I will run on. Do that, and you've got yourself an interview."

Murdoch agreed to the conditions and set the interview for the following night, on the six-thirty Nightly News.

"I thought you'd run as a Republican," Murdoch told Cotti.

"Well, my values and morals are Republican, but I'm also pro-Union. And that doesn't sit well with the

Republican Party," replied Cotti. "Although most of the time I vote Republican. But I just don't know yet. Forget about it!"

"Okay, Mr. Cotti. I'll have someone come by your house and drop off the questions; say, a little after eight tomorrow morning. If that's alright with you?"

"That's fine."

"Then we'll see you at the station at six tomorrow night."

"I'll see you then," Cotti promised.

Murdoch ended the call and hung up his phone.

***

Cotti was flying high and was the talk of the town. He loved it. His egotistical brain couldn't get enough. He was very happy and overjoyed at the outcome.

But not everyone was as tickled pink over Cotti's popularity. Napolie, Cotti's Capos, and his soldiers were utterly confused by this turn of events. Nearly everyone, from the Media Moguls, the Feds, and even the Commission had thought Cotti would be the laughing stock of New York and not the most popular guy. This just fueled Cotti's ego even more.

The next morning, at precisely eight, Cotti answered the door and was handed the questions for his interview. He thanked the delivery boy, gave him a fifty dollar tip, which the boy tried to refuse but Cotti would have none of it. So the kid figured it was better to take the tip rather than

58

take a chance that he could get whacked by the most famous gangster in the country. As soon as the nervous kid had left, Cotti returned to his desk and made a call to his Underboss.

"Hey, Johnny, come on over and pick me up," he said into the phone. "I need to go to the club and have some coffee and cannolis."

"Jack, what's going on? Fox News is saying that you're giving an interview tonight about your sudden popularity. Is that true?"

"Forget about it! But yes, it's true. I was just given the questions that they're going to ask so I can give answers that are rational and sound."

***

Napolie was even more bewildered by his boss's naiveté, and was sure that Cotti was gonna get himself killed before the interview was to happen. But he couldn't talk Cotti out of it. This was Cotti's *thing* and *his thing* only. Even though Napolie believed he would be hit along with his boss, he gave up trying to change his boss's mind.

"Jack, I wish you would have talked about this interview thing with Benny the Brain first before deciding to do it, but now that it's on, I wish you the best. I'll be over within ten minutes." He hung up the phone.

Napolie was true to his word and picked up his boss in nine minutes. Fifteen minutes later, they were sitting at their table at the club drinking coffee and eating their cannolis.

***

Benny the Brain came into the club and sat at their table, joining them in their coffee and cannolis. "Jack, what were you thinking?" he asked, clearly puzzled.

"About what?" Cotti answered. He looked over his questions for the interview and thought, *Hell, this will be a snap.*

"Jack, look at me. This interview thing is not a good idea." Bartolo's voice took on a worried tone. "I've already heard that a meeting with the heads of the Four Families is taking place tomorrow, over this thing of yours. It's not good, Jack."

"I've been trying to tell him this when he decided to get into politics," Napolie told Bartolo. "Boy, I'd like to whack that reporter that started this thing in your head, Jack. I never thought it would get this far."

But Jack wasn't hearing any of it. His head was in the clouds. He wasn't listening to anything they were saying.

***

The Feds, however, were listening to every word Cotti and his boys were saying. They were also listening to Don Talluchi's phone conversation with his Underboss concerning Cotti's interview. Talluchi wanted this nonsense to stop. Cotti was bringing attention to the Families that they didn't want or need. And the Families were right with their premonitions. Every time a reporter mentioned Cotti's name, they also mentioned the other Families and their bosses. The Commission was not a happy group. They couldn't wait for their meeting the following day. For the moment, though, they had to bite their tongues.

***

Talluchi was furious and told his Underboss Denneli his feelings over the phone. "That fucking Cotti. He's making trouble for everyone!"

"I know, Tommy," Denneli replied at the other end. "What the hell are they gonna talk about at that interview?"

"It won't be nothing good. I know they'll only talk about this *thing of ours*. It's fucked up."

"What'll we do, boss?"

"Come on over and we'll talk about it. But do you have everything ready for tomorrow's meeting?"

"Yeah, everything is set. I've got all the food and drink being delivered just before two. And I got boxes of cigars for everyone, including the Underbosses."

"Where did you get the cigars?" Talluchi asked.

"I got 'em from Denny Pavalo...from one of his high jacked loads out of Kennedy."

"Good enough. I'll see you when you come over." Talluchi hung up his phone and waited for his Underboss to arrive. They had much to talk over.

***

While Talluchi and others didn't want the interview to take place and wanted to stop it one way or another, the Feds and Fox News personnel couldn't wait for the interview to happen. Fox News believed they would get a ratings surge from it and the Feds believed that Cotti would be taken down a notch, fall flat on his face, and lose the people's trust.

Bob Campbell, who was to host the interview with Cotti, was a veteran and hardened reporter, having reported from many war-torn countries: Iraq, Afghanistan, and Syria just to name a few. He didn't back down or take any guff from anyone. He believed without a doubt that he could handle Cotti.

But Talluchi didn't want the interview to take place and when his Underboss visited with him at his home as ordered, he told Denneli his feelings and plans concerning Cotti.

"Angie," he said, "we gotta stop Cotti from doing this interview."

"How we gonna do that?" Denneli responded. "He'll be surrounded by his soldiers and the media will be all over him."

"Well, we gotta find a way. Hell, they're playing that goddamned Cotti interview advertisement nearly every break. This shit can't go on."

Just in case the Feds were listening in, Talluchi wrote down on a piece of paper the names of two soldiers he wanted to do a suicide hit. He passed it to Denneli.

Denneli quickly read it, nodded and then lit the paper on fire and set it into the ashtray.

"Tell them it's a favor to me that will be repaid one-thousand times," Talluchi said.

"Okay, Tommy. If that's what you want. But the other Families won't like it without giving their approval. You're playing with fire."

"Forget about it! Those guys won't say a word once it's over. I'll be doing them a favor. Hell, I'll be doing all of us a favor." Talluchi beamed.

"I better get going," Denneli said, reluctantly. "I got to set this thing up and don't have a lot of time to do it. Fuck, I don't even know where those guys are."

"Well find 'em. We gotta get this done."

***

Denneli left Talluchi's home disgruntled, but he would do as ordered. He headed to their club. He had to contact those two soldiers and do it quickly. He only had a few hours to put a plan together. He believed now that what Cotti had started and what Talluchi wanted to do was going to be the downfall of "*this thing of ours.*"

***

The Feds agreed with Denneli's thinking. They had listened in on the wiseguys' conversation. They just didn't know where or when the hit was to take place but knew that it would happen before the interview. So they would put tails on Cotti and stand guard outside the Fox News station an hour before. Afterwards, they would escort the boss of the Valoppi Family to his home.

The Feds believed the Commission was going to make their move on Cotti after their meeting the following afternoon. But this interview thing had stirred the pot and they now believed that Talluchi had decided to make the move sooner. They didn't know if the Commission had Ok'd the decision or if Talluchi was doing it on his own. In either case, the Feds knew a hit was coming…and coming soon. They just needed to be at the right place at the right time to stop it. But there were a lot of variables to that plan.

Would Cotti enter through the front door of Fox or the rear door? How would the shooter or shooters make their move? Would he or they shoot from close range or from afar? Or would they hit Cotti just as he was leaving his club or home? There were many questions to answer and not much time to figure it out.

After consulting with his crew, FBI Supervisor Arms had his crew divide and conquer. One group would follow Cotti until the interview was over and had been escorted home. The other group would stand guard at Fox studios, at both front and rear exits, along with New York's finest, the NYPD. Then it was up to Talluchi's shooters to make the first move. The Feds would make the second, hopefully killing the shooters before they could kill any of them—or for that matter, Cotti.

Agent Arms had everyone in place within an hour. There were only five hours to interview time. Everyone was on edge: the Feds, the Moguls, the Five Families, and especially Cotti and Talluchi. No matter what happened, there was sure to be a war between the Families: maybe one on one or four on one. Only time would tell.

Two hours before the interview, Cotti was at a nearby bakery picking up a box of cannolis to eat in the limo on the way to Fox studio. As he was coming out, he literally ran into Tommy Talluchi. This clearly wasn't planned. It happened by accident. The two wiseguys said their "hellos," but neither acted as though there was something wrong. The Agents tailing them waited nervously to see what would transpire, but for a few minutes the two men acted like best friends. Then Cotti brought up the fact that his Family had been left out of the window deal that would have made him over two million dollars a year for the next five years and wanted to know the reason why only his Family had been left out of sharing the wealth.

Talluchi refused to argue with Cotti. All he said about the problem that had ruffled Cotti's feathers was: "It's Parrissi's deal. The Lucchese Family runs that scam. He got the City contract. Talk with him about it."

With Cotti's big night ahead of him, he didn't start anything in the street. He just nodded, shook hands, and left it at that. Then, both men went their separate ways.

Chapter 5

The hour was at hand. Fox's limo came to pick Cotti up, along with his entourage that included Napolie, Bartolo, and a few close button men used for security. Within a few minutes, they had arrived at the station.

The Feds and NYPD were on alert as Cotti and friends got out of the limo. They weren't one hundred percent certain that a hit was going down, but kept their eyes and ears open just in case. Everyone was at the *ready*.

Cotti got out of the vehicle and was mobbed and encircled by reporters wanting to get a word with him. A second car came rumbling down the street, driving slowly past Cotti and his entourage. Suddenly, the passenger rolled down the window, pulled out a semi-automatic pistol, and fired.

Pop, Pop, Pop!

One bullet went through the front window of the limo. The others, God only knew. The Feds would have to find them. The Feds and NYPD returned fire as the car sped away.

***

The two Talluchi assassins had failed in their mission. The police finally caught up with them a few blocks away, but they were too late. The two thugs were sitting in their car, riddled with bullets. They were the first victims in the Cotti debacle. Talluchi was as good to his word. He had paid them back a thousand times.

***

The Feds escorted Cotti and entourage into the building.

One lone reporter found his way inside. "Mr. Cotti, Mr. Cotti," he said, trying to get Cotti's attention.

Cotti stopped to see what this young man wanted. "What can I do for you son?"

"Mr. Cotti, my name is Bobby Legend and I am an investigative reporter for an independent news organization." The reporter held his microphone near Cotti's face. "If you win the Presidency, can I call you the Godfather President?"

Cotti seemed to like the question. He thought about it for a few seconds. "Son, if I'm elected President, you can call me anything you want!" A big smile crossed his face. "But—hell, yes! I'd be honored to be known as the Godfather President."

The producer of the show directed Cotti and his entourage to their dressing room. Cotti, Napolie, and Bartolo went inside while his two soldiers stood guard outside the door, as did the Feds and NYPD.

***

The producer of Fox News came into Cotti's dressing room to see how Cotti was doing. The people at Fox were nervous as hell after the shoot-out between the police and wiseguys. He came to see if Cotti still wanted to do the interview.

"Mr. Cotti, let me introduce myself. My name is Don Gates and I'm the producer for your interview," he said. "I know you're probably shook up after the shooting, so if you want, we can cancel tonight's interview and do it another day. What do you think?"

"Are you kidding?" Cotti replied. "I'm fine. It's not the first time someone's tried to kill me. It's just another day to me. That's the *life*, Donny. Forget about it!"

"Ok, then. If you're ready, let's go to Studio 1-A. That's where we're doing the interview."

They walked down the corridor and Gates explained what would transpire during the interview. "Mr. Cotti, Mr. Bob Campbell, our top anchor, will be hosting and asking you the questions. He is a veteran of over twenty years here at Fox News. Oh, and here he is now."

Campbell came over to them and introduced himself. "Mr. Cotti, I'm Bob Campbell and I'll be doing the interview with you. There is water available, on the table next to you. And that's about it. We have about two minutes before air time, so let's take our places, shall we?"

"Forget about it!" Cotti replied.

He and Campbell took their seats directly across from each other.

Campbell began the interview. "Mr. Cotti, before we get started, I'd just like to thank you for allowing Fox to do this interview. And let me say this to my viewers: If it hadn't been for my boss, Rupert Murdoch, I doubt Mr. Cotti and I would be sitting here now. He had the foresight to ask the question to you, our viewers, which many in our profession refused to do. They didn't think it was relevant or a serious news story and thought Mr. Cotti was a joke. But we, at Fox News, did ask you, our viewers, 'Would you vote to put mobster, Jack Cotti into the White House?' And the majority of you said, *yes*. Now we see all the other news organizations are jumping on the bandwagon to get that question out to their audiences. And it seems their patrons also gave Mr. Cotti a *thumbs up* for President."

"Forget about it!" said Cotti.

Campbell turned from his viewing audience and to Cotti. "Let me ask you this question, Mr. Cotti: Do you believe that a Don or boss of the largest and most vicious Mafia Crime Family, with over thirty-two hundred members, should run for President of the United States?"

"Why? Is it a crime for a Mafia member to run for Political Office?" Cotti asked.

"Mr. Cotti, I'll ask the questions, if you don't mind," Campbell answered.

"So, ask away."

"Mr. Cotti, you are the head of a Mafia Family, are you not?"

Cotti snickered, then said, "I plead the fifth!"

"Mr. Cotti, what makes you think you can run the country?"

"Why not? The government is run just like a Mafia Family."

"Are you serious?" snapped Campbell. "Why would you say a thing like that?"

"I'll give you just one example, for now, Bobby boy. The Mafia uses its members as earners, where a percentage of their profits is kicked upstairs to the boss. The boss takes his cut and the rest is divided amongst the earners. The Federal Government does exactly the same thing, except they get a bigger percentage of the earners' money. In fact: The boss of a Mafia Family usually only gets fifteen, maybe twenty percent. When the Government takes their cut, they get thirty to forty percent."

"I see. You know, the way you say that...it makes sense. And simply put," Campbell mused.

"Forget about it!" Cotti retorted.

"Mr. Cotti, not to get off the subject—and we don't have a lot of time left—but I don't know if our viewers know about your near assassination attempt that happened right outside our studio not more than a half hour ago, in front of many police officers and FBI agents." Campbell looked directly into the camera. "So let me ask you this, Mr. Cotti: Someone tried to kill you as you walked up to the front doors of Fox Studio. Do you worry that the people who ordered the hit might not fail the next time?"

Cotti shook his head. "Not at all, Bobby. That's part of the *life*. I've had people try and kill me before and I'm sure it will happen again. I try not to let it bother me."

"Will you seek revenge?" Campbell asked, sheepishly.

"I plead the fifth!" Cotti replied, smiling.

"Mr. Cotti: If you do run and do well in the Primaries, and then get on the ballots, will you quit the mob?"

Cotti looked at him in disbelief at such a question. "You must be new around here, Mister. No one leaves the Mafia...alive, anyway."

"So you won't quit? Campbell asked again.

"Forget about it! If I become President, I'll take a leave of absence so I can concentrate my full time on the people of this country. Especially the poor and middle-class. The rich don't need no help."

Campbell looked directly into the camera again and talked to the viewers. "Well, that's about all the time we have tonight." He then turned to Cotti. "Can I ask you back at a later date, especially if this ***thing of yours,*** as you put it, takes on a life of its own? And it seems to be going in your favor. Never before has Fox News ever experienced such a phenomenon in the realm of politics. You've definitely gotten the people involved in the political process once again, which has fallen flat for nearly two decades. So, thanks once again, Mr. Cotti. It's been my pleasure."

The two men shook hands.

"Forget about it!" Cotti replied.

The two men left the set, and Gates came over to speak with Cotti.

"Mr. Cotti, we would like to invite you back in a week or so to see how you're doing in the political arena. You've got people's attention, especially the people who decide elections, the top dogs in their profession, which is hardline politics. You may become a thorn in their sides."

"Yeah, theirs, the Feds, the Media Moguls, the Commission, and last but not least, the politicians," interjected Rupert Murdoch, who had come by to shake Cotti's hand and wish him good luck.

"Thank you, Mr. Cotti," continued Murdoch. "Our ratings shot up over thirty points, which is the best we've done since nine-eleven. You've awakened a sleeping giant. Politics will never be the same."

"Forget about it!" spouted Cotti. "It was my pleasure."

Murdoch smiled. "But now, on a softer note, Mr. Cotti, the FBI, Fox security, and the NYPD will escort you from here to your home. We've had your limo moved to the private underground garage to keep away any threats. And thank you once again. I'm sure we'll be talking to each other again."

"Mr. Murdoch, if I can ever return the favor, just let me know. I'm deeply grateful for your help in getting my word out. The response has been overwhelming. Forget about it!"

They all shook hands once again and escorted Cotti and entourage to the limo. Once the car was safely loaded, the limo was accompanied by three police vehicles in front and three following in the rear.

***

As the cars sped away, Rupert Murdoch had a few things to say to Gates about Cotti. "Cotti today proved that he is fearless. Nothing fazed him. Not even an assassination attempt. The Presidency and running the country would be a snap for him."

***

Cotti was anxious to get to their destination. He had a few words to say to his Underboss.

"Johnny, we gotta find out who ordered the hit. It couldn't be the Commission because they gave me their word that I could have this time to do my thing without any interference from them. So if I find out that one or all ordered the hit, shit's gonna hit the fan. Get me?"

"Sure, Jack. I'll see what I can find out," the Underboss replied.

"I mean, the Commission Ok'd my run. Why would they try and hit me now?"

Napolie replied emphatically, "I told you, Jack. They don't want the publicity. And now that you're everyday news...and big news, at that...they evidently changed their minds."

"Yeah, they tried to stop my interview. They thought the people wouldn't support a Jack Cotti Presidency. But now that they have, the Commission doesn't like it. Hell, I told them that if I became President, we'd run the country."

"But they already run the country. They told you that," Napolie reminded him.

Two minutes later, the limo pulled up in front of Cotti's house. The FBI did not allow Cotti and his entourage to exit, until they were standing guard over him, making sure that he was safe. As Cotti, Napolie, and Bartolo entered the home, the rest of his entourage stood guard at the front and rear doors. The cops and security detail, on the other hand, left the premises and returned to their duties.

The three wiseguys went directly to Cotti's office to figure out what had to be done to alleviate the situation, before it blew up into an all-out war between the Families.

***

As they were discussing their problem, Talluchi was on the phone discussing his problem with the other three Dons concerning the Commission's problem and to remind them of the meeting the following afternoon. But Talluchi found that he was in trouble with his peers for putting out a contract on Cotti without full approval from the Commission.

"You broke the rules, Don Talluchi," said Parrissi, in anger. "We gave Cotti our word and allowed him to try his hands at politics...and you broke that promise. We have much to talk about, Don Talluchi."

***

Parrissi hung up his phone. He wasn't certain that Talluchi was the culprit, but after speaking with the other Dons and hearing their complaint about a hit that wasn't sponsored by them, he figured it had to be Talluchi. And when the names of the dead assassins were announced, he knew for certain that Talluchi had ordered it. This failed hit would now shine the light on the Commission even more than Cotti's insane run for President.

***

On his way to the meeting, Napolie met Talluchi unexpectedly outside the same bakery Cotti had visited the day before. They didn't have very nice words to say to each other.

"Tommy, we know what you did," snapped Napolie.

"Did what?" he retorted, standing chest to chest with Napolie.

"What do you think? That we're stupid?" Napolie backed a few feet from Talluchi, not wanting to start something that might get out of hand. "When the Sally brothers were found in their car, riddled with bullets, not five blocks from where the hit took place, we knew you sent them. So if I was you, Tommy, and don't want any backlash, I'd let the Valoppi Family share the wealth on the window deal."

"Well, that's Parrissi's deal. He got the contract."

Napolie nodded. "Yeah, but you speak for the other Families, just like at the meeting. So, you see that it gets done and things may stay peaceful. And remember, we had the Commission's word that Jack could see his thing through. But instead, you try to **whack** him!" Napolie shouted. "You broke the rules, Tommy. I just hope the other Families didn't approve the hit, too. That would create trouble that couldn't be overlooked."

Their conversation ended and the two parted ways without any more hassle.

***

The Feds were still tailing Talluchi, so they heard the whole conversation between him and Napolie.

Agent Arms had a different slant on the Cotti hit and told his brother agents, "Hey, guys. You know Talluchi may have tried to hit Cotti over this window deal. They did Ok Cotti's run. And if Talluchi put out the contract without Commission approval for either reason—the window deal or bringing too much heat to the Families—Talluchi broke the rules of *this thing of theirs*, no matter how you look at it."

The others nodded in agreement.

"Yeah," said Lundy, "he may be in trouble with the Commission too. We'll see in less than an hour."

***

Not long after the Talluchi-Napolie run-in, Talluchi and his Underboss, Denneli, sat in the conference room at the Selsor Hotel. The other three Bosses showed up, slowly waddled in, and took their seats. Pens, pencils, and small sheets of notebook paper were placed in front of them to use to cast their votes silently, just in case someone unwanted was listening. This would make it tough on the FBI to know exactly what was said at the meeting. The Dons lit cigars, and Talluchi stood up to begin the meeting.

"First of all," Talluchi said, "I'd like to thank you all for coming here on such an unhappy day. We have some important decisions to make." His tone was half-hearted.

The three Dons nodded in unison.

"You all know," he continued, "what was said the other day at our meeting here. Our dear and old friend, Don Cotti, wants to do a foolish thing...a foolish thing. He wants to bring attention to *this thing of ours*, to make fools of all of us in this room. We must solve this problem. It is a hard decision to make. But we must rid ourselves of this problem. Do you agree?" He looked at each member; he wanted their answer.

Giving a concerned and stout look, Parrissi nodded...agreeing to rid themselves of this problem that Cotti had created. Each of the others also nodded in agreement to the problem at hand.

"Then, it's settled," Talluchi exclaimed. "We'll decide when and where and who and what Family will be responsible for the hit: When they will do it. And where it will take place. If you're all in agreement, we'll have another meeting in two days from today and decide these questions."

This time, all four nodded together in agreement.

Don Parrissi spoke up. "I would like to ask Don Talluchi and the rest of you about the hit on Cotti last night at Fox Studios. I want to know who gave the orders." He looked directly at Talluchi. "Did you give the order, Don Talluchi? It was your two soldiers that were found shot to death in their car just a few blocks away. And the Feds said it was the same type and color as the one seen leaving the crime scene. When they view the security tapes, they'll know for sure. But it's better if you tell us, Don Talluchi."

Talluchi, now nervous, remained silent for a good minute before answering. "I think those two guys did it on their own. Neither I nor Denneli gave the order to whack Cotti. I swear on my mother's grave and the heads of my children," he exclaimed. He hoped his lie would keep him and his Underboss alive for at least the next two days.

But Parrissi wouldn't let it go. "Don Talluchi. If we find out differently, it will be you that pays the penalty. We will not be able to save you...or Denneli," Parrissi promised.

All Talluchi could do was look down at the floor and nod. He knew his fate was also now in the hands of the Commission.

The meeting ended and each went his own way.

***

The Feds, listening in, thought the spurts of silence were intentional on the part of the wiseguys. But later, after listening to the tapes, they found that apparently the main bug had a bug of its own and had sputtered to a halt. They would have to replace it before the room was used again by the mob.

***

As the Feds were struggling with a plan to fix their *bug* problem without getting caught planting a new one, Cotti and Company were struggling with their Commission problem, trying not to get killed in the process. Not long after the meeting of the Four Families, Napolie had been given the meeting's minutes from Parrissi Underboss, Petey "Boy" Vattoli.

Napolie told Cotti about the meeting when the two met outside their club that day. "Jack, the word's gone out."

They walked around the block so the Feds couldn't listen to their conversation.

"The Commission voted to whack you," Napolie said. "They haven't decided which Family will take on the job. They are gonna have another meeting in two days."

"I can understand Talluchi doing the hit without Commission approval," Cotti replied. "He could use the window deal as his excuse. But I can't understand why the Commission would take a contract out on me now? I've come too far in such a short time that I can't stop now. I gotta see this thing through to the end. And if that means going on the offensive, then so be it! What will be, will be."

"Jack, maybe they changed their minds when they saw how quickly your popularity soared? I mean, your name, over this *thing of yours,* has spread all over the country. Did you see the papers today? You were all over the headlines. The Times read: New Powerhouse in Politics: Don Cotti. The Herald: Political Hottie—Vote Cotti! Another had: Political Fireball—Mobster Cotti. The Huffington Post called you the Political Don Juan. Fuck, Jack, you're all over the news and that's not good. We're gangsters. Not celebrities," Napolie reminded him.

***

Napolie wasn't the only one reading the papers. So were Talluchi and the other head wiseguys. They, and especially Talluchi, were outraged over the headlines. It seemed to bother him the most and he told his Underboss just how he felt, as they sat around his office table in his home "*shooting the shit.*"

"I can't believe this fucking Cotti. The media thinks he's god's gift to politics. The papers are having a field day over Cotti's fiasco. Now, I hear he's getting calls from news affiliates from all over the country, wanting interviews. This *thing* of Cotti's is getting way out of hand. I don't think we can wait for our next meeting. I think the time has come to finish the job we started. I want Cotti dead…and I want him dead today!" He slammed his fist on the tabletop.

"But Tommy, we broke the Commission's rules once,"

Denneli reminded him. "We can't do it again or we'll be on the contract with Cotti. We have to be very careful...or we could be the ones that end up dead."

"I don't give a fuck! Parrissi and the others will be thanking me if we get this thing done right. And this time, we won't miss."

Denneli just shook his head in disbelief, knowing the actions that could be taken by the other Families if Talluchi went ahead with his plan. And if they missed—and without the approval of the Commission—that would seal their fates. But what could he do? If he went against his boss, he could end up dead before Cotti. He was ***damned if he did, and damned if he didn't.*** He was definitely caught in the middle.

***

The Feds had heard nearly every word between Talluchi and Denneli and were very concerned at Talluchi's threat against Cotti. This could get messy and have deadly ramifications. The Agents were still tailing both Talluchi and Cotti but would not be much longer because their funding would run out at midnight.

"How are we going to keep the tails on those wiseguys if we can't pay for it?" Lundy asked Arms.

"We don't. I'll have to pull the guys off surveillance and hope Congress passes our new budget tomorrow," replied Arms.

"Boy, what a time to lose our surveillance," said

Meadows. "If they start a war amongst themselves, there'll be lots of dead bodies to investigate."

"Yeah, a war is about to erupt and we won't be able to stop it. Should we tell Cotti?" Bailey asked Arms.

"Of course," Arms replied. "Lundy, you and I will go to Cotti's house and tell him about what we heard. But I'm sure he already knows. He didn't get to where he's at by being stupid."

"Is he still at his home?" Lundy asked.

Bailey still had his headphones on and was listening for any conversation from the bugs hidden in Cotti's home. "Yeah, he's there. But for how much longer, I don't know."

Lundy and Arms quickly left the surveillance room and headed for Cotti's place. Ten minutes later, they were in Cotti's living room, sitting on the sofa and giving him the news.

"Mr. Cotti," said Arms, "Agent Lundy and I apologize for showing up like this, but we need to tell you about a conversation we heard earlier today between Tommy Talluchi and Angie Denneli about you."

"Does it have anything to do with the assassination attempt the other day?" Cotti asked.

"Yes, and we believe there is about to be another hit out on you. Talluchi's still gunning for you. He wants it done before the day is out. We don't know where or when, but we're pretty sure he'll send his soldiers after you again."

"Why don't you arrest him? Hell, you're good at that. At least with me," Cotti chided them.

"We would if we had any good evidence against him," replied Arms.

"You just told me you listened to Talluchi's conversations. And you're here telling me he's gonna whack me. What more evidence do you need?" asked Cotti.

"We need corroborating evidence, Mr. Cotti. We're going over the tapes now. But we don't have enough to arrest him. We are just surmising the outcome...because Talluchi didn't really say that *he* was going to kill you, just that he wanted you dead. That's why we're here, especially after what happened at Fox Studio."

"What more do you need?" Cotti asked him.

"More than what we have, I'm sorry to say. Unless we can catch him or his soldiers in the act, then we got nothing. I just wanted to warn you to be on your toes."

"I'm always on my toes. I've even got eyes in the back of my head," Cotti replied, sarcastically.

"Mr. Cotti," interjected Lundy, "you should have as much security around you as possible. That way, if Talluchi does come after you, he'll have a harder time of it."

"Why, you guys will be tailing me, won't you? That's all the security I'll need."

"Usually, that's the case. But we have lost our funding until Congress passes a new budget, so we've had to discontinue our surveillance on you. So, basically, you're on your own. Sorry," said Arms, apologetically.

"You mean to tell me I won't have you guys tailing me

for a while?" Cotti asked them.

The two agents nodded in unison. "We don't usually tell the people we have under surveillance that we're pulling our surveillance crew," Arms explained, "but under the circumstances we felt we had an obligation to tell you. When it comes to life or death, we always prefer *life!*"

"You'd be happy if Talluchi killed me," said Cotti.

"No," Lundy replied. "We want to put you in jail for life. Killing's too good for you."

"Well, Mr. Cotti," said Arms, "we came here in good faith to tell you our fears about your future. And we wish you good luck."

The two agents shook hands with Cotti and went on their way, back to their surveillance headquarters.

During the drive there, Lundy had a few things to say to Arms. "Dennis, why did you tell Cotti that we pulled his tails? That wasn't very smart."

"It was my duty to tell him, so now he can be responsible for his own security."

"But he won't have us as backup."

"Can you keep a secret?" asked Arms.

"Why? What's up?"

"What I said back there, about our surveillance being lifted?" Arms replied. "It wasn't. We still have tails on Cotti."

"Are you kidding me? Why the charade?"

"I want to catch these guys. You think Cotti's just gonna stand around and do nothing? I don't think so. I believe a war is about to begin and I want us in the middle of it, arresting them as we catch them in the act. Even if Cotti gets killed, we'll still have his killers."

"Yeah, but if Cotti gets killed and we can't stop it before it happens, we'll make him a martyr for every wiseguy in the country," Lundy said. "But, at least there will be one less political powerhouse in the country," he added.

"Yeah, Talluchi may be trying to kill our future President," Arms replied, sarcastically.

"That's funny," Lundy answered.

***

Arms didn't know just how prophetic his words would become. But right at that moment, Cotti wasn't thinking about his political future; only about his future. If he stayed alive, then he could think about politics. If he was dead, *Forget about it!*

So, Cotti and Napolie put a plan together. Napolie would get two or three of his top hitters and take out Talluchi and his bodyguards.

***

Denneli had already given the contract to two of his more experienced soldiers. Cotti was to be hit as he entered his club, and any others that got in the way.

Fifteen minutes after getting the "go ahead," Talluchi's shooters were in place, waiting in a barber shop across the street from Cotti's club.

***

Cotti's shooters would be riding in a car directly behind his. That way, if anyone were to come after Cotti and entourage, they could be neutralized.

Chapter 6

Cotti knew that if what Agent Arms had told him about pulling their surveillance was true, then he would have an opportunity to hit first, before Talluchi could make his move.

What Cotti didn't know was that Denneli had sought out Napolie earlier that day and asked him to **take out** his boss or take the chance of getting hit himself along with Cotti.

***

"Johnny, you gotta clip Cotti," Denneli told Napolie. "His time has come. And you know it's gotta be done."

"Sorry, Ang," Napolie replied. "Can't do it. If I hit him, then I'll have a big bull's eye on my forehead."

"If you don't, you could get clipped too."

"I'll take my chances."

Denneli gave up trying to talk sense with Napolie and they both went their separate ways.

"Good luck!" Denneli said to Napolie as he walked away.

But it wasn't Napolie who turned on his boss; it was

Denneli who ratted out Talluchi to Parrissi.

***

The Feds had told Cotti to be very careful when leaving his home and to have as many bodyguards as possible surrounding him at all times until his Talluchi problem was fixed. But living on the edge was nothing new to Cotti. He feared no one. And most assuredly, nothing would stop him from going to his nightly watering hole: the Dergin Hunt and Fish Club.

***

Cotti's car pulled up in front of the club's entrance, and with his bodyguards in the car following close behind. Cotti waited for them to open his door. As they did, Talluchi's hitters came running at Cotti and entourage with guns blazing.

But shooting while running wasn't very accurate. Cotti was thrown to the ground by one of his bodyguards, as the bodyguard and his partner returned fire. Then, without warning, three other men also began firing at Talluchi's shooters. Both assassins were shot and killed, by either Cotti's bodyguards or by the three men—who were FBI Agents assigned to tail Cotti. Cotti and his bodyguards were unharmed, other than a few scrapes and bruises.

***

Napolie sent his two top hitters to Talluchi's club,

Dante's Inferno. His orders were to whack Talluchi, either coming out or going in. The hitters waited in their car for any sign of their **mark**. They watched a light red Cadillac pass by two or three times over a fifteen minute period; they knew wiseguys were inside. But the questions of who they were and what Family they belonged to went unanswered.

The same red Cadillac drove slowly by just as Talluchi was exiting through the front door of the club. The car suddenly stopped in the middle of the road, stopping the traffic behind it. Two men jumped out and began firing at Talluchi, emptying their guns.

Napolie's two gunmen sat stunned, in disbelief. This was their hit! They didn't know others were out to get Talluchi. And just when they thought the shooting was over, two other men dressed in black came running from down the street, now firing their weapons at the two hitters from the Cadillac, just as they were getting back into the red car. Both men were hit and fell into the street, dead.

The two men in black ran over to check the men's injuries. Then they checked to see if Talluchi had been hit. Talluchi was lying face down on the sidewalk. The men in black turned him over. Napolie's men could see blood trickling down from Talluchi's forehead to his chin. He apparently had been nicked in the head by one of the hitters' bullets. They saw Talluchi open his eyes.

The men flashed badges: even at a distance, Napolie's men knew they were FBI. They put their car into gear and drove away slowly, without making themselves look suspicious.

***

It was another failed mission for professional hit men. That was *three* failures within as many days. Four, if you counted Napolie's men's failure.

***

An ambulance arrived and took Talluchi to the hospital to get checked out. His wound wasn't serious, it was only a scratch. However, he was admitted overnight for observation, which gave the Feds a chance to question him. Agents Lundy and Arms did the honors.

They entered the room and stood before Talluchi.

"Mr. Talluchi, this is Agent Lundy." Arms pointed to his partner. "And I'm Agent Dennis Arms. We'd like to ask you a few questions about your near-death experience."

Lundy snickered.

"What near-death experience?" Talluchi asked.

"You know, your assassination attempt," Arms responded. "I was just being facetious about the near-death experience comment. But we identified your shooters; they belong to the Lucchese Family and are Parrissi's soldiers. Do you have anything to say?"

"I got nothing to say to you or anyone else," snapped Talluchi. "Now please get out of my room. I need my rest."

A nurse entered the room to give Talluchi a sleeping

90

pill and chased away the two Agents. "Please, gentlemen," she said, "you'll have to leave now and come back tomorrow. Mr. Talluchi must get his rest. He's got a nasty head wound."

The two agents left the room and headed for their headquarters.

***

Talluchi, on the other hand, lay thinking about who had tried to kill him. Was it the Commission who ordered it? Parrissi? Or Cotti? He had many to choose from who wanted him *dead*. He wondered if *his* hitters had gotten rid of Cotti. The Feds hadn't brought it up, so he was anxious to find out. But where was his Underboss? The only ones around were the medical crew and the two cops that were planted at the door for protection, just in case another try was made. Denneli was nowhere to be found.

***

Cotti was back at home, also wondering where his Underboss was. He hadn't heard from Napolie all day long. That wasn't like him. Now he wondered if Napolie had anything to do with the *hit*. Or was he lying dead somewhere?

Cotti began making phone calls to find his Underboss. Within just a few minutes, he found him. Napolie was sitting at home, listening to the news about the assassination attempts on two Godfathers.

The media was blasting the story all over TV and radio. The newspapers would tell their readers the following morning.

All week, Cotti had been the biggest story of the year. He had gotten more press than the wars, the President, and Putin combined. He was the biggest thing, at least for the media, since the first Moonwalk.

But there was an even bigger story on the horizon. The Commission had heard the news too and were even more upset that two Dons would take it upon themselves to put hits on each other at nearly the same time, and then to have another Don take it upon himself to get caught up in the melee. That was a *slap in the face* to the other Family Heads.

The Commission had voted to pick the Family that would take care of the Cotti problem the following day. But Talluchi had disobeyed Commission rules and had taken it upon himself to hit Cotti for a second time, again without Commission approval. And now they found out that Parrissi had tried to hit Talluchi, also without Commission approval. All Hell was breaking loose. If things didn't get straightened out and straightened out fast, this Family *spat* could get out of hand and become Family against Family. All because Jack Cotti wanted to get into politics.

***

Cotti contacted Napolie and instructed him to come to

his home. He needed Napolie to answer some important and pertinent questions.

***

Talluchi, on the other hand, would have to wait until the following day to contact his Underboss. He was sure the Feds were listening to his conversations. He decided to wait until his release from the hospital, although he hoped that Denneli would visit him there. That didn't happen. Talluchi learned from Fox News that his Underboss had been found dead from a gunshot wound to the back of the head.

"More news tonight on the war going on between the New York Mafia Families," exclaimed Commentator Campbell. "Angie Denneli, Underboss for the Genovese Crime Family, was found dead today with a gunshot wound to the back of the head. That's seven wiseguys dead within the last few days. And now, in other news—"

Talluchi was beside himself when he heard the news. He wanted to get out of his bed and find the ones responsible in the killing of his Underboss. He figured if Parrissi had ordered *his* hit, then he'd probably ordered the hit on Denneli, too. But his thinking drifted to Cotti. Cotti had ample reason to hit both him and Denneli. He could have hired Parrissi's soldiers to whack them to make it look like Parrissi had ordered the hit.

Talluchi was tired, confused, and angry. Cotti had started this shit! Now all the Families were involved. Just like they knew they would be. What was to come of them was anyone's guess. It was too soon to tell if these two skirmishes would turn into an all-out war between the Cotti and Talluchi Families. But both Talluchi and Cotti knew that this could be the start of a much bigger war. The *War of the Five Families*!

The Media, Feds, and Five Families were on the phones making contact with their people. The media personnel found that more and more people were on Cotti's side and still in favor of him running the country. In fact, that morning, the New York Times headline read: *Godfather President? Maybe!* Other papers had similar headlines. The New York Herald read: *Cotti 2, Hitters 0!* Another smaller paper's headline read: *Cotti: Fearless!*

The media were falling all over themselves to keep Cotti in the news. But Cotti was doing that all by himself. He was becoming the Paul Bunyan of men: Bigger in legend than in life. They couldn't get enough of him and his life story. "Poor guy makes good" was the gist of the stories written or spoken about him. His Mafia ties were barely mentioned anymore, if at all. The media commentators and writers were now making him out to be just a "*regular*" guy.

But the Feds didn't think Cotti was just a "*regular*" guy. They weren't selling newspapers, or TV and Radio ads, and they knew Cotti for what he was: a cold-blooded killing machine. No way would they sugar-coat it. No matter what the voters thought of him.

In fact, that night, ex-Mayor Giuliani gave his opinion on Cotti to Bill O'Reilly on The O'Reilly Factor. O'Reilly asked Giuliani the question that had captured the interest of all the people around the country: "With the two assassination attempts against Jack Cotti and all the Mafia killings lately, would you still vote for mobster Jack Cotti for President?"

Rudy was adamant against a Jack Cotti Presidency, and answered rather angrily, "Are you kidding? Cotti is a mobster, a killer, a thief, a hijacker and just a plain thug. If I was a prosecutor again, I would put him jail for life."

"You tried!" O'Reilly exclaimed. "Two times! And he beat you both times. He was acquitted and found 'not guilty' in both trials."

"Yeah, he got lucky," Giuliani quipped. "But I know the guy as he is. He's not some political *Don Juan,* as the papers call him. He's a murdering thug."

Many other political celebrities jumped in to downplay Cotti's sudden rise in popularity. Even John McLaughlin and his four political pundits of the McLaughlin Group gave Cotti some attention. McLaughlin asked them, "With all the negative comments and the seven killings within the last three days of Mafia members in New York City, do you think that will help or hurt mobster Jack Cotti's run for President? I ask you, Pat Buchanan."

Buchanan laughed, then said, "John, Cotti's popularity is nothing more than a *freak show.* He's a joke! The people aren't voting for him but against the establishment, the old guard. He's still got a ways to go to get into the Primaries. That is, if his enemies don't kill him first." All the pundits laughed at that one.

McLaughlin looked to Eleanor Clift. "I ask you the same question, Eleanor."

"Pat's right, John. Jack Cotti is nothing more than a conversation at a party. But you have to admit, John, he does have a snappy personality."

"Oh, come on now, Eleanor," snapped Buchanan.

"He does, Pat," replied Eleanor. "He comes across, at least on TV, as a likeable guy. But I see his run for President of the United States as a non-starter. There's more to running in a political election than being popular."

"So you do like him, don't you, Eleanor?" asked John.

"You better say *yes.* If you don't, he may have you whacked," joked Mort Zuckerman of World News. They all snickered and laughed at Mort's sick joke.

"Tom Rogan of National Review, do you have an opinion on this Mafia madness and Cotti's run for President?" asked McLaughlin.

"Yes, I do like him. But he's fooling himself if he thinks he can run for President. He hasn't even given a hint at which party he'd run for. It takes a lot more money to run in a Presidential election than his illegal enterprise can make. I don't think he'll even have the money to run in the Primaries."

"And now to you, Mort Zuckerman of World News. Give us your opinion on this Jack Cotti *thing,*" John said.

"Well, I like this guy too, John. I mean, look. They voted in George Bush and Obama. Why not Cotti?"

The rest of the panel gave him a stunned look.

"But seriously, John," Zuckerman continued, "how can conservative Republicans vote for a guy like that? I mean, he's a thug; he's a mobster who's in the Mafia, organized crime. Get real."

McLaughlin gave the last opinion of the show. "I say Jack Cotti has no chance in politics and won't get to first base when the running starts. That's all. Bye, Bye."

That was pretty much how all the news shows went that day. Many of the media commentators were now against Cotti. Oh, how soon they forgot. One day they were raving and saying good things about him and the next, bad things. They just couldn't make up their minds. Except for one— Rupert Murdoch and Company again stood up for Cotti and praised him for being a "tough and wise man."

***

Nearly everyone in the FBI and media thought all the negative comments against Cotti and his way of life, especially from the pundits, would bring him down. Later that night, however, they found out differently.

People again were calling and texting the stations and newspapers to disagree with the pundits. Jack Cotti was still their number one pick for President.

"He's someone you'd like to have a beer with at your favorite bar," opined a male viewer.

97

"He's handsome and a good husband," a female texted.

"You can't keep the man down. He gets shot at, hits the ground, and bounces right back up. I mean, even though he's in his seventies, he acts and looks like he's in his fifties. We need a tough guy like that in the White House," another male caller said.

The majority of the opinions were still for Cotti, despite his so-called failings in life. His popularity continued to rise. Fox News Commentator, Bob Campbell called Cotti: "A bright new star forming."

The Feds didn't care what the political pundits had to say about the **Mafia God**. They wondered how Cotti would react to his assassination attempts.

***

Cotti really didn't care. He wondered what had happened to his Underboss, and finally saw him when Napolie came to his home two days after being contacted. They sat in his office and talked.

"Where in the fuck were you when I got shot at?" Cotti asked.

"I'm sorry, Jack. I was taking care of some very important business."

"What's more important than my life?" Cotti asked.

"It's your life I *was* thinking about," Napolie snapped. Then he whispered to Cotti, in case someone was listening, "I wasn't around because I was the one that whacked Denneli."

The Godfather President

"You what?" bellowed Cotti. "What have you done?"

"Jack, when I explain, you'll understand."

"Start explaining!"

"Denneli ran into me on the street and told me to whack you or I could get hit too. So I played like I was gonna do it and followed him back to a storage locker where he kept some guns. He picked one out and gave it to me, loaded, and when he had his back turned, I shot him in the back of the head. I was gonna tell you...but when I saw the cops and Feds outside the club, with the two shooters lying dead on the street, I hightailed it out of there and laid low until now."

Cotti digested Napolie's excuse. The phone rang and he answered it. "Yeah."

"Don Cotti, this is Scarfino. The Commission requests your presence at an emergency meeting at the Selsor Hotel tomorrow afternoon at two. It is important that you be there."

"Yes, Don Scarfino. I will be there," Cotti replied. He hung up the phone.

Napolie looked to Cotti for the reason Scarfino had called. "What's up, Jack?"

"Forget about it! The Commission wants another meeting tomorrow at two."

"Where?" Napolie asked.

"Where else? The Selsor Hotel."

"Fuck, Jack. The Feds will be all over that place. We might as well plant our flag that says, 'the Mafia meets here every chance we get'."

"Forget about it! It's not the Feds I'm worried about. I'm just wondering if I'll get out of there alive."

"Don't show up," Napolie suggested.

Cotti shook his head. "I have to show, Johnny. If I don't, it's a guarantee that they'll kill me."

"Well, at least let me go with you."

Cotti nodded. "Okay, you can come along. Just don't mention anything about Denneli or the hits. If they ask, we don't know nothing. *Capisce*?"

"Forget about it!" Napolie replied.

Cotti knew that Commission usually held a meeting once every five years, unless there was an urgent matter to contend with. Now they were about to have their third meeting in a week. All thanks to him, Jack Cotti.

"What do you think it's about?" Napolie asked.

"What else? The hits. They know a war is about to erupt and they want to nip it in the bud before it starts. Forget about it!"

"I hope you're right. I'll pick you up at one."

"Just make sure that Travano's crew follows us. Let them guard the exits just in case. We don't make it out alive, neither will they. If they kill me, I want every one of them motherfuckers DEAD!"

"See you tomorrow, Jack," Napolie said, and he walked out the front door and to his car.

***

Napolie was true to his word. He picked Cotti up precisely at one o'clock and then drove to the Selsor Hotel, with two cars of hitters following close behind.

Cotti and Napolie entered the hotel. The eight gunmen, strapped to the hilt, secured both the front and rear exits. The gunmen knew what had to be done in case their boss didn't make it out alive.

Chapter 7

The meeting started right on time, with all five Family Heads sitting around the conference table, smoking their cigars and eating fruit. There was no joking around with one another and no friendly chats, as everyone, including the Underbosses, was in a somber mood.

The room remained quiet for nearly five minutes before Scarfino, the eighty-three-year-old boss, stood and began the meeting. "We are here today to see if we can put an end to this fighting, this bloodshed," he said, slowly looking around the room to each Don for their cooperation with their problem.

"Fighting? Hell! Talluchi tried to kill me...Twice!" shouted Cotti.

"Don Cotti, Don Cotti, please! *Calma, Calma,*" begged Don Scarfino, in his broken-English. "There's been too much killing, too much bloodshed. The Feds are tailing all of us and interfering in our business. This can't continue."

"You tell Talluchi that!" snarled Cotti. "Unless he tried to hit me on Commission's orders and you were all part of it, then we have nothing more to say. But if Talluchi took it upon himself to whack me, then that problem is between me and Talluchi."

"Fuck him," shouted Talluchi. "He whacked out my Underboss, Angie Denneli, who was like a brother to me." He suddenly looked at Parrissi. "And what about Parrissi? It was his soldiers that tried to kill me and were killed themselves by the Feds."

"I had nothing to do with that, Tommy, I swear," whined Parrissi.

OK. Enough!" yelled Scarfino, looking tired, frail, and weak. "We came here today to try and settle our differences."

"Yeah, but to do that, Cotti has to stop his *fucking* Politics!" snarled Talluchi, chomping on the cigar clenched between his yellowing teeth.

Cotti answered his new nemesis. "You guys sitting here at this table promised and allowed me to try my hand at Politics without any interference. But since that meeting...that's all I've had. You all said that I'd be 'laughed right out of politics.' That everybody would think I had lost my mind. But look what's happened. The people *love* me. The polls say that if the election were held today, I'd win by a landslide. A LANDSLIDE! I've made liars out of the political pundits and pollsters. Or *fools*. Take your pick."

"Yes, Don Cotti. The people love you," interjected Don Farcano, "but they are not the ones that count right now. We are! You must put politics aside and listen to your brothers sitting at this table."

"Quit pussy-footing around," Talluchi told the others. "Cotti's the reason we're having this meeting." He looked at Cotti and pointed his finger at him in anger. "You're the one who started this problem. We shouldn't have allowed you to get into politics. So this Commission was also at fault. All of us here, sitting at this table, approved Jack's political career. But now it must stop. It must end," Talluchi demanded, pounding his fist on the tabletop. "We cannot allow this to go on!"

"Fuck you! I will not stop," Cotti bellowed. He jumped up from his chair. "I will fight to my last fuckin' dying breath." He looked at his peers. "You sitting here are friends of mine, in this thing of ours, but if you go back on your words, then all bets are off. The streets will be flooded with the blood of our Cosa Nostra brothers. You decide how this will end."

Talluchi and Cotti continued their heated argument, blaming each other for the debacle. They stood nose to nose, ready to start a new bloody war.

Scarfino intervened. "Boys, boys! That's enough!" he yelled. Suddenly, his body wobbled and he keeled over.

The argument between the two Dons stopped as they looked at Scarfino lying on the floor. Scarfino's Underboss, Carlo Lambino, sat his boss up, loosened his tie, and slapped his face to get a reaction. Scarfino moaned and moved his head slowly from side to side. He was out of it. But nobody at the meeting remembered to call an ambulance.

***

Fortunately, the Feds were listening in on the meeting and had an ambulance there before any of the wiseguys dialed nine-one-one.

Scarfino was wheeled out of the hotel, with his Underboss in tow, and the meeting continued as if nothing had happened. Talluchi and Cotti continued yelling at one another, but this time from their chairs.

"Talluchi, I didn't start this shit. You did!" Cotti barked. "You gave me your word that I could do this thing of mine. And then you try to whack me! If I killed you now, no one sitting at this table could deny me my revenge."

All but Talluchi nodded in agreement.

"You had Denneli whacked," snarled Talluchi. "I know it was you!"

"I had nothing to do with his murder. You blamed Parrissi for trying to whack you. Maybe he was the one who had Denneli killed!"

"I didn't have anyone whacked," shouted Parrissi. "I...."

Parrissi suddenly stopped when a desk clerk came into the room and handed him a note. Parrissi read it. "I'm sorry to say...," he said, "but Don Scarfino passed away before reaching the hospital."

"That's your fault," Talluchi told Cotti.

"Fuck you!" Cotti yelled. "Fuck all of you! I'm gonna

do what I'm gonna do. And if any of you get in my way, all bets are off."

Cotti stormed out of the meeting and Napolie followed.

***

Nothing was settled. The three Dons were stunned and very pissed off at the outcome of the meeting. But they stayed to talk about their next move. Talluchi, as always, took over the meeting.

"I'm sorry to say that our dear friend, Jack Cotti, has left us with only one decision, one which we should have made the minute we heard about his idea to get into politics. But we didn't believe it would get this far. Now that it has, we can't allow it to go on any longer. We must stop this...this cancer from growing any bigger. This cancer within our midst. Let us now take a vote either to stop Jack Cotti or allow him to continue in this *wave of destruction*." Talluchi looked to his peers. "Do any of you have anything to say before we vote?"

The room was quiet for a good minute. Then Parrissi stood up and spoke. "I want to make certain that Talluchi won't go to war with me. He thinks I tried to clip him and he may want revenge. Let Don Talluchi promise me, before we leave here today, that all past aggression is forgotten."

"I don't have to promise a fucking thing," Talluchi replied. "We are here to solve a bigger problem."

"Talluchi, *you* are a problem to *me*," Parrissi

acknowledged. "I want your word."

"Fuck you! You sent your hitters to clip me. You know and I know. So don't try to make excuses."

"You tried to hit Cotti without Commission approval," Parrissi barked. "You broke the rules."

"Maybe I did," Talluchi admitted. "I only did it because I didn't want Cotti to do his interview. I was doing it for all the Families."

"You couldn't have waited one more day?" Farcano asked. "That's when we would have had the meeting we're having now...about this very problem."

"I thought it...too...important. We didn't need the publicity," Talluchi replied. "But that doesn't excuse Parrissi for admitting that he was the one that sent the hitmen."

Parrissi's face reddened and his demeanor turned ugly. "So what if I did," he snapped, glaring deep into Talluchi's eyes.

"Then you did it without Commission approval. So if I'm guilty of breaking the rules, you are too," Talluchi snarled, giving Parrissi the evil eye.

***

While Talluchi and Parrissi were arguing, Cotti and Napolie planned their attacks on their enemies.

Cotti was going on the offensive. "We're gonna take out all my enemies. Anyone that's against me...for *anything*—the window deal, my running for President—I want

DEAD!"

"But Jack—" whined Napolie.

"Don't **but Jack**, me. They're gonna hit me and maybe you, too. I won't let that happen. I'll get them first."

"Don't you think you're taking this a bit too far? You're talking about taking out all Four Families."

"No, we'll go after the Capos and Dons. We just kill one or two in each Family and they'll crawl back to me, begging me to stop the war."

"I hope you're right," Napolie replied.

"I want you to get every hitter we got and tell them who to hit," Cotti ordered.

"We'll have to dig a lot of holes out at the marshes," Napolie quipped.

"Then get the dockworkers on Pier 7 and have them use the bodies for fish bait."

Napolie just shook his head in disbelief and continued driving with a helpless look on his face.

***

Cotti and Napolie continued their conversation, one that the Feds couldn't hear because the two wiseguys had the radio turned up loud enough to neutralize the bugs. The meeting with the three Dons broke up, with nothing getting solved. Talluchi, Parrissi, and Farcano left as Cotti had: all pissed off at each other. Now it was a free-for-all.

If a war did break out, it would be among all Five Families; and the Feds believed it would happen sooner rather than later. Trust among the Dons no longer existed. Each Family was now against the others. They were no longer partners in crime. Only for themselves. And all because Jack Cotti wanted to run for President.

***

The Feds were still waiting for their new budget, Agent Arms was worried that he didn't have enough agents to tail all the wiseguys that needed to be tailed, in order to stop any premeditated killings in this volatile situation. And they still needed to figure out what Napolie and Cotti had talked about in the car.

***

Meanwhile, Cotti and Napolie put their plan into play. Cotti went into hiding while Napolie gave his shooters the go-ahead to hit the Talluchi Capo, Nicodemus Pravachi.

Cotti knew that the Feds were tailing him, so he got lost and stayed hidden for the next few weeks. The Feds tried finding him by honing in on his phone calls, but Cotti was now using throw-away phones that weren't traceable, so the Feds had no idea where Cotti had gone. Only Napolie knew where Cotti was hiding.

While Cotti laid low, he used his time by returning calls from TV and radio affiliates for more interviews, and made calls to the Chairs of the Republican, Democratic, Independent, and Green Parties to speak with them about joining their party, if they'd have him.

Cotti's first call was to National Republican Party Chair Reince Prebius. The switchboard operator wasn't going to allow his call to go through, until she was told the caller's name.

"Jack Cotti!" she gleefully exclaimed. "Are you the gangster that wants to run for President?"

"Yes, that's me," Cotti replied, somewhat surprised that she had heard of him.

"Mr. Cotti, I just want to say that you have my vote."

"Thank you, Ms. I appreciate that."

"Just a second and I'll put you through to Mr. Prebius. And you have a great day, Mr. Cotti."

A few seconds later, Mr. Prebius answered his phone. "Yes, this is Mr. Prebius."

"Mr. Prebius, this is Jack Cotti. I'd like to set up—"

"Excuse me, who are you?"

"I'm Jack Cotti. I'm wanting to run for President and I haven't yet chosen a Party. I would like to set up a meeting with you and talk it over."

"I'm sorry, ah, Mr. Cotti, but you'll have to speak to one of my underlings about that. I don't get involved with people I don't know. Are you a donor?"

"No, sir. I'm the guy that did the interview on Fox about a week ago. I'm getting a lot of publicity about wanting to run for President."

"Wait a minute. You're not that gangster from New York City, are you?"

"Yeah, that's me. Forget about it!"

"Well, Mr. Cotti. Neither I, nor the Republican National Committee, want any involvement with you and your kind."

"Get off your high horse, Mister. You do not disrespect me. Do you understand?" Cotti warned.

Prebius just realized who he was talking to and didn't want to end up missing, so he changed his tune. "I'm sorry, Mr. Cotti. I didn't mean to sound demeaning," he said apologetically. "So, what can I do for you?"

"First, I want to know what demeaning means? It sounds dirty and disgusting. So what does it mean?"

"Are you being facetious, Mr. Cotti?" asked Prebius.

"What does facetious mean? I don't like the words you use," Cotti snapped.

"I'm sorry, Mr. Cotti, but if you're planning on running for President, you better learn how to use the dictionary."

"Fuck the dictionary. I want you to meet me at Sparks Restaurant in New York City."

"But, Mr. Cotti, I live in Washington, DC."

"Well, take a plane. And when you get to New York, I want you to go straight to the Selsor Hotel and wait to hear from me. Your room will be reserved. I'll contact you within minutes of your arrival. Then I'll meet you at Sparks Restaurant."

"What time? When?"

"I can't tell you that right now. I have to be very careful. A lot of people in my community are not too fond of politics or politicians. If you get my meaning?"

"I'll leave tomorrow morning," Prebius promised.

***

Prebius was shaken after talking with Cotti. He wondered if he should go as promised. He talked with a few of his assistants and they suggested in the strongest of terms that *he go*.

Prebius was now afraid. If he refused Cotti's demand to run on a Republican ticket, he might not leave New York alive. He had two of his security team tag along.

But he didn't know that Cotti was one step ahead. Prebius's security guards worked for a company that a Cotti Capo owned. So when Prebius and company landed at JFK airport, the two security guards suddenly got lost and walked away while Prebius gathered his luggage.

Prebius saw that his security team was nowhere to be seen. After waiting more than an hour, he flagged down a cab that took him straight to the Selsor Hotel. He checked in and called Cotti, and then took the Hotel's limousine to Sparks. The clock was nearing eight pm when he entered the restaurant. He wasn't looking forward to the meeting with Cotti, but he knew he had to attend.

Cotti was already sitting down at his reserved table and had the headwaiter bring Prebius to him. He stood up and introduced himself. "Mr. Prebius, I'm Jack Cotti."

They shook hands.

"I'm glad to meet you, Mr. Cotti," Prebius said, his voice shaking. "I'm Reince Prebius. It's nice to meet you."

They took their seats. Cotti remained silent for a good minute, just staring at Prebius. He suddenly came out of his daydream and began telling Prebius the reason why he had asked him to New York City. "Mr. Prebius—"

"Call me Reince, Mr. Cotti. We don't have to be so formal."

"And you can call me Jack," answered Cotti. "The reason I asked you to this meeting is that I'm looking for a Party to back me for my run for President of the United States."

Prebius snickered. He stopped laughing when he realized Cotti wasn't joking. He was serious. *Dead* serious. "I'm sorry, Jack. You were saying?" Prebius asked, between sips of water.

"Well, that can wait," Cotti replied. "We'll talk business after we eat."

The waiter handed them menus, but Cotti was a regular so he wanted to order for Prebius. He ordered linguini with clams for both of them.

"I'm sorry, Jack, but I'm allergic to clams. I need to order something different, like spaghetti and meatballs."

Cotti didn't want to hear it. He was adamant that Prebius try his favorite dish. Prebius tried to refuse Cotti's selection but Cotti would have none of it. He gave his guest the evil eye, the killer look.

Prebius quit complaining and just sank silently back into his seat.

When their food arrived, Prebius again tried to object,

although half-heartedly, to his dinner.

Cotti held up his hand, wanting Prebius to remain quiet and eat.

Prebius reluctantly began eating his linguini with clams.

About ten minutes into the meal, Cotti noticed big red blotches on Prebius's face. "Hey, Reince, you got some big red blotches on your face."

Prebius began to scratch like crazy, so Cotti began feeding him wine, and lots of it. In fact, in less than an hour, Prebius had drank over three bottles of red wine and was nearly falling asleep. Cotti had Prebius loaded into his limousine and taken back to the hotel.

There, he had friends undress Prebius and then took lewd photos of him with a number of male and female prostitutes doing the "*Wild Thing*." Cotti wanted them for leverage, in case he needed a "favor" at a later date, especially if he decided to run on the Republican ticket.

The next morning, Cotti met Prebius at the hotel restaurant, where they ate breakfast and continued their conversation from the night before.

"Damn, I've got a headache," exclaimed Prebius.

"Yeah, you were pretty drunk last night. Forget about it! You drank three bottles of wine in less than an hour."

"Please, I hope you're not ordering breakfast for me. But if you do, make sure you don't order clams."

Cotti laughed. "Forget about it! You can order your own breakfast."

And Prebius did. After eating very little, he asked Cotti why he was there.

"I want to see what the Republican National Committee can do for me if I decide to run on a Republican ticket," Cotti replied.

Prebius didn't know what to say. He was stuck between a rock and a hard place. He wouldn't be Chair very much longer if he backed Cotti on a Republican ticket. Then again, if he denied him, he might not leave New York City alive—either that, or he could go missing. Prebius asked Cotti the only question he could think of at that moment. "Mr. Cotti, why do you think you'd make a good Republican candidate?"

Cotti thought for a good minute and then replied, "My morals and views about business and life are of Republican values. I'm a Republican at heart. I mean, people have called me ignorant, mean, egotistical, and that I have no conscience and only care for myself. Those are pretty much the same qualities of most Republican politicians in Washington. Are they not, Reince?"

Prebius sat stone-faced, not believing what he had just heard. He shook his head. "Mr. Cotti, are you serious? *You* have no morals. You're a gangster, a killer."

Cotti nodded. "Even so," he answered, "the voters seem to like me. I mean, they voted your guys into office, didn't they?"

Prebius didn't know how to answer Cotti.

So Cotti answered for him. "Hey, those politicians are

crooks like me. They are no better. I mean, they blackmail the lobbyists to give them money, homes, stock tips, whatever they're asked to give. And if they don't, they're ignored and the politicians vote against their bill. Just because they make the laws to protect themselves from jail doesn't mean they're not criminals. I mean...Forget about it! That's America. We have the most corrupt politicians and government in the world. So how are they different from me?"

"Mr. Cotti, they are not criminals," Prebius retorted.

"Reince, if you believe that, then I've never killed anyone in my life and am not a member of the Mafia," Cotti shot back.

Prebius became nervous. He drank his glass of water in one gulp to quench his thirst. He didn't know how to get out of the predicament he was in. He was flabbergasted by Cotti's defamation claims against his Party's politicians. Even though Cotti could be right, Prebius just didn't want to believe it.

"So what do you want me to do, Mr. Cotti?"

Cotti looked him straight in the eyes with an evil glare and said, "I would like you to tell me that if I decide to run as a Republican, you and the Committee will back me."

Prebius swallowed hard, scratched his head, and said something that he would regret. "I'm sorry, Mr. Cotti, I can't back you. And I don't think the Republican Committee can endorse a Cotti Presidency. Although, if you do decide to run as a Republican, I can't stop you. You just won't get funding."

"Well, I thought you might say that, so I want you to take a close look at something you and your wife might be interested in." Cotti snapped his fingers.

One of the dozen soldiers who were guarding Cotti from harm came over and handed Prebius a dozen or so eight inch by ten inch photographs—the ones that had been taken the night before in his hotel room.

Prebius looked at a few of them and threw them on the table. "What the hell are these?" he snarled, looking at Cotti with hatred in his eyes.

Prebius now knew how it felt to really want to kill a person; to hate someone so much that the hatred permeated out of every pore in his body. He thought that if he had had a gun in his possession, he might well have used it at that moment on Cotti.

"Now, now, Reince," Cotti quipped, as he grabbed the photos and motioned for the soldier to return to his seat. "These will never get out if you do as I say."

"I'll see you in jail first," Prebius promised Cotti.

Cotti snickered. "Reince, I don't think you're thinking rationally. You have a big family and I wouldn't want any harm to come to them. So, you might wanna think this thing out."

"Fuck you!" shouted Prebius. He couldn't believe the words that just left his mouth. He was a bible-thumping, religious man and had never sworn. He figured that he was just so upset and angry that those words had just come out on their own, without coaxing from his brain.

Cotti tried to calm the situation. "Hey, easy, Reince. Don't get so upset. It's just business. Listen, I have many values that are Republican virtues. Then again, there are some that I can't get behind. I mean, you guys, for some reason, can't see reality. Take abortion. I mean, I'm against it, but hell, I'm not the one having the baby. Ultimately, the woman decides that question, not some lying politician that cares nothing for the fetus, only for the Christian vote. Forget about it!"

"How can you say that?" replied Prebius.

"Easy. If these politicians cared about those unwanted lives, then they would go and adopt a half dozen of them. But do they do that? Hell, no! They're all talk and no action."

Prebius didn't want to agree with Cotti, but he did. "Yes, you may be right."

"Well, hell, even if the Republican Party wanted to back me, I don't know if I could, in conscience, accept their offer. I just might have to start my own party," Cotti joked.

Prebius was relieved when he heard Cotti say he wasn't right for his Party. "Well, Mr. Cotti, if we're finished here, I ought to be getting back to DC."

They finished their coffee, stood, and shook hands.

As Prebius was walking away, Cotti barked, "I'll let you know the Party I will run on within a month or so."

***

While Cotti was busy eating breakfast, the Feds were busy trying to track him down. They had no idea where he had gone, even though his name was ringing loud and clear over most airwaves of the many TV and radio stations. His name was already synonymous with mobster; now, it was becoming synonymous with politics. And Cotti was going to give the people much more to talk about.

***

Cotti returned to his hideout, went right to his phone, and contacted Debbie Wasserman, the Democratic National Committee Chair. He wanted a meeting with her as he had with Prebius, wanting to see if *they* would help him in his bid to jump into the political arena.

The operator put him right through to the Chair. Wasserman was taken aback, like Prebius had been, when she found out who she was speaking with.

"Excuse me," Wasserman said, "who are you?"

"I'm Jack Cotti from New York City and would like a meeting with you."

"You're not the mobster that's been all over the news lately, are you?"

"Yes, Ma'am, that's me. I need to speak with you about my run for President."

She gave nearly the same answer as Prebius had. "Mr. Cotti, are you serious? It takes a lot of money and organization to run a campaign. That is no easy task."

"That's why I'm calling you. I'm thinking of running on

a Democratic ticket and thought maybe your organization could help me."

"I very seriously doubt it. I don't think the Democratic Party and a mobster have very much in common."

"Mrs. Wasserman, you are not being very helpful. It would be in your best interest to meet with me as soon as possible."

"Why? Are you going to bump me off if I don't meet with you?"

Cotti laughed. "I think you're getting ahead of yourself. I'm not threatening you. All I'm asking for is a sit-down; a meeting to talk over my reasons for wanting to run on a Democratic ticket and to see if our values are similar."

"What values? You kill people."

"Ma'am, you're very antagonistic. I am not your enemy," Cotti replied, adding, "Not yet!"

That last sentence stunned her. She was taken aback by Cotti's bluntness. She then decided it was better to hear what he had to say, rather than ignore him and possibly make her his enemy.

"Ok, Mr. Cotti, you win. But we'll have to set it up for..." She looked in her appointment book. "Let's see, do you want to have the meeting here in DC or someplace else?"

"I can't travel that far," Cotti told her.

"How in the hell are you going to run a campaign if you can't leave the state?"

"I guess I didn't make myself clear. It's not that I can't;

it's just that a few people would like to see me dead."

Wasserman thought, *Yeah, and I'm one of them*.

"I would be taking too many chances if I left the city," Cotti added. "So let's have the meeting here, in New York City."

Again, Wasserman looked in her appointment book. "I have to be in New York a week from today. How about we get together then?"

"Good. I'll contact you the day before and let you know where to meet me and the time."

"Very good. But let me say this, as bluntly as possible, Mr. Cotti: I am not looking forward to this meeting at all. You're not the kind of person I want to be involved with."

With that said, she hung up the phone, as did Cotti.

Cotti heard a knock on the door. It was Napolie. He came to give Cotti an update on the *War of the Five Families*.

Chapter 8

Napolie was clearly upset when he entered the room.

"Jack, we just hit Nicodemus Pravachi. One of our guys was killed too. I gotta feeling *shit's gonna hit the fan*. All hell's gonna break loose. What do we do now?"

"What are we gonna do? We hit 'em harder. We hit 'em until they say '*Uncle*.' I want this war to end sooner rather than later."

Napolie shrugged and changed the subject. "I heard about your meeting at Sparks. Whatever you do, don't go back there anytime soon. Parrissi and the others have been checking *it* and other favorite places of yours."

"I figured as much. I have to keep a very low profile if I don't want to end up dead. But I can't stay hidden too much longer. In fact, on Sunday, I'm doing a live interview with the guy on Meet the Press. What's his name?"

"How in the fuck would I know? Forget about it!" Napolie snapped.

"I think his name is Chuck Todd."

"So, who gives a fuck?" Napolie replied. "You better take lots of bodyguards with you 'cause I won't be coming with you. I'll be taking care of business. Forget about it!"

"Well, if I do, they'll have to follow behind the limo that NBC is sending. I'll take a few of the guys with me and the rest can follow. But no one knows where I'm at. And I told NBC to pick me up two blocks away, at the coffee shop."

"Well, you just be careful," Napolie said, leaving the hideout.

Cotti waited patiently for his interview with NBC.

***

Talluchi hit back against both Cotti and Parrissi. Two wiseguys came up to Sal Vichenzi, the Cotti Capo, and two of his crew and gunned them down before they knew what hit them. At nearly the same time, two others from Talluchi's Family were also hitting the Parrissi Capo, Pauli Gilanti, killing him and an innocent bystander and nearly hitting Parrissi himself.

That was three Family Heads nearly assassinated by rival Families within the last couple of weeks. They were all breaking Cosa Nostra rules.

***

The Feds were up in arms over the *War of the Five Families* and weren't sure how to handle it. They wanted to speak to Talluchi and Cotti, but did not know where they were. With no budget money left in FBI coffers, Supervisor Arms was also hard-pressed to use any new personnel and had to continue using agents already in the field to search for and find both Cotti and Talluchi.

It seemed as though the two Dons had suddenly disappeared into thin air. His agents were disgruntled, overworked, underpaid, and just tired of following these thugs around. They were happy the thugs were killing each other. But that changed when an innocent man was killed for being in the wrong place at the wrong time.

The politicians that ran government also wanted these senseless killings stopped. And Cotti's name kept coming up among the TV and radio commentators, who were giving editorials against the mobsters and especially political wannabe Jack Cotti.

***

So, when Sunday came around, Jack Cotti was at the NBC station without incident, and ready to speak to his "public." He would give this interview without being given the questions beforehand, and anything was fair game.

Cotti and his two bodyguards met with Chuck Todd. Cotti and Todd then sat face to face for the live interview. Cotti felt cool and confident, like the owner of Secretariat after winning the Triple Crown. Nothing could stop him from giving this interview. No one, that is, but the FBI.

Todd had just asked Cotti which Party he would run on, when the room suddenly filled with FBI agents.

Agent Arms came up to Cotti, who was still sitting in his chair, and introduced himself. "Mr. Cotti, I'm FBI

Agent Dennis Arms. I'm sorry, but you'll have to come with me to FBI headquarters for questioning."

Cotti actually looked shocked. "You've got to be kidding me," he exclaimed. "Can't you see I'm giving an interview?"

"I'm sorry, Mr. Cotti, but you must come with us."

"Am I under arrest?" Cotti asked.

"No. We just need to ask you some important questions concerning some murders."

Cotti shrugged, apologized to his host, and stood up to leave with his nemesis. He was used to FBI harassment. He didn't act crazy or put up a fight; he went quietly, as if he had done it many times before.

Cotti's bodyguards hailed a cab and had the driver follow the Feds to FBI headquarters. There, they stood guard outside the building, waiting for their boss to return.

In custody, Cotti cooperated and answered as many questions as he could without incriminating himself. Nearly two hours later, the Feds decided to kick him loose, knowing they had nothing on him that could stick and not wanting to blow another case—especially after already losing three Federal cases against Cotti.

Cotti left the building and was confronted by his bodyguards and his lawyer, DomAchelli. He and his attorney talked for a few minutes before leaving in DomAchelli's car. One of the bodyguards noticed a car following it and determined it was the Feds. They were tailing Cotti, evidently not wanting to lose him again.

***

Cotti ordered DomAchelli to lose the tail. "Dom, lose 'em."

DomAchelli sped up and started driving recklessly until he was nearly one block ahead of the Feds.

Cotti suddenly yelled, "Dom, turn here!" He pointed to an underground garage where, coincidently, he had a car stashed there. It was owned by Napolie's mistress, but used by Cotti for secret and romantic rendezvous.

Cotti directed DomAchelli to his ride and ordered his lawyer to stop. He and his two bodyguards jumped out and quickly got into the unlocked car. Cotti got behind the wheel and a few seconds later, both cars sped out of the garage parking lot and headed in separate directions. No Feds tailed either of them. Cotti had lost them—for the time being, anyway.

Cotti drove to his hideout. He parked the car and went inside. The two bodyguards stood outside, securing the area.

Cotti made some important phone calls. First, he summoned his Underboss to his place for an update on the war. The second call went to the NBC station and Chuck Todd. Cotti wanted to ask him for another interview, seeing that the first one had never gotten off the ground.

"I can promise you that the Feds will not interfere with this interview," Cotti said.

Todd was apologetic but wasn't sure if the producer

would allow another interview when the first one had gone so badly. "I don't think the producer will allow it," he told Cotti.

"Please, go ask him. I'm sure he'll say yes. I'm good for the ratings. Forget about it!"

Todd agreed and did as Cotti asked. A few minutes later, he spoke to Cotti about the interview. "Mr. Cotti, I did get permission to do the interview but I'm not certain when we can do it. I will have to get back with you for a date and time."

"It will be in the next few days, will it not?" Cotti asked.

"I really don't know. It will be up to my producer. Let me get your number and I will get back to you as soon as I have an answer."

"Forget about it! No one has my number. I'll call you back tomorrow. Have an answer for me!" Cotti hung up the phone in disgust.

Cotti was fuming with anger at not getting an answer for his interview. He lit a cigar to calm his nerves. He sat down to enjoy it, when gunfire erupted outside his hideout. He ran to the front door, thinking that his bodyguards were taking lead or returning fire.

He opened the door to déjà vu all over again. Three of Talluchi's men were shot and killed: two lying in the street and the other sitting in the driver's seat of the getaway car. One of his own bodyguards lay dead on the sidewalk and Napolie, shot in the shoulder, was sitting against Cotti's building, bleeding.

"What the fuck happened?" Cotti shouted. He looked at the dead bodies and then to his Underboss. "How ya doing, Johnny?" He kneeled down and placed his handkerchief on Napolie's wounded shoulder. "What the fuck did you do? You led the motherfucking shooters right to me."

"Sorry, Jack," was all Napolie could say.

***

Cotti was so busy with Napolie he failed to recognize the FBI agents in his midst. They had followed Napolie, hoping he would lead them to Cotti. Evidently, they had guessed right.

It was the Feds that had done most of the damage. Cotti's bodyguards did defend themselves when confronted by Talluchi's shooters, but the Feds, five of them, also opened fire seconds after the shooters began firing their weapons. They wouldn't know for sure who killed whom until the coroner dug the bullets out of the bodies and ballistics matched them to the guns. But the Feds believed that their agents had shot and killed all that were dead and believed it was their bullet that had also wounded Napolie, even though Napolie had no gun. He was simply collateral damage.

The police arrived and put tape around the crime scene. Reporters began arriving as well; TV commentators and crews took pictures of the scene while trying to get Cotti's attention.

"Mr. Cotti, Mr. Cotti," shouted a female correspondent,

holding a microphone. "Can you tell us what happened here?"

Cotti ignored her. He was still kneeling and trying to calm his Underboss as the paramedics placed him on a stretcher and then into an ambulance. When Cotti stood up, the media people began waving their hands to get his attention. When they asked him questions about the shootings, he ignored them. When they asked him about his run for the Presidency, however, he smiled and strolled to one reporter he had spoken to before.

"Mr. Cotti, Bobby Legend here," the reporter said. "Can I ask you a few questions about your political ambitions?"

"Yeah, I remember you. You're the reporter that called me the Godfather President," Cotti exclaimed.

"Yes, sir. How is your political career going?"

Cotti smiled and gave him a look of concern. "Right now, I'm more concerned about my friends and their families. I'll be going to a few funerals soon. And possibly my own, if this killing keeps up."

"Everyone saw what happened to you on live TV. You didn't get to do your interview. Will you do more interviews in the future?"

Cotti nodded. "I hope to. That is, if they'll have me. But right now, I'm having a little Family problem that I need to resolve, and in a hurry."

"Is that what's happened here? Was this a Family dispute?" Legend pointed to the dead bodies being loaded into the coroner's van.

"You could say that," Cotti replied.

Just as Legend was about to ask Cotti another question, an FBI Agent came strolling over and whispered into Cotti's ear: "Beware of the man in the pin-striped suit."

Cotti gave him a look of bewilderment. "What the fuck are you talking about? I'm supposed to beware of a New York Yankee?"

Cotti was confused. The man who was really synonymous with a pin-striped suit was Scarfino, but he was dead. It was actually Talluchi who was Cotti's biggest enemy at the moment. Or so he thought. Cotti decided that while his Underboss was in the hospital having surgery on his shoulder, he needed to speak with his Consiglieri. But Benny "the brain" Bartolo was in Miami doing business with Carmine Batalia, an associate of the Family.

Once the Feds had completed their investigation at the scene, Cotti was allowed to leave with his bodyguard. Cotti knew he couldn't stay at his hideout any longer so the two wiseguys went to their club. There, Cotti contacted his Consiglieri.

"Get your ass back here *now!*" he ordered into the phone. "Johnny's been shot and I need you here with me. And when you get here, you and I will go see Johnny."

Bartolo told Cotti that he'd meet him at the club the following morning.

***

Cotti then phoned the NBC studios and spoke with Tom Holt, the producer of Meet the Press.

"Yes, Mr. Cotti," said Holt. "I'm looking forward at doing another interview with you—"

"When?" Cotti replied, rather abruptly.

"As soon as possible. I haven't really had time to set it up yet."

"Well, find the time. My time is valuable, and other stations are wanting to do interviews with me. I can't wait forever."

"What other stations are you talking about, Mr. Cotti?" Holt asked.

"Forget about it! Do we do the interview or not?"

"When are you available?" Holt asked nervously.

"Look, Mr....Mr...."

"Holt. My name is Tom Holt." Holt had a squeamish feeling go through his body. He'd just given his name to a guy that could make him disappear. So, if by chance he made Cotti upset, Cotti's people could track him down and kill him.

"Listen, Holt, I'm available any time. Just tell me WHEN!"

"Well, we won't be able to do it live. We can tape the interview and then show it Sunday."

"Can we do it two days from today?"

"I'm sorry, Mr. Cotti, but that's impossible. It would take a miracle to get it done then."

"Hey, just make it happen!" Cotti ordered. "You'll

thank me for it," he added.

What could Holt say? He wasn't about to argue with Jack Cotti. So he took the easy way out. "That's fine," he answered meekly.

"See. You're a miracle worker." Cotti laughed.

"Can you come in at six a.m.?"

"I sleep in. I'll be there at ten."

Holt hung up. He quickly dabbed his sweating forehead with his handkerchief and heaved a quick sigh of relief.

***

Cotti hung up the phone and then ate a full plate of spaghetti and meatballs. Afterwards, he returned home to relax.

The next morning, he and his half-dozen bodyguards were at the club by nine. While Cotti's soldiers were busy standing guard outside and in, Cotti was busy drinking coffee, eating cannolis and smoking his cigar. An hour later, Bartolo was sitting at the table doing the same.

Cotti gave him an update on the situation. He'd figured Bartolo was in Miami and didn't get the local news down there.

Bartolo, however, told Cotti differently. "Jack, I know what's been going on here. Forget about it! You were all over the news down there. Hell, you might be just as popular there as you are here."

"Are you serious? Did they talk about the Family war?"

"Jack. They talked about that and much more. You're a

very popular guy. And that's not good for a wiseguy."

"Forget about it! I've got an interview at NBC tomorrow. Then I'm going to start my campaign. I'm running for President of the United States." He pumped up his chest and held his head high as he spoke those last few words.

"*Not for nuttin'*, Jack, but you're crazy. You do this and you're liable to get all the Families a war that could last for years; that is, if we're not dead before then. I mean, Parrissi, Talluchi, and you...and now Napolie. Come on!"

"I don't give a fuck what you say! If I can win the Presidency, we'll control the whole fucking country!"

"Yeah, but Jack, it takes a lot to get up to that point. Don't get me wrong. I hope you can do it. But it's just not *logical*."

"I don't want to hear it!" Cotti barked. "I'm gonna find a way to get funding, either from a major party or through donations. That's how Colombo funded his political campaign."

"Jack, he started an organization for Italians."

"Yeah, and isn't Cosa Nostra an organization for Italians?"

"Yeah, so? What are you getting at?"

"I'm saying: We have the organization to start our own Party...and it spans the entire country!"

"Do you hear yourself? You want to start your own Political Party? Jack, be realistic."

"Hey, if I can get the backing of one of the main Parties,

then I'll choose them. But if not, I'll first ask for funding from the Five Families."

"Oh, the Five Families that want to kill each other. Those Five Families? Right now, they wouldn't give you a dime."

"No, not yet. But this war will end soon and they'll beg me to take their money."

Bartolo shook his head in disgust. He just couldn't get through to Cotti. Nothing he said changed Cotti's mind. He just gave up and figured Cotti would fall flat on his face without his help. So he changed the subject. "Jack, are we gonna go see Johnny or what?"

"Forget about it! Yeah, let's go."

Cotti gathered his six bodyguards, and the wiseguys left the club and headed for the hospital.

***

Cotti and Bartolo got into Bartolo's car, while the six bodyguards followed close behind in their car. Without their knowledge, the Feds were following close behind them, just in case there was another assassination attempt on Cotti. But what the Feds hadn't realized was that they too were being followed. A car full of Talluchi's soldiers was following Cotti's caravan, hoping to hit him whenever he stopped and got out of the car. They would kill him and as many of Cotti's men as necessary. Talluchi told them that "all's fair in love and war." And nothing would stop them from getting the job done. Except maybe the Feds.

Cotti's car reached the hospital parking lot. A car screeched to a halt in front of Cotti's car and three wiseguys got out, with guns drawn, pointed at Cotti and Bartolo.

Another car full of Talluchi hitters screeched to a halt behind Cotti's bodyguards' car and its shooters also got out, with guns drawn. What the wiseguys didn't notice was the two cars of FBI agents that had surrounded both parties of shooters, along with agents that were coming out from behind parked cars, trees, and bushes. Before anyone fired a shot, the Feds arrested all involved with the attempted hit.

The Feds had preempted this hit by again by listening to the conversations of Cotti, Bartolo, Talluchi, and Talluchi's Consiglieri, Pete "Sideburns" Tolato, from their bugs and wiretaps hidden in the Dergin Club and near Talluchi's hospital bed.

After a few short minutes, Cotti and company were allowed to leave. But instead of leaving the hospital grounds, Cotti and Bartolo, under the protection of their bodyguards and a few FBI Agents, went to do what they had planned, which was to visit with their childhood friend, Johnny Napolie.

***

The three wiseguys had been friends forever, since their childhood days. They'd grown up just doors away from each other in the same crumbling, twelve-story apartment building in the projects in Queens and had hung around together since the age of five. They all came from large families and were born a year before the bombing of Pearl Harbor.

Cotti had grown up in a family of thirteen children: eight boys and five girls. He was the second youngest of the boys and grew up getting beaten up and giving beatings. He had to be tough in his neighborhood. The people there settled arguments with their fists...sometimes pipes, bats, maybe knives, but rarely guns. Cotti was swearing by age five; smoking and drinking at eight; fucking at twelve; and doing crime just after his eleventh birthday. By his early teens, he had quit school and shortly thereafter had become the leader and muscle of his two to four man crew—and sometimes a five man crew, when he had to babysit his younger brother, Donny, and would take him along on jobs to act as the lookout. Napolie and Bartolo also went along. They called themselves the "Park Boys."

Bartolo lived directly across the hall from Cotti, and Napolie lived next to Bartolo. Bartolo came from a family of ten: seven boys, three girls. He was the youngest of the brothers. He, like Cotti, smoked, drank, fucked, and became a criminal at a very young age. He quit school at age twelve to try other endeavors, which included armed robbery and running numbers. Bartolo was the instigator of the gang. He started fights with others and Cotti, having a psychotic personality, finished them, and finished them brutally.

Napolie grew up in the same type of two-bedroom apartment as Bartolo and Cotti and had nine siblings: seven boys and two girls. He was the oldest of the boys. He was good friends with both Cotti and Bartolo by the time they entered Kindergarten.

Cotti was the biggest and toughest and protector of the group. He didn't let anyone mess with his friends, especially his close friends. Bartolo was the smartest, but Napolie was the most educated of the three. He didn't quit school until age fifteen, his sophomore year of high school. Even though Napolie swore, smoked, drank, and fucked beginning around the same age as the others, he had hoped to graduate. But trouble followed him and, going against his father's wishes, Napolie finally quit school just before graduating to the eleventh grade. He then spent most of his time with the "Park Boys."

The "Boys" wore black silk jackets that they'd stolen from a Queens Department Store and then had the words *Park Boys* sewn on the back in printed letters. They helped themselves to other accessories also, including boots, hats, rings, watches, and anything else that caught their attention.

Benny was the thinker; he set up and planned robberies and shoplifting escapades. Napolie, most of the time, was the lookout and Cotti the muscle. They were first arrested, convicted, and sent to a juvenile facility at age eleven. The three did one month in Juvenile detention and were released to their parents, who were basically alcoholics, except for Cotti's father, who was a workaholic and adamant about providing for his large family.

After their first stay in Juvie, Cotti became the leader of his crew. Neither Napolie nor Bartolo disagreed and would follow their close friend and leader to the ends of the Earth.

They were all quite handsome kids. But as the years passed by and as they grew older, the scrapes and fights took their toll on Bartolo's and Napolie's looks, mostly in the form of large scars on their faces and arms.

Cotti somehow made it out unscathed. By adulthood, he was still a very handsome guy with a head of wavy black hair and not overweight at all. He was five feet, eight inches of hard muscle and stocky build, with a Jack Kennedy smile. Bartolo, on the other hand, was five feet, six inches and two hundred pounds of fat with a balding head. Napolie was five feet four inches, with a stocky build, greased back black hair, and a slight limp from a bullet wound in his right thigh.

The three wiseguys came up the ladder together. Cotti was the first to be indoctrinated as a "made" member of the Valoppi Family. One month later, Bartolo and Napolie got their badges together. Cotti walked around with his head held high and a sense of confidence; he would protect his friends at any cost. He would lay down his life for any one of them.

***

Now that his close friend and Underboss had been shot and nearly killed, Cotti felt guilty that it was his fault and he wanted revenge; and wanted it badly. He and Bartolo were on their way to Napolie's hospital room to discuss the problems at hand. Because Napolie was out of circulation, Bartolo would have to fill in.

Two FBI agents entered Napolie's room and gave it the "once over," while two of Cotti's soldiers stood guard at the door. The agents left the room and Cotti and Bartolo entered.

Luckily, Napolie was awake and smiling when he saw his two friends. "Jack, Benny, I'm glad you're here."

The two wiseguys took their seats and made fun of their wounded friend.

"Did little Johnny get a booboo?" Bartolo asked in a baby's voice.

Cotti laughed. "Did Johnny fall down go boom?" he asked, also in a baby's voice.

"Alright, alright. That's enough of that shit. So how's the war going, Jack?" Napolie asked.

"Forget about it! They just tried again in the hospital parking lot. But the Feds got 'em first, before they could fire a shot."

"Jack, this is getting too close for comfort," Napolie told him. "This has got to stop." Napolie motioned for Cotti and Bartolo to come closer. He whispered, "Jack, either they're going to kill you—I mean, they've tried three times already—or we gotta hit them so hard, all at the same time, that they'd want to stop the war."

Cotti nodded. "Yeah, we know. Benny's gonna take care of it."

"You know what to do, Benny?" Napolie asked.

Benny nodded. "Forget about it!"

Napolie added, "It's gotta be done right for this thing that *we* started to be over. If not, we might as well dig our own graves. Forget about it!"

A nurse came into the room to give Napolie a shot of morphine for pain and sleep. She ordered the two wiseguys out of the room and they decided it was time to go.

"We'll see you, Johnny," Cotti said as he and Bartolo left the room.

Cotti and his entourage were then escorted by the FBI to Cotti's home, where he had his soldiers stand guard, completely surrounding his home. He had to get some much needed rest for his morning interview.

Bartolo left to take care of business elsewhere.

Chapter 9

As Cotti was busy getting dressed for his interview, Bartolo was busy planning four different hits simultaneously in four different places with sixteen of the Family's most experienced shooters. The aim was to finish the *War of the Five Families* as quickly as possible, with as little collateral damage as possible. The hitters were definitely out for blood and would take no prisoners.

Bartolo had made some inquiries the night before concerning certain Capos' eating habits. Now he knew where they would be and what time they would be visiting their favorite restaurants.

***

A few hours later, Cotti entered the NBC Studio. His hitters were primed and ready at their designated destinations, waiting patiently for their targets to arrive. However, they would hit after the targets had eaten their meals—their last meals before taking a dirt nap. The groups of four were sent to four different cities: one to Brooklyn, one to Bensonhurst, another to the Bronx, and the last to Manhattan.

The shooters took their positions and the leader of each group, using a throw-away phone, contacted Bartolo to await orders.

"Hit 'em when able," Bartolo told each caller.

They had more than an hour to wait, so the plan called for two hitters to wait in the car, while the other two of each group waited in the rear of each restaurant. They sat around, smoking cigarettes and bullshitting.

***

Cotti was halfway through his interview with Chuck Todd.

"So, Mr. Cotti," Todd said, "as President, you'll have to deal with leaders from other countries. What foreign policy experience do you have?"

"It's all about negotiations and alliances. And I'm a good negotiator," Cotti told him, a big smile crossing his face. "In my line of work, I've negotiated with the Russians, Chinese, Colombians, Cubans, Jamaicans, Albanians, and Israelis. Forget about it! I deal with people from all over the world. And I guarantee the Heads of States will be a snap compared to the people that I've dealt with. Forget about it!" Cotti nodded his head confidently and waited for his next question.

"Mr. Cotti, Presidents have to deal with the terrorist situation. What would you do as President?"

"Well, I don't want to put all my eggs in one basket. I should save these kinds of answers for the Primaries. But to answer your question, the terrorists don't know what real terror is until they mess with me. They kill one of mine, we kill ten of theirs...and not in a nice way. If they want to fuck those seventy-two virgins that Allah's got waiting for them, well, they'll do it without any dick or balls."

"Mr. Cotti, you're a funny guy. But you can't swear on TV. Thank god this interview isn't live or we'd have been fined by the FCC. At least now, we can edit this part of it."

"Just delete *fuck* and replace it with *screw* or *have sex*. And erase *dick* and *balls* and replace it with *private parts*, for Christ's sake."

"Well, that seems all the time we have for today. Thank you once again for coming today, after we were rudely interrupted during our last interview. I wish you the best on you endeavor, Mr. Cotti." Todd turned and faced his viewing audience. "And we'll be right back, after this message from our sponsor."

Cotti and Todd shook hands, then Cotti shook hands with producer Holt and thanked him for the interview.

"My interview will be shown Sunday, right?" Cotti asked Holt.

Holt didn't know what to say. He hadn't thought about running it on Sunday or even running it at all, but Cotti wasn't *asking* him, he was *telling* him. He really didn't know how to respond. All he could say was "Yes."

Cotti added, "I hope you do another interview with me when I reach the primaries."

"If you get that far," quipped Holt, before being called

to the set.

***

Cotti and his entourage left the studio near noon, without incident; the Feds followed. They arrived at his club and broke out the cigars and brandy and martinis.

Cotti's shooters were still nervously awaiting their targets. The Capos finally showed up at their favorite restaurant, to eat what they didn't know would be their last meal. As each was exiting through the front door, with cigar in hand, Cotti's soldiers hit their marks. Capo Frank Casone, of the Genovese Family, was first, hit as he was coming out of a Brooklyn eatery with two associates. The two hitters came up from behind; one stabbed an icepick into Casone's brain, and the other shot the two associates at close range in the backs of their heads. Then the two jumped into their car, picked up the other shooters near the rear of the building, and escaped unscathed. No Feds or Police were anywhere to be seen.

At nearly the same time, Cotti's other groups of shooters were hitting their targets, again without incident. In Manhattan, Capo Pete Collato of the Lucchese Family and a friend were hit by gunfire and died on the spot in a big pool of mingled blood.

Outside an eatery in the Bronx, Capo Gene Talinni of the Bonnano Family was hit, along with his fifty-two-year-old son. Talinni was stabbed in the neck and shot in the back and head, while his son was also shot in the back of the head. They lay where they fell, also in a big pool of their mingled blood.

The last killing, outside a restaurant in Queens, didn't go as planned. Louie Catania of the Colombo Family came out of the restaurant alone and was shot in the shoulder, but was able to pull out his gun and return fire while running down the street trying to get away. Cotti's shooters had to run him down before emptying their clips into his limp body. He took more than twelve shots to different parts of his body. His life ended the same as the others, lying in a pool of his own blood.

All hits went off without a hitch and all the shooters got away without incident. Again, using their throw-away phones, the leaders of the four groups called Bartolo and gave him the news.

"All's well." They all used the same code word.

"Good work," Bartolo told the leaders. "Now lay low until I say otherwise."

***

Bartolo and company were happy and proud of the outcome of their plan. No shooters had been lost, while all the Capos targeted were dead as doornails. But not everyone was happy with the outcome. The Feds, upon reaching each murder scene, were livid at what they saw.

Supervisor Arms and his Agents, outside the Brooklyn eatery, investigated the crime scene. Agent Arms was **up in arms** as he watched the dead bodies being loaded into the coroner's van.

"What the fuck is going on here?" he asked his agents. "This killing has gone on long enough. We got to stop it and nip it in the bud."

"What are we going to do, boss?" asked Agent Meadows.

Arms's face was beet red with anger. "I'll tell you what we're going to do. We are going to hit every bookie joint, every chop shop, and any and every criminal enterprise that we know about. We're going to hit them harder than ever before. They're going to cry 'Uncle' and finally put a stop to their damn war, or we're going to be picking up dead wiseguy bodies all over the whole fucking city."

***

As the Feds planned their next steps to quash the killings, Cotti, at his club, changed into an outfit that he hoped would fool the Feds and prevent them from following him to his new hideout. To lose his FBI tails and to get to a new hideout without being noticed, Cotti dressed as a homeless man. He carried a bag of aluminum pop cans and wore a dirty and torn ankle-length coat, dirty baseball cap, and scuffed tennis shoes. He walked away without any one the wiser.

A few blocks away from the club, his daughter's boyfriend, Pat Downey, picked Cotti up.

"Get out of the car," Cotti ordered. He got behind the wheel. "I'll call you to let you know where you can pick up your car," he yelled out the open window as he drove away.

Cotti parked the car a few blocks away from his new hideout in Brooklyn, not far from the club where his nemesis hung out on most days. Cotti figured that nobody would think of looking for him there, especially not among Talluchi's friends and neighbors. But he still had to be extra careful. He had no bodyguards surrounding his new hideout. He felt that they would only call attention to himself.

He entered his new digs and changed into a new suit, lit a cigar, and sat down on the couch to relax and look over the place.

***

The Feds were busy all over the five Burroughs, busting in doors of bookmakers and betting parlors. They arrested seventeen people, including two Capos and two Lieutenants, from four businesses that were believed to be owned by the Valoppi, Lucchese, Farcano, and Parrissi Families. Scarfino's Family businesses weren't hit on that particular day, but over the next few days, with the Feds busting every illegal mob business that they could find, the Five Families' earning power slowed to a trickle, which pissed off the Dons enormously. They wanted to put an end to the Feds' revengeful ways and the only way to do that was to stop the killings.

The Dons all had the same idea, except for one: Jack Cotti. He wanted to make another big splash against the

Families to get them on his side and allow him to try his hand at politics. So, using another pre-paid phone, he contacted his Consiglieri once again. "Take care of business," he ordered.

Bartolo knew exactly what Cotti meant and quipped, "Will do. Forget about it!"

Nearly a week after Bartolo and the Family's soldiers had "taken care of business," the same shooters were awaiting their second big splash against the Families. But now they were about to hit two Underbosses and two Dons. These would be the hits of the century, if all went according to plan. And to allay suspicion on Cotti, Bartolo ordered his soldiers to hit one of their own, Capo Sal Catallia. He was believed to be skimming money from the profits of an Atlantic City Casino that Cotti had an off-the-books interest and part ownership in. The death was ordered, but would be made to look as though another Family had ordered it.

Three bullets to the back of the head was the trademark of a Parrissi ordered hit. The other Families considered that one bullet to the back of the head was enough; Parrissi loved overkill. So, three bullets to the back of Catallia's head were essential for this particular hit. So far, the other Families had not retaliated or initiated any killings against the Valoppi Family since Talluchi's hospitalization; he was still recuperating from his wounds.

If the hits worked out as Cotti and Bartolo planned, these would be the last of the killings and the start of a political career for Jack Cotti.

***

The Feds knew that something was going down all over the five Burroughs again. And they wanted to be ready when it did—maybe with a pre-emptive strike. But things were tough on Agent Arms and his Boys. The budget cuts and agents being transferred to Homeland Security left Arms with only enough people to tail the Dons—the ones they could find, anyway—so surveillance was limited.

***

Cotti was one step ahead of the Feds. He and Bartolo figured that the Feds would be tailing at least the Dons, but probably not the Underbosses. So they put shooters armed with hunting rifles, with scopes attached, on the roofs approximately three hundred feet away from the hangouts frequented by Don Parrissi and Don Farcano.

Again, four groups of four hitters each were set to clip their designated targets, hopefully, without FBI interference. Each group going after an Underboss waited in cars in both the front and rear of the intended target's building.

Cotti Capo Sal "Sonny Boy" Catallia was the first to be hit. The Cotti soldiers walked up behind him, in broad daylight, and popped three caps into the back of his head; his knees buckled and he dropped like a three-hundred pound lead weight. Ten seconds later, Sal's killers were gone in a puff of smoke, as the tires on their car burned rubber when the accelerator was pushed to the floor. They sped away, with not a cop or Fed in sight. Catallia's hit went off perfectly and without a hitch.

The second wiseguy killed was Scarfino's Underboss, Vincent Mongano, who had not stepped into his deceased Boss's shoes fearing revenge from other Family members. The shooters in that murder also got away without interference from anyone, not even from Mongano's bodyguards, and definitely not from the NYPD nor the FBI.

The shooting of the two Dons was a different story.

***

Don Farcano exited through the front doors of his Queens hangout, Sadie's Tavern. Two shots rang out. The first hit Farcano in the right leg, knocking him to the ground. The second hit the building, just inches above his head as he was falling.

The sound of the shots brought Feds out from cars and buildings in every direction, with weapons drawn.

"Shots fired! Shots fired!" a number of agents yelled, as they looked in every direction for the shooters and huddled over Farcano to see if he was still alive.

He was.

The Feds radioed for an ambulance and by the time it had arrived, the NYPD were all over the scene, looking for the shooter and keeping onlookers away.

***

Another group of lawmen was cleaning up a crime scene in Manhattan. Don Parrissi had been shot and wounded in the neck and shoulder; one bullet had missed his carotid artery by a half-centimeter. Although both wounds were minor, Parrissi too was taken by ambulance to hospital for observation. An associate walking next to Parrissi was not so lucky; he'd been shot once in the back and killed, the bullet penetrating his heart.

Again, the shooters got away without so much as a glance from a Fed or Cop. Even though the rooftop shooters left their weapons behind, the Feds wouldn't be able to trace them to anyone. They'd been stolen from an Armory just weeks before and rubbed with fingerprint-proof oil-type material, although it wasn't needed because the shooters wore gloves—even while filling their clips.

All four groups of shooters got away clean and then went their separate ways, as ordered, to hideouts designated all over the five Burroughs. Before going to their stash houses, they abandoned their stolen vehicles and burned them to the ground.

***

The Feds were very angry and disgruntled, to put it mildly, at the events that had transpired. They knew who was behind the hits but couldn't prove anything. They needed more evidence just to get warrants for the people allegedly involved in the hits. In the meantime, they were busting more of the Five Families' businesses.

When the two hospitalized Dons got wind of more of their businesses being brought down by the Feds over the killings of many Family members, they summoned their Consiglieres to their respective hospital beds for conferences concerning Family business. This was meant to signal to the rest of the Commission members their willingness to stop the war, including allowing Cotti to follow his dream for a run in politics without Family interference.

***

Cotti, however, surrounded by his soldiers at nearby tables, sat at his favorite table at Sparks Restaurant, waiting to have brunch and talk politics with Democratic National Committee Chair Debby Wasserman.

After an hour of waiting, his guest finally arrived. As she neared the table, Cotti stood up and introduced himself. "Ms. Wasserman, I presume. I'm Jack Cotti. I'm glad to meet you." He shook her hand. "Please, sit."

Wasserman took her seat, and the waiter poured her a cup of coffee. She sipped her coffee and then spoke. "Now, Mr. Cotti, what can I, and the Democratic National Committee, do for you? I mean, that is why you asked me here, isn't it?"

"Yes, it is. But please...call me Jack."

"That's out of the question. Mr. Cotti, I am not your

friend. You're a gangster and murderer. I came here today because I felt threatened and didn't want to end up on the news as a murder statistic if I didn't show up. So, Mr. Cotti, why am I here?"

"First of all, Ms. Wasserman, I was acquitted of murder. And second of all, you have nothing to be afraid of. I asked you here because I'm thinking of going into politics and need a major Party to back me."

"So you want to run on a Democratic ticket?" she asked.

Cotti nodded. "I'm thinking about it."

"Why do you want to run as a Democrat? I don't see you as a Democrat, but more of the Republican type," Wasserman opined.

"Lady, I'm just a blue-collar guy who grew up poor, along with twelve brothers and sisters, in a crumbling two bedroom tenement apartment. Now I'm running a billion dollar enterprise. I'm also a Union man, and I believe in Global Warming and scientific evidence like Darwin gave us. I also believe in a clean environment. That's why I would make a good Democratic candidate instead of a Republican candidate, although I must say there are some things about Republicans that I like."

"Like what?" she asked, between sips of coffee.

"Well, for one thing: Guns! I could be a poster boy for the NRA. Forget about it!" Cotti exclaimed.

"What else don't you like about the Democratic Party?"

Cotti thought for a minute, sipped his brandy, and said,

"Well, for one, you let the Republicans in Congress step all over you. You gotta be tough!" He shook his fist and pumped his chest as he said those last few words. "You get the upper hand and you keep it. You can't be soft with those Bastards. Some of those Republicans are truly nuts; their views are so out of touch with reality. In fact, I wondered if some from the South were still members of the KKK; either that, or they're from another planet."

Wasserman laughed. "I think some are from another planet also."

Cotti gave her a funny look and shot back, "I might add, some Democrats in Congress aren't quite playing with a full deck, either."

"But what do you want from me?" she asked.

Cotti leaned forward, staring into Wasserman's eyes. "I need your list of donors," he said. "If I'm running for President, I need the big money behind me."

She was taken aback. The way he was looking at her, staring into her eyes, she felt threatened. But for some reason, she wanted to please him. He had that type of mesmerizing power over people.

"But, Mr. Cotti, you said that you run a billion dollar enterprise. I'm sure you must know some rich people that could help you fund your candidacy."

"Not enough. That's why I need your help."

"Mr. Cotti, you run a criminal enterprise. I can't be representing a gangster," she replied, hesitantly.

"Ms. Wasserman, I'm sorry but you are mistaken. All

my dealings are legitimate. If the people that work for me do illegal things, I have no control over that. I tell them the rules and if they don't follow them, then they lose their jobs. I tell them to earn, not how to do it. I believe they do it legitimately. If not, that's on them. And they suffer the consequences."

The waiter came up to the table and handed Cotti the day's newspaper. "Excuse me for a minute," Cotti told Wasserman as he read the headline: *Cotti Making Power Play to be Capo di tutti i Capi—Boss of Bosses*.

Cotti folded the newspaper in half and slapped it hard on the table, making a loud pop. In a split second, his bodyguards, nearly ten of them, stood up, some with guns drawn. Cotti looked around and motioned his men to sit.

"What's wrong, Mr. Cotti?" asked Wasserman, disturbed by his actions and those of his bodyguards.

He slid the paper across the table to her. She picked it up and read the headline. "Oh, I see," she said, stunned by what she had just read. She sat back in her seat and pondered her fate, wondering how the meeting with Cotti would end. She pushed the paper back over to him.

He picked it up and again read the headline. But this time, instead of becoming angry, Cotti smiled. It was still publicity, he thought. And it kept his name on everyone's minds.

"Mr. Cotti," Wasserman said, snapping him out of his daydream, "I must be leaving now. I think we've said all there is to say, don't you?"

Cotti started to answer her, but he noticed two soldiers from the Parrissi Crime Family sitting at a nearby table, watching him very warily. One made a phone call and Cotti, believing it might be a hit, spoke quietly to his guest. "Ms. Wasserman, you're right. It's time for you to leave. I'll call you in a few days for that list." He then motioned one of his bodyguards to walk with her for safety's sake. "Get her safely to a cab," Cotti told the bodyguard.

Cotti stood up to leave, with his bodyguards surrounding him so that nobody would have a clear shot at him. He moved towards the front doors and the two soldiers followed him.

Once outside, one of the Parrissi soldiers yelled out, in broken English: "Don Cotti, Don Cotti, I have a message for you from Don Parrissi."

Naturally, the bodyguards pulled their weapons and pointed them at the messenger. Cotti came out through the crowd. "Yeah, what do you want?"

"We have a message from Don Parrissi," the soldier replied.

"Yeah, you said that already," Cotti quipped.

"Don Parrissi says he wants a meet. Like before. All the other Dons will be there. He said you would know the day, place, and time. Do you have an answer for Don Parrissi?"

"Forget about it! Tell him I'll be there." With that, Cotti got into the back seat of a limo and drove off; his bodyguards following in their vehicles.

***

Cotti pondered his fate if he were to go to the meeting. Would he walk out alive or dead? If alive, his prophecy had come true. If dead, he wanted the people responsible for his death caught. Killed would be too quick. He wanted the killer or killers to be locked up in a cage for the rest of their lives. So he decided then to return to his home and not to his hideout. He figured the Feds would finally locate him and tail him wherever he went. And he wanted them to tail him to the meeting. Just in case!

***

By the time Cotti returned home the Feds were hot on his trail. And they were happy.

"We got him!" Agent Lundy yelled into his radio to Supervisor Arms.

"You found Cotti? Great!" Arms exclaimed. "Stay with him and don't let him lose you. He's the only Commission member without so much as a scratch. I don't think his luck will last much longer."

***

How wrong he was. Cotti's luck was about to get even better, but not if the current US President had anything to do with it.

"Get Cotti," he ordered the FBI. He wanted Jack Cotti off the streets and in jail.

"Take the gloves off," he told the FBI Director. But the

President would learn that getting Cotti was easier said than done. The Feds needed evidence against Cotti. Hard evidence. They figured they would get it through wiretaps and bugs. And through those, they became aware of the meeting of the Commission members, when they overheard the Lucchese Family Boss, Don Parrissi, tell an underling, "The Commission needs another meeting to take care of business, once and for all."

***

The Feds also heard Don Cotti tell his Underboss, in a tapped phone conversation, "I've been sent for."

"When?" Napolie asked; he was still in his hospital bed.

"Same day and time as before."

"Where?"

"The Selsor," Cotti replied.

"That doesn't sound too good, Jack. When someone gets sent for, they usually end up dead. You better get Benny to go with you."

"Can't. Benny's in Florida taking care of Family business."

"Well, call him back," said Napolie. "You need him with you at the meeting. I wish I could be there with you, but they won't let me leave for at least a week."

"Forget about it!" Cotti replied.

A nurse walked into Napolie's room with a syringe, interrupting the phone call. "The nurse is here, Jack. She wants to give me a shot. I gotta go. Good luck." With that,

158

the phone call ended. Napolie got his shot lying down and Cotti also lay down, trying to figure out his next move.

***

After pondering the situation, Cotti decided to "*ride the storm*." He was going to let the "*chips fall where they may*," to a point. He set it up within his Family that if he didn't come out of the meeting alive, he wanted his soldiers to fight to the last man. There was to be *no peace* among the Five Families. However, if the Commission members finally yelled "*Uncle*," and bowed down to his demands, then the world would be his to take. That is, if he played his cards right. He still needed the *People* to back his play.

***

The big day arrived. The Feds were nearby and ready for any outbreak of violence and to step in to defuse the situation, if need be. They were sure something big was about to explode and weren't about to sit back and *watch the volcano erupt*. They were even thinking about a preemptive strike, but reconsidered it. They wanted to get the hard evidence that was needed to get these guys off the streets *once and for all*, as the President had ordered. They didn't know which way the meeting would turn, but they would stay very near as the meeting went down. Regardless, they still were betting that Cotti wouldn't make it out alive...*again*.

***

Cotti arrived at the meeting alone. He knew, of course, that the Feds would be nearby and listening in. There wasn't any food, fruit, or cigars being handed out this time around. This was not business as usual. This was a showdown. Who would blink first? Cotti or the others?

A wounded and bandaged Parrissi started the meeting. "Don Cotti, thank you for coming here today on such an urgent matter."

"Forget about it!" Cotti exclaimed. "Now, why am I here, Don Parrissi? Is this to be my last day walking this Earth? Or am I here for some other reason?"

"Don Cotti," interjected a crippled Farcano, "this war must stop. A lot of good men have died. And for what? For nothing! We blame you for this, Jack Cotti. This didn't have to happen. But with the Feds busting down our doors and shutting down our businesses and throwing our earners in jail, we've reached an agreement among ourselves and decided to allow you to throw your hat into the political arena. We, here, sitting at this table, pledge—in order to bring peace and harmony once again to our Families—that you will have our complete cooperation in every way to help you in your endeavor, including contributing to your campaign. And we anxiously wish you good luck."

The rest of the Dons nodded in agreement. Then, they walked up to Cotti, bowed, and kissed his hand.

Cotti smiled. He had solidified his power. They had caved, just like he knew they would. He was now *Capo di tutti i Capi*: *Boss of Bosses*. They would now do what he ordered. And they knew the consequences if they didn't.

Cotti had prophesized the outcome of that meeting before the war even started. Now he had to act fast to get his campaign up and running before the Commission changed their minds.

***

The Dons walked out of the meeting, smiling and happy, Cotti included. But the Feds weren't quite as jovial with the outcome.

"Fuck! They did it again," shouted Agent Meadows, after listening in on the meeting. "They're gonna let Cotti get into politics and cooperate with him any way they can, even donating money. Unbelievable!"

"Keep your cool, Greg," said Arms. "We got plenty of eyes and ears on him and his buddies. They'll slip up, sooner or later. And if you really want to know, I believe the Dons are lying to Cotti again. I think they're waiting for just the right moment before bumping him off."

"You could be right," retorted Agent Brunson.

The Feds wondered what Cotti would do next. They knew he was serious about this politics thing, but believed he wouldn't be able to get the backing he needed to run a Presidential campaign.

***

But Cotti had other ideas. *Big ideas*. He needed to

speak with Rupert Murdoch for a favor. A *big favor*. For a slot on Fox News to make his announcement about running for President.

Cotti made the call and was put through to the man himself.

"Yes, this is Rupert Murdoch."

Cotti said "hello" to his good friend and put the question to the test. "Will you let me do it, Rupert? It will only take a minute."

"Are you sure you know what you're doing, Jack?"

"Forget about it! Ba Da Bing, Ba Da Boom, and it'll be over. I'll have said what needs to be said and then we'll leave it to the *People*."

Murdoch gave his approval. "Why don't you come to the station, say, at five-thirty tomorrow night, and we'll get you on the air to give your statement. I'll send the limo for you."

"Forget about it!"

"Are you sure? The limo's not a problem."

"No. I mean, yeah, the limo's fine," Cotti said, having confused Murdoch with his words.

"I'll see you when you get to the studio, Jack."

The phone call ended and the two went back to what they'd been doing before the call. Murdoch returned to fine-tuning his billion dollar business, and Jack Cotti did the same, trying to figure out just how much money he would need to get his political career going.

Cotti had already prepared his statement to be read over

Fox News channel. He owed a debt of gratitude to Rupert Murdoch for allowing this to happen. He would find out the following night if he still had the *People* behind him in his quest to be President of the US of A.

***

The time rolled around and Cotti was ready as ever.

Rupert Murdoch met him as he came through the station's doors. "Nice to see you, Jack."

The two shook hands.

"Thank you, Rupert. And thank you for giving me this opportunity. I owe you. If you ever need a *favor*, I'm your guy."

They walked into the studio.

Anchorman Bob Campbell came out to greet Cotti. "It's good to see you again, Mr. Cotti," he said, as they shook hands. He showed Cotti to the anchor desk, where they took their respective chairs.

Producer Gates stood next to the camera and, holding up three fingers, counted down—three, two, one—and pointed to Campbell.

"Good evening, viewers," Campbell said. "I'm here tonight to introduce you to someone I interviewed here not too long ago. I think all of you know who this guest sitting next to me is. He's mobster Jack Cotti and he has something to say. I think you will be surprised by his announcement." He turned and looked at Cotti. "So, go ahead, Jack Cotti. Fox viewers are all yours."

The camera focused on Cotti's handsome face as he made his announcement. "First, I'd like to thank Mr. Rupert Murdoch for giving me this opportunity, and to Mr. Campbell for allowing me to take time away from his segment of the show. Thank you. And now, to all you viewers: Hello, my name is Jack Cotti and I'm here to tell you that I'm definitely throwing my hat into the ring of politics. I am campaigning to run for President of these great United States. If I can get your help, we can truly change this country from one of stalemate and stagnation to one that prospers again, especially for all hard-working Americans. You deserve a fair shake and a decent wage. Thank You. And good night."

The camera went back to Campbell. "And that was Jack Cotti. You heard it here first. Jack Cotti is running for President. He needs your help. And now, to other news."

Cotti was all smiles when he left the anchor desk. As he walked off camera, Rupert Murdoch approached him.

"Do you know what Party you'll run for, Jack?" Murdoch asked.

Cotti shook his head. "No, not yet."

"You should consider running as a Republican."

"I haven't made up my mind. Although I did have a meeting with Reince Prebius, the—"

Murdoch interrupted him. "Yes, I know Reince. He's the Republican Chair. He's a good friend of mine."

"I see," Cotti replied.

"What Party are you registered with?" Murdoch asked.

Cotti told him he wasn't registered with any party. "But I've registered over the years as both a Democrat and Republican. I just haven't voted the last few years."

"Well, I'll tell you what. I like you. You've got balls. I believe you can do anything well if you put your mind to it. So let me see if I can get you a few people that help politicians get elected and see if they can help you. On one condition..."

"And what's that? I already owe you one big favor. Am I gonna owe you two?"

"You have to give Fox exclusive rights to your interviews. When you want to say something new, we want first crack to interview you. You promise me that, and I'll help make you President of the United States. That is, if you can make it through the primaries, and then win the convention. And that's a long road to ride. But I think the People are wanting a big change and are tired of all the professional politicians. And I think you'd make a great Republican."

"Well, thank you, Rupert. I'll need all the help I can get. Now, if you'll excuse me, I need to get home and plan my campaign with my Consiglieri."

Murdoch told Cotti that he'd keep in touch and find him the right people to help him in his endeavor. He then had the limo driver return Cotti to his abode.

***

Cotti entered his home and sought out his wife to tell

her what Murdoch had promised him. She listened intently and then he asked her what she thought about his announcement. She gave him an answer that he wasn't expecting.

"Jack, I think you've cracked up," Maria exclaimed, angrily. "You've really lost it. You really believe that the People will vote for a mobster as President? Get real, Jack!"

"Come on, hon, be happy for me."

***

The Feds heard Cotti's conversation with his wife and they were livid and disgusted by what they had heard also.

"What the fuck is Murdoch thinking?" Agent Lundy bellowed, for all his fellow Agents to hear. "He's taken the bait and played right into Cotti's hands and doesn't even know it."

"I don't know about that, Ken," interjected Agent Meadows. "Think about it. I think Murdoch's making Cotti look like a fool and Cotti doesn't even realize it."

"Of course he doesn't. He's a narcissist," opined Agent Brunson.

"Ok, guys. Let's take this investigation up a notch! Let's find some hard evidence to get Cotti off the street and in jail before he can get anything organized," barked Supervisor Arms. "And let's pay particular attention to his donations. When he starts bringing in money from donors, I'm sure him and his people will be skimming those donations left and right. And if he does, we'll nail him to the wall."

***

While the Feds were planning their next move, so was Cotti. And so were the media. After his announcement, Jack Cotti's name was once again being broadcast around the country. He was in everyone's conversation, including John McLaughlin of the McLaughlin Group.

"Ok, people," McLaughlin said to his panel. "I'm sure all of you heard Jack Cotti's announcement...that he is campaigning to become President." He held up the front page of the New York Times Sunday newspaper to show the most recent headlines about Cotti. "They say Jack Cotti is now the Capo di tutti i Capi: Boss of Bosses for the Mafia. Do you think he can be the Boss of Bosses for the country? I ask you, Pat Buchanan."

"John, you gotta give the guy credit. Nobody thought he'd get this far. But he has. And he seems to have found a friend in Rupert Murdoch."

All the pundits snickered and nodded.

McLaughlin asked Eleanor Clift the same question.

"As I've said before concerning Jack Cotti," she replied, "he's a conversation piece at a dinner party. Nothing more."

Mort Zuckerman chimed in. "John, I think it's safe to say that nobody on this panel expected Cotti to get this far. I think most of us here thought Cotti would be *sleeping with the fishes* by now. But, according to the New York Times, Cotti won the war with the other Mafia Families. I guess all one can say is ***more power to him***."

"Well, let me ask you this, Mort Zuckerman: We know Cotti is in organized crime. But does he have the organization to run a major campaign?"

"We'll find out, won't we, John," Zuckerman answered.

McLaughlin asked Pat Buchanan. "Pat, will Jack Cotti have the organization to run a political campaign?"

"John, you know the guy's got power and loads of money behind him. But will it be enough without help and backing from the main Parties? We'll just have to wait and see."

"John," interjected Eleanor Clift, "we don't even know what Party he's running for. He's still got a lot of work to do."

"Tom Rogan, what do you think," asked McLaughlin.

"John, I'm with Eleanor. I think Cotti is a lost cause. When push comes to shove, Cotti will fall to the wayside. He has no chance."

"Well, that's all for now. Bye, Bye," said McLaughlin.

***

Now it was up to Cotti to get his campaign started. He had no political connections or political organization to back his play, other than the promises Rupert Murdoch had made to him. And Murdoch was keeping his promise. He made a telephone call to an old and dear friend, Carl Rove, the main man behind Republican Presidential Campaigns.

"Carl, Rupert here."

"Rupert, and how the hell are you?"

"Fine, Carl. You're probably wondering why I'm calling you."

"That did cross my mind. What do you need?"

"Are you sitting down?"

"Yes, Rupert. Now, what's up?"

"I would like you to do me a big favor. I would like you to help Jack Cotti with his Presidential campaign."

"You want what?" Rove yelled.

"Carl, calm down. I want you to get a hold of Jack Cotti and do whatever you can to get his campaign in gear."

"Rupert, are you drunk? Is this a joke?"

"Carl, I'm very serious."

***

After some long discussion on the subject, Rove relented and agreed to do what he could for this new and raw talent in the political game. Rove would have to start from scratch.

Hell, he forgot to ask Murdoch which Party Cotti belonged to. Although he figured, if Murdoch was behind the Cotti push, then he had to be a Republican. That was hard to swallow for Rove, but hell, it was politics. There was quite a lot one had to swallow when it came to politicians.

But Cotti had at least one thing going for him: He

wasn't a politician. He was only a mobster, a thug, possibly a killer, that Rove had to turn into Presidential material in a very short time. He had done it before for someone that didn't seem too bright; that couldn't put two sentences together correctly if his life depended on it. Rove knew that the People had voted for a General for President, an actor, a physicist, a redneck: hell, why wouldn't they vote to put a mobster in the Oval Office?

At first, it sounded absurd. But the more Rove thought about it, and had looked over videos of Cotti's interviews, and learned of his popularity amongst the voters, he figured, with the right campaign strategy and enough money behind him, Cotti had a chance to at least get pretty far in the Primaries, but a long shot at the Presidency. But, as Rove knew, anything could happen.

Chapter 10

Rove was planning a campaign for someone he hadn't met yet. He wasn't even sure Cotti would accept his help if offered. So, using the telephone number he was given by Murdoch, Rove telephoned Cotti to introduce himself.

Cotti's wife answered the phone. "Hello."

"Is this the Jack Cotti residence?" Rove asked.

"Yeah, and if you're a reporter, GO TO HELL!" she bellowed. "Don't call here no more!" She went to hang up the phone but heard loud yelling from the other end.

"Wait, Wait. Don't hang up! Don't hang up!"

"What?" she asked.

"Excuse me, ma'am. But I'm calling Mr. Cotti as a favor for Mr. Rupert Murdoch, a good friend of Mr. Cotti's. I'm calling to help him with his campaign."

"Just a minute." She handed her husband the phone.

"Yeah," Cotti answered.

"Mr. Cotti? Jack Cotti?"

"Yeah, who is this?"

"Mr. Cotti, I'm Carl Rove. Rupert asked me to contact you to help get your campaign started. There's lots of work

171

to get done and we need to start *yesterday*."

"Mr. Rove, I take it you're experienced in politics."

"Yes, sir. I helped George W. Bush with his campaign for Governor and President."

"I see." Cotti didn't really know what to say about that. He'd hated Bush as President. But then he realized that if Rove could get GW Bush elected, then he, Jack Cotti, was a shoe-in. "Great. What do we need to do?"

"Let me ask you a few questions now. We'll set up a meeting either here in DC or in New York and get to know each other. How does that sound, Mr. Cotti?"

"Please, call me Jack. You say Mr. Cotti; I look for my father."

"Ok, Jack. What do you say, two days from now we get together for a meeting?"

Cotti agreed.

They decided to meet in New York City at the same place Prebius met with Cotti: Sparks.

Rove then asked the questions that were on his mind. "I take it, Mr. Cotti, you are a registered Republican?"

"Ah, no. Didn't Murdoch tell you? I'm not affiliated with any Party. That's what I've been looking for: a major Party to back me."

"You're going to have to make up your mind within the next two days. I want to know your answer at our meeting."

"I'll see what I can do."

"And you'll have to quit the mob," Rove demanded.

Cotti was silent for a good minute.

"Mr. Cotti, are you there? Mr. Cotti?"

"You must be new around here, Mister," Cotti replied angrily. "Nobody quits the mob. I might be able to take a hiatus, but the only way you get out of the Mafia is in a pine box."

"Mr. Cotti, I want people to forget that you're a gangster."

"Forget about it!" Cotti exclaimed, explaining, "Remember when Nixon told the People that he wasn't a crook. Well, I'm not gonna lie to them. They're gonna know what they get when they vote for me. I **am** a crook and they know it. Furthermore, they like it."

"Well then, we'll work your campaign from that angle. It looks like it hasn't hurt you so far."

"We'll talk about it at the meeting."

"I'll meet you in two days at Sparks Restaurant at two in the afternoon," Rove promised.

***

During those two days, Cotti received a number of phone calls from Murdoch and Prebius, who were hoping to talk him into running as a Republican. But Cotti left them unsure which way he would turn. The Feds had no idea either.

The Feds were able to listen to all Cotti's phone calls with the Republican bigwigs. They wondered why the Republican Party would choose Cotti as a possible candidate for President.

"What the fuck's wrong with these guys?" bellowed Agent Meadows. "Are they trying to bring down the Republican Party?"

"Remind me to never again vote Republican," interjected Agent Brunson.

It just didn't make sense to them. And it didn't make sense to John McLaughlin of the McLaughlin Group when he heard Rove tell the media that he was heading Jack Cotti's campaign for President. He asked that question to his guests.

"Reince Prebius, Rupert Murdoch, and Carl Rove have all asked Jack Cotti to run on a Republican ticket. Will the Republicans reel this new fish into the Party? I ask you, Pat Buchanan."

Buchanan shrugged. "I don't know, John. I honestly don't know."

McLaughlin asked Eleanor Clift the same question.

"They're flirting with the Devil, John," she quipped. "He might be handsome and smart, but we know what lurks behind that pretty face."

McLaughlin's pundits all felt the same about the prospect of Cotti running as a Republican. They weren't at all happy about it. When the Democratic National Committee Chair, Debbie Wasserman, heard the news, however, she was overjoyed. She said to her circle of friends over brunch, "Damn, I can't believe Carl Rove and others are trying to talk Jack Cotti into running as a Republican. That really takes a load off my mind. If the

Republican Party wants to endorse a gangster for President...more power to them."

Wasserman was truly hopeful that Cotti would choose the Republican Party to back him in his run for President. But Rove, on the other hand, wasn't sure how Cotti would respond. So when the meeting finally rolled around, Rove wanted some extra ammunition and he brought Reince Prebius with him, just in case Cotti needed a little coaxing.

Cotti also brought some big guns with him too. He wanted his two close friends, Napolie and Bartolo, sitting in on the meeting to hear what Rove had to say.

***

With introductions completed, the meeting started in earnest. They sat at Cotti's favorite table in the back room.

Rove began the conversation. "Jack: Prebius and I think that you can go a long way on a Republican Ticket. We have the organization, donors, and the money it takes to put you in the White House. And with your popularity with the People, let's just see if we can keep that going."

"And if I say yes?" Cotti asked him, lighting his cigar.

"Then we'll begin at once to get funding," Rove replied. The rest of the group all lit cigars that Cotti had given them. This was truly a smoke-filled back room.

"Ok. I want one of my guys keeping track of the money. Understood?" Cotti told Rove.

"Yeah, well, we'll talk more about that at a later date," Rove answered.

***

The Feds couldn't believe what they were hearing.

"Did you hear how Cotti reacted when Rove mentioned **money**? His greed button lit up," Agent Meadows told the other agents.

Their electronic bugs were working perfectly, so they then went back to listening to the conversation between the mobster and two political powerhouses.

"So, Mr. Cotti," Prebius was saying, "are you willing to run as a Republican? Rupert and I and Mr. Rove think you'd make a great President."

***

The two President-makers pulled out all the stops and stroked Cotti's ego, hoping he would take the bait.

Cotti thought for a minute. "Only if you do as I say. And I want to Okay every facet of my campaign. Remember, what they see is what they get. I won't lie to them. If you agree to those terms, then I'll try my hand as a Republican."

"Alright then," said Rove. "Our next step is to get you some good security."

"Are you kidding?" Cotti replied. "Hell, between the FBI tailing me, and my soldiers, I mean, bodyguards, I got all the security I need!"

Rove nodded and didn't argue. "Then the next thing that needs to be done in our adventure is to speak with the money men; the people that fund political campaigns. These are billionaires, like yourself, Mr. Cotti."

Cotti laughed. "If you think I'm a billionaire, I got news for you. It goes out as fast as it comes in. You know, bribing cops, politicians, city workers, and payroll takes the brunt of the profits. But I'm not complaining. My family lives pretty good."

"I guess you can't believe everything you hear. I'll get a meeting together where you will have to talk with the donors and answer their questions," Rove told Cotti.

Cotti came back with a quick answer. "As long as I don't incriminate myself," he joked.

But Rove and Prebius weren't sure if Cotti was joking or not.

"Good. Well, Reince and I have to get back to DC and get this campaign started," Rove said. "Stay close to your phone. I'll be calling you all times of the day and night, with schedules, meetings and up to date results with funding and other things."

The two political powerhouses got up to leave. Cotti shook their hands and thanked them for their time.

Rove nodded. "I'll send you a schedule for your campaign trips and interviews."

Prebius and Rove left the restaurant and headed back to DC.

***

Upon arrival at his DC home, Rove called Doug Long,

his man at the DC Fox News Station, requesting air time to give a quick statement and interview. Long gave Rove his approval for the following evening on the six o'clock news. Rove then immediately phoned his contacts in the political arena to get them on board with Cotti's campaign.

***

While Rove was busy speaking with his friends, Cotti was busy contacting Crime Families across the nation to get their soldiers on board to help collect signatures to get him on the ballot. He also called all the New York Dons and asked for their help with volunteers and money and mentioned that he was running for President as a Republican. The Dons reluctantly agreed and wished him the "best."

The next day, Cotti ordered his Underboss and Consiglieri to his home to help plan his next moves.

***

Rove sat on the Fox News set, giving his interview with host Tony Perkins.

"I'm sitting here with Carl Rove, the brains behind George W. Bush's campaigns," said Perkins to his viewers. "Now, I hear he has someone in mind for a Presidential run. So, Carl Rove, it's good to see you."

"Thanks for having me, Tony."

"I know you're aching to tell the viewers who this person is that you're helping."

"I am. The man I'm about to tell you about has been very popular lately. The People seem to **love** him. It seems his past doesn't bother them, or his chances as a possible Presidential Candidate. I'm talking about Jack Cotti. He's campaigning as a Republican and hopes to win it all in this coming Presidential Election."

"You heard it here first, viewers. Carl Rove is running mobster Jack Cotti's campaign for President."

Rove cringed when he heard the word **mobster** come out of Perkin's mouth, but then he remembered that Cotti being a mobster running for President was appealing to the voters.

***

But it had no appeal to the Feds. Or the President. When the President heard and read about Rove's decision to help Cotti's campaign run as a **Republican**, he had two different feelings on the subject: First, he couldn't believe that a mobster actually had the gall to run for President, and second, he was actually giddy that the Republicans had no qualms in backing a mobster for President. The President, a die-hard Democrat, believed that that the mobster angle alone could bring down the Republican Party—**for good**!

***

The President and Feds weren't the only ones frustrated by Rove's actions. John McLaughlin also had something to say about it on his show.

"Well, on our last show," he said to his viewers and four political pundits, "we wondered if Carl Rove could reel his fish into the Republican Party. And we found out a few days ago that he had. Mobster Jack Cotti is now running for President as a Republican. Will he win the Primaries? I ask you, Pat Buchanan."

"It's unbelievable, John. I don't understand what Prebius and Rove were thinking. This may well bring down the Republican Party. But to answer your question, John. Win the Primaries? Never happen. Not in a million years."

"Yeah, John," interjected Eleanor Clift. "It's unbelievable. I never expected anything of this sort. He has no chance against a Bush or Christie. Cotti will fade after Iowa. He's still just a good conversation piece at a cocktail party."

Zuckerman chimed in: "Better watch what you say about Jack Cotti, Eleanor. He may have you whacked."

The pundits snickered and McLaughlin ended his show. "It looks like we'll have more to talk about on the Jack Cotti subject as the race goes on. Bye, Bye!"

***

Cotti's name came up once again on many of the news programs and newspapers. And Rove, being the master at his craft, got his boy two scheduled appearances: The first, an interview with George Stephanopoulos on ABC News; and the second, with Republican donors in Washington,

DC.

Evidently, Rove didn't know about the deal Cotti had made with Rupert Murdoch, to give Fox News the first chance at a Cotti interview. It was Murdoch who had given Cotti the chance to blossom as a political powerhouse and he was furious when he found out. But he didn't find out until it was too late, nearly three days after the interview.

Cotti's interview was *short*, but not very *sweet*. Stephanopoulos pulled no punches and went straight for the gut.

Stephanopoulos introduced his guest to his viewers. "And for those of you who haven't heard about my guest, I'd like to introduce mobster Jack Cotti, who is now running for President as a Republican. Mr. Cotti, I thank you for giving ABC this opportunity for an interview."

Cotti smiled. "Forget about it!"

"Mr. Cotti, how can a mobster and murderer run for President? I mean…to get into the mob one has to kill, do they not?"

"I can't answer that. But what I can tell you is that if I had murdered someone, I'm sure the Police or Feds would have arrested me and locked me up. They tried three different times and struck out each time." Cotti leaned forward and gave Stephanopoulos an antagonizing look, adding, "So be careful of accusing an innocent person."

Stephanopoulos sat up with a startled expression on his face. "I didn't mean to upset you, Mr. Cotti. Let's carry on with the interview. You are running for President as a

Republican. Why do you think you'd make a good President?"

"Why? Because I'm tough," Cotti replied, in his deep gruff voice. "And you need a tough President to get things done in Washington these days. As Ricky Nelson used to say: 'I don't mess around, boy!'"

"Mr. Cotti, we know mobsters are tough. But those politicians in Congress are no pushovers. They mean business."

"Hey, if I can handle four thousand crazy wiseguys, a few hundred politicians will be a snap. Forget about it!"

"It might be harder than you think," Stephanopoulos said. He added, "Well, I and ABC wish you well. But before we go, we here at ABC play a little game with our guests. Would you care to play?"

Cotti shrugged. "Sure, why not?"

"If you were going to kill an animal to extinction, which would it be?"

Cotti leaned back in his chair and thought for a few seconds, before saying: "Ted Nugent!"

Stephanopoulos looked shocked and wondered if he had heard correctly. "Excuse me?"

"Yeah, I'd like to see Ted Nugent extinct. He loves killing innocent animals that can't fight back. But I can."

"Is that a threat against Nugent?"

"I don't threaten," Cotti said with a smile. "I don't have to."

With that said, the interview was over. Off camera,

Stephanopoulos shook Cotti's hand and wished him 'good luck' in his endeavor. "Mr. Cotti, you are quite the character. I don't think I've ever interviewed a potential Presidential candidate like you. This is one for the books."

Cotti just shrugged and went on his way. His entourage of bodyguards followed behind, as did the Feds.

***

When Nugent heard what Cotti had said about him, he was livid. He couldn't believe that a mobster would threaten him like that. He bragged to friends on a TV hunting show that he also carried a gun, twenty-four/seven. "If Cotti wants to try and make good on his threat then let him come and get some!"

Well, Nugent's words didn't set too well with Jack Cotti and his followers. In fact, nearly four thousand Valoppi members were now out to *get* Nugent.

Cotti knew that Nugent was a die-hard Republican and they were sure to meet up one day for a Republican Party Conference, like CPAC. He planned to say "hello" to Nugent and set him straight about who was the hunter and who was being hunted.

Chapter 11

The first Donor Party went well for both Cotti and Rove. The money men enjoyed Cotti's frankness and cavalier attitude and gave his campaign more than two million dollars.

That was just the beginning. Things only got better over the following weeks and months, especially, when the Conservative Political Action Conference, or CPAC, came around. This was where all the Republican Political Presidential Hopefuls were to give a speech to their audience and answer questions posed by the host, Sean Hannity.

While Rove was giving pointers to his "boy," Ted Nugent strolled by. Nugent stopped in his tracks when he saw the person he recognized as Jack Cotti. He was startled at first, but then got brave and stood nose to nose with Cotti.

Rove grabbed Nugent by the arm and stopped him from doing something stupid that the man would regret later. Rove knew the reputation Cotti had and wanted to stop a volcano from erupting. He needed to nip it in the bud before Cotti lost his temper and a fist fight ensued. So Rove introduced Cotti to Nugent.

Cotti and Nugent shook hands, but Nugent said, "I heard the threat you made against me."

Cotti smiled. "Forget about it! It was just talk."

"That kind of talk could get you hurt," Nugent replied.

That was the wrong thing to say to Jack Cotti. But Cotti just snickered and let it slide.

Rove jumped into the conversation. "Come on, guys. Let's not get physical in this place. Not now!"

Cotti nodded and let go of Nugent's hand. "Forget about it!" Cotti exclaimed. He watched as Nugent walked away and into the restroom. A minute later, he too headed for the restroom. Cotti entered, catching Nugent with his pants down.

Nugent was standing at the urinal with his back to the door. He turned to see who had come into the room. Seeing Cotti, he pulled his gun from the holster hidden under his jacket.

Cotti reacted and grabbed Nugent's gun in one hand and wrapped the other around the back of his enemy's neck. He threw Nugent down to the ground and into an empty stall, where he picked the man up by the back of his jacket and dunked his head into the pungent, urine-smelling toilet. He then smashed Nugent's head a number of times with the seat.

Nugent just moaned as he lay on the dirty floor. Cotti threw Nugent's gun into the trash container. He left the restroom, and just in time, because two armed security guards came through the door just seconds later.

The guards asked Nugent if he knew his attacker and wanted to press charges. Nugent thought for a long minute and finally said, "No!" One of two thoughts alternated in his mind: Either he would settle things with Cotti on his own at another place and time, or he knew Jack Cotti wasn't someone to mess with (as he had just found out). It was most likely the latter. Nugent was crazy, but not that crazy.

The crowd that had gathered was listening to what was being said between Nugent and Security. It seemed the people were quite happy and content that the great, egotistical, arrogant, and narcissistic Rock and Roller had just gotten his ass whipped by a possible future President. That didn't sit well with Ted Nugent, and he vowed revenge.

***

Cotti couldn't have cared less. To him, Nugent was nothing more than a sissy and coward.

Rove cornered Cotti and continued giving his "boy" political lessons for his short speech. Cotti didn't have anything written down to read from and would play it by ear. His turn finally came; he went on right after Rand Paul and Ted Cruz.

The audience gave Cotti light applause as he stood at the podium.

"Thank you for this opportunity," Cotti told the audience. He smiled a slightly nervous smile, rubbed his hands together, and then proceeded to give the audience something they'd never forget. Something they'd never heard before; such a breath of fresh air.

They were listening to a *man's man*. Not a politician. A guy that had come up from the gutter and who'd made a name for himself the hard way: in the streets. He had made it onto the front covers of Time and People magazine, made headlines in newspapers and TV editorials across the country, and was now speaking to the people that could make or break him on this very night. These audience members would vote in a straw poll to see which Republican speaker leaned closer to their views.

Hannity introduced Cotti to the audience: "And now, I'd like to introduce all of you to a rookie politician who has just joined the Republican Party: Jack Cotti."

"Thank you, Sean, for that great introduction." Cotti cracked his knuckles. "For those of you who haven't heard of me, my name is Jack Cotti and I'm running for President of the United States. I want to tell you a little bit about myself. Some people call me a criminal. Others, a mobster. But I'm just a smart businessman."

The audience clapped, hooted, and howled to Cotti's words.

Cotti continued. "I'm just a businessman who doesn't like paying taxes to the Federal Government. I mean, what do they do to deserve my money; money that I worked hard for?"

Again the audience went crazy: whistling, clapping,

and hooting. A few even yelled out: ***"Cotti for President."***

Cotti went on. "I guarantee that I can get this economy going again. And I also guarantee that no more jobs will be sent overseas to countries that use slave labor. I'll get the top CEOs of the Fortune Five Hundred Companies and persuade them to keep the jobs in this country. And believe me, I'm a man of persuasion. I can get people to listen to me. I mean, I could stand up here and talk about all the bad things our President has done. I could talk about all the mistakes made. I could talk about the Affordable Health Care Act. But I won't. I want to talk about the future and going forward to find the best solutions to mounting problems to keep America the best country in the world."

The audience gave Cotti a standing ovation. By the time they had quieted down, the red signal light went on and it was time for Cotti to end his speech. "Thank you!" Cotti yelled. The crowd again broke out into nonstop applause for nearly five minutes, with echoing shouts of ***"Cotti for President."*** The incredible response held up Rick Perry's turn at the podium. Cotti came off like a rock star. He knew he had done well. And he hadn't had to threaten anyone.

Cotti left the stage. Passing by Rick Perry, he quipped, "Top that, fuckhead!"

Rove was overjoyed with Cotti's performance at that prestigious event. Cotti was bound to get millions of dollars more from the big Fat Cat donors, like the Koch Brothers, the Adelsons, and others, not to mention the

NRA, and Americans for Prosperity, just to name a few. Rove was counting on getting the *big bucks* for his contender.

***

Rove might have been happy, but the Feds and Rupert Murdoch were not. Many of the Feds stationed in the audience and around the convention center just looked to the floor and shook their heads in disgust at the thunderous applause. Cotti was more popular now than when he'd first started on his political endeavor.

Everyone, including the Feds, had believed Cotti would fizzle out and return to criminal life. How wrong they'd been. The Feds now knew that if they couldn't dig up the evidence to put Cotti away soon, they would most assuredly have to protect him instead of tailing him. That outcome didn't sit too well with the agents at all and brought out the anger in them.

"Damn!" said one agent. "I should have shot the guy myself when I had the chance. We could have blamed one of the Families."

Rupert Murdoch had Rove in a corner and reprimanded him over the interview quagmire.

"I'm sorry about that, Rupert," Rove said. "Had I known about the deal you had made with Cotti, I'd have given Fox the interview."

Rupert just grumbled. Now he didn't know who to be pissed off at.

Rove tried to console him with an idea. "Hell, let's see how the poll comes out and if he does as well as I think he will, Cotti's next interview will be yours."

"We'll see," said a grumpy Murdoch.

Cotti came up and stood between the two political monarchs. Murdoch gave him a dirty look, turned, and walked away.

"What the hell was *he* pissed off at?" Cotti asked Rove.

"How the hell should I know? Something about a deal he had made with you regarding interviews. He said the interview you did with ABC should have been with Fox. But I'm sure he'll get over it, especially if you win tonight's poll."

"I hope so. I owe Murdoch a lot. He was the only one who believed in me. To tell you the truth, I just forgot about the interview thing," Cotti admitted.

"Well, we're done here," said Rove. "I want you to get back to the hotel and rest up. We have a long day tomorrow. We'll be meeting with some big donors and we have to get ready for our big debate."

"What debate is that?" Cotti asked.

"It'll be with most of the guys who spoke tonight: Perry, Paul, Cruz, Bush, Walker, and Christie. If we win tonight's straw poll and the debate, then soon it's Super Tuesday. If we win Iowa, New Hampshire, South Carolina, and a few of the others, then we should have enough delegates in our pocket to win the convention."

Cotti just smiled. "Great!"

***

Cotti returned to his hotel room while Rove stayed behind to meet with the people most likely to give Cotti money.

Rove walked into a conference room where he was met by Sheldon Adelson, Harold Simmons, Robert Perry, Peter Thiel, and Robert Mercer. These men were the big money players for the Republican Party. They took their seats around a huge oval table, nearly all lighting Gurka cigars.

Rove started the meeting. "Now, gentlemen," he said, addressing the **Men of Means**, "we are here to put a winner in the White House. And I have the man we're looking for. Jack Cotti is a tough and wise businessman who could be a big help to you in all your endeavors. He is more popular now than when he started his quest for the Presidency, and his popularity only gets stronger as the days pass. The people seem to love this guy—"

"But Carl," interjected Peter Thiel, the head of Clarium Capital Management and always a multimillion dollar donor for the cause, "Cotti's a mobster. When it really comes down to it, who is going to vote for a mobster?"

Rove's response was interrupted by the arrival of an attendant, who handed Rove a note. Rove thanked him and then read the note. A big smile crossed his face. "I'll be goddamned!"

"What's up?" asked Adelson, owner of the Las Vegas Sands Casino and Hotel, among other holdings.

"Cotti won the straw poll, with seventy-two percent of the vote! The runner-up got fourteen percent. I think that tells you what the voters think of Cotti. I'm telling you, it's time to jump on the bandwagon. Let's get this campaign out of first gear and into second!" Rove looked around at them. "Cotti's a fundraiser's dream."

They all laughed, sipped their scotches, and smoked their thousand dollar cigars. They were one big happy family. Rove hoped they would soon become happy Cotti Family members.

***

"Carl," said Robert Perry, owner of Perry Homes and home developer, "you might think you've got a winner, but we don't think you do."

All the men around the table nodded in response to Perry's comment and some stroked their chins, thinking about their commitment to their good friend. They just weren't quite sure whether to fund Rove's *new boy* in the political arena.

"But guys, Cotti's got a unique personality that hasn't been seen before in a politician," Rove said. "I mean, look what he did tonight in the straw poll. He blew the others away. Hell, Rand Paul only got fourteen percent of the vote. And he was the second place finisher. What does that tell you?"

"Yeah, but it's early yet," interjected Harold Simmons, owner of Contran Corp. "What's going to happen when the going gets tough? Will he fold?"

"Hell, no!" Rove shot back. "This guy put his life on the line when he went against the other Crime Families' wishes. They've tried to assassinate him more than once since he threw his hat into the ring. Jack Cotti has brass balls. And I might add, they're bigger than anyone's sitting at this table."

The men snickered at Rove's remark. But they knew it was true.

"So, Carl, what do you need from us tonight?" asked Sheldon Adelson.

"I'd like you to get on board and help fund Cotti's election campaign," replied Rove.

"I don't know..." Simmons replied.

"Hey, we still have a way to go," Rove admitted. "We've got a debate coming soon and then Super Tuesday. Let's see how well Cotti does and take it from there. But I'm telling you, we've got something here and we need to ride the wave all the way. And I need your help. Please, help me to help you."

"Carl, where in the hell is Cotti?" asked Perry. "Why didn't he come to this meeting? I'd like to ask him a few questions concerning his views on some important issues."

"Well, that's my fault, Robert," Rove answered. "I had him go back to his hotel room to get some rest."

"Cotti's just not the type of politician I want to invest in, for crying out loud," exclaimed Thiel. "He's still a mobster, in my eyes."

Rove nodded in admission that his **political wonder** had a criminal background. But what he said next had the big money boys scratching their heads: "By tonight's vote, the people seem to want a change in our political system. They're tired of professional politicians."

"You may be right about that," quipped Adelson. "Hell, I've been sick of them for years."

"Carl, I'll write you a check—on one condition," said Perry.

"What is that, Robert?"

"I want to ask Cotti about his values. Hell, it seems his being a crook doesn't scare the voters away. In fact, they seem to be in **awe** of the guy. But I want to see if his views on important issues are similar to mine."

"Not a problem," Rove replied. "I'll set up a meeting with him at my place sometime next week. But I can tell you now, his views are like mine, and I bleed Republican values. I know he won't let any of you down."

"Fine," said Perry. "I'm taking your word on it, Carl. Don't let us down."

Before the meeting broke up, the money men took a gamble. They all wrote checks to Rove and his American Crossroads fundraising company, for a total of more than three million dollars.

***

Rove was incredibly happy the way the night had turned out. Cotti had taken home his accolades by beating his peers in the straw poll and Rove had received his accolades by check from his peers.

Two days after the CPAC straw poll results, everyone in the media, and especially the McLaughlin Group, was talking about Jack Cotti and his political upset over the well-known and established Republican politicians. The headline of the New York Times read: *CPAC UPSET WINNER: JACK COTTI.*

John McLaughlin asked the four political pundits on his show, "You've all heard about the CPAC straw poll results, won by none other than that political newcomer, Jack Cotti. He won by the largest margin ever and beat the man that was picked to win, Rand Paul. How in the world did Cotti win?"

"John," answered Pat Buchanan, "I think all of us here are dumbfounded by the results. We keep telling the viewers that Jack Cotti doesn't have a chance to become a Presidential Candidate, but yet over and over he's made liars of us. Look, John. We think of him as nothing more than a gangster, a mobster. Evidently, the CPAC voters undeniably think of him as a viable Republican Presidential candidate."

McLaughlin repeated, "Eleanor Clift, I ask you the same question. How in the world did Jack Cotti win the CPAC straw poll?"

"How he got seventy-two percent of the vote is just inconceivable, John, while Rand Paul only received fourteen percent. I just don't get it. Those voters evidently see something in Jack Cotti that I just don't see. I still say he's just a good story at a cocktail party."

"Yeah, John," interjected Mort Zuckerman, "I don't know what's happening to the Republican Party, but I don't think it's healthy, first of all, for a mobster to be backed by the Republican Party. I believe I said this on last week's show. And I'm disgusted by the results of the CPAC voters. I mean, the Party's got to have a better Presidential candidate than a mobster."

"Watch it, Mort. Cotti may have you whacked for disrespecting him," quipped Tom Rogan.

"Well, I must say, I also am disgusted…and dumbfounded…by the outcome. Jack Cotti for President! Please!" said McLaughlin, sarcastically. "Bye, Bye."

***

McLaughlin wasn't the only one who was disgusted and dumbfounded by the voters at the CPAC convention. So were the Feds.

"I don't believe this shit," said Agent Arms. "I'll be damned if I'm going to allow a mobster to become President."

"There's not a whole hell of a lot we can do," said Agent Lundy. "When Cotti makes a wrong move, then we'll nail him."

"If Cotti ends up becoming the Republican Presidential Candidate, I will hang up my gun. Or use it on him," quipped Arms.

"You know, that may not be a bad idea. We could make it look like another gangster killed him," remarked Agent Brunson.

"That's enough of that talk," replied Arms. "I was only speaking hypothetically."

"So was I," retorted Brunson.

"Let's get back to work," ordered Arms.

***

As the Agents returned to their surveillance work, Cotti was also busy. Rove had set up speaking engagements across the country for his political **Wonder Boy,** visiting Super Tuesday States to give the voters there what Eastern Seaboard voters had already seen: A look-see at mobster and now political powerhouse, Jack Cotti.

Over the next five days, Cotti visited Iowa, Illinois, Missouri, Oklahoma, and Kansas. His receptions were unlike any ever seen before. They came to see the **new boy on the block.** Cotti made nonbelievers into believers with his honest personality and his unbelievable speaking qualities.

After visiting the five Midwestern states, Cotti returned to his home in Queens and waited for further instructions from his mentor.

Rove called a few days later and gave Cotti instructions and schedules for his visits to five Western states: Arizona, Utah, Montana, California, and Idaho. He would then have a meeting with the Fat Cat donors, and soon after, he would participate in the first debate of the Republican Primaries.

That was a lot on Jack Cotti's plate. After all, he still had to oversee his organization, take care of his family and children, and on top of that, make appearances all over the country. But he loved every minute of it. And the people loved him back.

He made new friends wherever he went. Black, white, brown, red, Chinese, people of nearly every ethnic background, wanted to see this guy, this mobster, to shake his hand in the hope they had shaken the hand of a possible President. Cotti was a political phenomenon. The crowds became bigger and bigger as the days progressed, swelling to over fifteen thousand at times, blocking traffic so that the police having to shut roads down to appease the crowds. At times, things became hectic and difficult, but Cotti handled it like a pro. And he never became impatient and upset and reverted back to that inner thug mentality. He was very professional about his image.

Cotti traveled with only a few of his bodyguards but knew he was being closely watched by FBI Agents. They were wandering about the crowd and following his every move, waiting for that moment when he would slip up and they could pounce on him and put him where the President wanted: in jail.

But Cotti wasn't giving the Feds any reason to arrest him. He was now acting the role of a politician and not the *gangster* that he was known for.

Chapter 12

Cotti's visits to the five Western states were no different than his Midwestern visits. The crowds swelled to nearly unmanageable sizes. His appearance in California was held at Angel Stadium, where the crowd swelled to over twenty thousand. No one in politics had ever seen such large crowds of people just wanting to see and hear a politician who was running for President. Hell, they'd never seen crowds that large at a President's inauguration. This was unheard of. It was overwhelming.

But the media ate it up. They couldn't get enough of Jack Cotti. They stopped calling him *Gangster* and began calling him a ***bona fide*** candidate for President of the United States.

Over the next three weeks, Cotti visited seven Southern states that would participate in Super Tuesday and gave speeches in competition with the other Republican candidates. During a respite in his stately visits, Cotti had to visit Rove in DC for a donor party, which included those donors from the CPAC Convention. The donors wanted to hear, in person, what Cotti had to say. They wanted to question him on issues that were important to their own personal and business needs.

During the party, Cotti "made nice" with all those involved. After nearly an hour of introducing himself and being introduced to the Fat Cat donors, the meeting started in earnest. The donors sat around a big table while Cotti stood on a stage behind a podium.

The first question was asked by Sheldon Adelson. "Yes, Mr. Cotti. What do you think about guns?"

"Why? You want to buy some?" Cotti answered. "I know a guy who has a whole truckload for sale. He's got Glock pistols to AK 47's. I could get you a great deal on quantity."

The crowd laughed and snickered.

"No, I don't need to buy any," Adelson replied. "I just wanted to know if you were a gun enthusiast."

"Yes, I am, Mr. Adelson. Guns are used in my business. If you get my meaning."

"Yes, we do, Mr. Cotti," interjected Peter Thiel. He began to ask a question, but Simmons beat him to it.

"Mr. Cotti," Simmons asked, "what do you think about torture? Many say it is wrong to torture your enemy. What do you say?"

"Well, I'm for it," Cotti said. "And without a rule book."

The Fat Cats nodded to each other with that answer.

Cotti continued. "I've seen it myself, firsthand. I know torture works and I'll tell you why. A friend of mine—we'll call him Charlie—had a guy who'd tried to kill him tied up to a chair in his basement. It was Christmas Eve and the guy wouldn't tell him who else was in on the hit and who'd ordered it, so Charlie cut out the guy's nuts, put them on the end of an icepick, and roasted them over an open fire. Then he made the guy eat his own roasted nuts. When the guy was through eating, Charlie put that same ice pick through his ear canal and into his brain, which killed the guy instantly. But before he did that, Charlie'd gotten the answers to his questions. See, the thing about torturing is: if the guy has something to lose, he'll tell you whatever you want to know. But if the guy believes in an ideal, forget about it! You might just as well kill him, 'cause he ain't giving nothing up. Usually, those kind of guys are proud of what they've done for their cause and will tell you everything they know if you just ask nicely. I hope that answers your question."

Robert Perry jumped into the fray. "This might be off the subject, but I've wanted to ask Mr. Cotti this question since he started his political career. I want to hear it from the horse's mouth." He looked directly at Cotti and asked, "Is it true that before one becomes a member of the mob, a person must kill first?"

That question took Cotti aback. He really didn't want to respond to such a stupid question. He thought about it for a minute and replied, "Did you know that in the Sioux Tribe of Indians, before one could become a Warrior, they had to first kill one of their enemy? That law is similar to Mafia law. Before becoming a member, it is true one has to make his *'bones,'* as we like to call it. To show his loyalty to his Family, he has to kill one of their enemies. Then his induction begins. But I am no longer in that life. I have taken a leave of absence, to pursue a life in politics." He then added, "Hey, *not for nuttin'*, but is this the kind of questions you want to ask me? If it is, I can tell you some stories that would curl your toes."

Before anyone could ask another question, Rove jumped in. "Maybe another time for that," Rove told Cotti. "I'm sure our guests have the answers they were looking for. Now, let's see if they're going to help get us into the White House."

Cotti went around the table shaking hands with the **Money Men.** He thanked them for their confidence in his ability to go all the way.

***

Shortly after, Cotti was on a plane heading for home to take care of business there. Even though Napolie was running the Family, Cotti continued to oversee the operation.

So far, the truce was holding. But Napolie had some news for Cotti that might put a whole new light on the subject. A light that had been shining brightly for now, but could soon be flickering out.

Cotti and Napolie met at Cotti's home to talk about the Family. Sitting in the den, Napolie began to explain about the troubles that lay ahead.

Before Napolie could speak, Cotti asked, "What's up?"

"Well, it could be trouble."

"So, spill!"

"Jack, I heard that your boy, Petey, is being courted by the Luccheses. They want to make him."

"Forget about it!" Cotti shouted. "I don't want any of my kids to get into the *life*. And they know it. Especially, Petey! He's my oldest and I expect him to obey my wishes."

"So what do you want me to do?"

"Go see Parrissi. Tell him that he would be doing me a big favor if he'd tell my kid to fuck off. Tell him I don't want my kid following in my footsteps. You tell him that."

"What if Parrissi refuses?"

"Then do what you gotta do," Cotti lit a cigar. "Even if you gotta break my kid's legs. That'd put him out of commission for a good six months, at least."

"What about Parrissi? You want him hit?"

"Hell, no!" Cotti exclaimed. "I don't want nothing breaking the truce. Nothing!"

"Right, Boss."

***

After another half-hour of small talk, Napolie left to take care of business. And take care of it he did. Within just a few days, Napolie had taken care of Cotti's problem without much repercussion from the Lucchese Family. But he came up against a wicked tornado when he confronted Petey. So much so that legs had to be broken: Petey's legs. That would give Petey a good six months to recuperate and lick his wounds, and think about his future. Now he was a problem no more for his father.

***

Cotti was home for two weeks before he got a call from Rove. "Jack, we got our first of nine Primary debates before Super Tuesday. They'll be held here in DC in seven days, so we have to get you ready. We need to go over some of the questions that will be asked and find the answers that you need to give to get the voters on your side."

"I already got the voters on my side," Cotti replied confidently.

"You might have them in your corner for now, Jack. But there's still plenty of time left for one of your opponents to go up in the polls. Especially, if you're not prepped correctly. That's why the question and answer session is so important."

"No problem. When do you want me in DC?"

"Two days before the Primary. You can stay in my guest bedroom. I'll see you then."

"Hey, before you go, how's our funding? Is the money still rolling in?" Cotti asked.

Rove didn't know what Cotti had in mind, or how to answer him, but he tried. "So far, so good. Soon, we'll have money coming in from all corners of the world and from all organizations that favor Republicans. But it will dry up if we don't do well in the Republican Primaries. Let's just concentrate on that, and leave the money worries to me.

204

Okay, Jack?"

"Not a problem. Forget about it!" Cotti answered. He hung up the phone.

***

Cotti had a few more days to relax and be with his family before traveling to DC. During those days, he had time to think about the money that was rolling in from donations and why he wasn't getting his cut off the top. He needed to set Rove straight and show him *how things were done*. He wasn't going to take "no" for an answer. He believed he deserved a percentage of that money. After all, if it wasn't for him, those millions wouldn't have materialized. He fell asleep on the couch thinking about that money.

By the time he had awakened, he was on a jet plane heading for DC, sitting in first class, and giving autographs to people around him, including the co-pilot.

A few hours later, Cotti was sitting around Rove's dining room table, having a cigar and drinking a beer. It had been a long day for him, so they retired to bed early that night, to get up bright and early the next morning and start prepping for the debate.

After a breakfast of cannolis and coffee, Rove and Cotti went through a long and frustrating practice session. Rove was satisfied with Cotti's answers, so tweaking wasn't necessary.

Rove asked Cotti question after question on topics that

he thought would be asked.

***

Rove had thought of every question that was asked that night at the debate—but one. And Rove was more than surprised when it was asked:

"What ethnic race do you belong to?" asked Fox Host, Chris Wallace.

Cotti seemed to be taken aback by the question, but the others were quick to answer:

"I'm of the White Race," quipped Rick Perry. The audience erupted in applause and whistles.

Wallace jumped in to take control of the question. "Jeb Bush, I ask you: What ethnic race do you belong to?"

"Mr. Wallace, I am Caucasian. I, too, belong to the White Race." Again the audience erupted in applause.

Rand Paul, Chris Christie, and Ted Cruz all answered the same as the two politicians before them.

But when Cotti was asked that question, he answered differently. "I am of the Human Race," he exclaimed. A sudden hush came over the crowd. They didn't know how to react to that one.

Wallace took control of the silence and asked Cotti to expand on his answer:

"I know of only one Race, Mr. Wallace. And that's the Human Race. There is no other, as far as I'm concerned. Black, White, Red, Yellow, Pink, Blue, who gives a fuck. We are one world, one people. We're just gonna have to live together...Peacefully."

Wallace gave out a sickly laugh. "Mr. Cotti, you can't curse. Your profanity just went over the airwaves to twenty-two million people. We're LIVE! This is the first time I've ever been embarrassed by one of my questions."

Fox quickly went to an advertisement, as the producer came over to the group of politicians and told them in explicit terms that profanity was prohibited and wouldn't be tolerated.

Cotti felt like all the weight was falling on his shoulders. He was being belittled like a little school kid and didn't appreciate it. In fact, he wasn't on stage to answer the last question, which was on the use of profanity. The ones still standing on stage swore that they never used profanity.

"It isn't allowed in my house," stated Ted Cruz.

"Nor mine," added Perry.

"My wife would skin me alive if she ever heard a dirty word out of my mouth. It just doesn't happen," replied Jeb Bush.

"I rarely swear," admitted Christie. "I might say 'damn' or 'pissed off,' but nothing like we heard out of Mr. Cotti's mouth. Never!"

Rand Paul was the only one who admitted swearing, but under extenuating circumstances. He explained how he swore once when he had a mishap while doing eye surgery on a lady patient.

"Would you elaborate on that answer, Rand Paul?"

Wallace asked, surprised by Paul's admission.

"While I was scraping her retina with a scalpel, I suddenly sneezed and the scalpel plunged through the eyeball and into the brain, paralyzing her for life. I swore then and only one or two other times last year."

"Is that it?" asked Wallace, smiling.

He was thinking, then blurted out: "And a few times the year before, but that's it." He thought some more. While scratching his head, he admitted, "I did have a few mishaps in surgery three years ago, similar to the incident I just mentioned. I can't remember further back than that. But I try not to swear. Only under trying times."

Once Rand Paul had given his answer, the debate ended. The politicians walked off stage.

Cotti was already in his dressing room getting reamed by Rove for his answer to the Race question.

"Jack, what the hell is wrong with you?" Rove barked. "You had the audience in your pocket until you gave your damn answer to the race question. What were you thinking?"

"Hey, **fuck you**, Carl. I gave them my honest answer. I told you. I will never lie to the People. They can love me, hate me, despise me, I don't care. But I will not lie to them. I told them just how I felt. Period!"

"Okay. Forget about it!"

"Hey, that's my line," Cotti quipped. They both laughed.

"So let's get out of here and get ready for next week's

debate. We have a long ways to go before election time. Let's see who won tonight's debate. Let's hope you didn't go down in the polls."

"And what happens if I do?" Cotti asked.

"Well, we won't worry about that now. I'm sure if you do drop, it won't be much. You're so far ahead of your closest opponent, a few points lost won't matter."

They quickly closed up shop and returned to Rove's home to await the polling results the following morning.

***

After a breakfast of a half grapefruit and one three minute egg, Cotti and Rove retired to the den to digest their meal and smoke a cigar. While relaxing, Cotti told Rove what he thought about breakfast.

"*Not for nuttin'*, Carl, but I think you should eat a healthier meal for breakfast."

"Jack, a half a grapefruit and a three minute egg is only two hundred calories," Rove told Cotti.

"That's what I mean. You need to eat healthier. When I'm home, I try and eat three or four eggs, a slew of well-cooked bacon, toast, cannolis, and coffee, which is well over two thousand calories. Now that's a healthy meal."

Rove just laughed at Cotti's thought process, but his laughter was interrupted by the rings of a phone. He took the call.

Cotti didn't know who was speaking on the other end until the conversation was over and Rove said: "Thanks,

Rupert. I'll see you tomorrow."

"What's up?" Cotti asked him.

"That was Rupert Murdoch on the phone. He gave me the results of last night's poll."

"Well, how did I do?"

"I got some good news and some bad news. Which would you like first?"

"Fuck that, Carl. Just tell me what you want me to know."

"Okay, Jack. Take it easy. The good news is that you won last night's debate with fifty-five percent of the vote. Jeb Bush took second place with thirty-two percent. Then Rand Paul with eight percent, Christie had three percent, Cruz had two, and Perry got nothing. And it seems, according to Rupert, Perry dropped out of the race and Governor Walker will take his place for the next debate."

"So what's the bad news?" Cotti asked, puffing on his cigar.

"The bad news, Jack, is that you're down seventeen points from the last poll that was taken. And it was all due to the comment about your race. We would have won by a landslide otherwise."

"Hey, I tell it like it is. Forget about it!"

"Yeah, I know. You don't lie to the People. You know, this is politics. And you'll have to be kissing babies, too," Rove told him in no uncertain terms.

***

210

The Feds were listening in on the conversation between Rove and Cotti and were inebriated with happiness over the fact that Cotti was finally losing his charm with the voters. They had bugs throughout Rove's house and had been listening to his conversations for more than a decade.

"Next debate, Cotti will drop another seventeen points," surmised Agent Arms.

"Yeah, my bet's on Jeb Bush," said Brunson, before returning to his surveillance duties.

***

Rove wasn't worried. Cotti still had a rather large lead. Rove knew Cotti could never stay in the seventy-plus range. But if Cotti could just use his charisma to retain the voters' confidence, he could stay above fifty percent in the polls. And Rove was satisfied with any spot between fifty and sixty percent.

It was getting late and Cotti needed to get home before his wife started worrying about him. So he asked Rove if he could get him to the airport. "The wife gets angry if I'm late for dinner."

A few hours later, Rove had his limo driver take Cotti to the airport so he could return to his life in Gotham.

***

Cotti was in a good mood when he left DC and in a better mood when his wife picked him up at Kennedy Airport. He was in a romantic mood when he got home and was ready to throw his wife in bed and do the "*wild thing*," but the ring of a phone interrupted his sexual motor.

"Shit, whoever it is, you sure picked a bad time," Cotti snarled as he picked up the phone.

"Jack, Johnny. I need to speak with you. Can you meet me at the club?" It was Napolie's voice on the line.

"Is it really that important? I just got in the door from DC. Can't it wait?"

"I wouldn't have called this late if it wasn't important," Napolie replied.

"I'll see you in two hours."

The two wiseguys met at the club and then walked outside to talk, hoping the Feds weren't listening in on their conversation. When they were a good two blocks from the club, Napolie told Cotti about his concern.

"Jack, we got a problem."

"What now?" Cotti asked.

"Parrissi made Petey."

"He what?" Cotti yelled. "I thought that was taken care of. Are you sure that Petey's been made?"

"Yeah, Jack, I confirmed it. I thought we had that thing straightened out too, but Parrissi lied to me. It's been less than three weeks and he's already broken his word. He promised that he wouldn't make Petey."

"How could he make Petey? The boy's lying in bed with two broken legs. He can't go nowhere."

"Parrissi and the boys made him at Petey's place."

Cotti just shook his head in disgust and disbelief.

"Fuck!" he muttered under his breath.

"I'm sorry, Jack. Want do you want to do?"

"Nothing," Cotti snapped.

"Nothing? Jack, if we don't do anything, that'll make the Family look weak. Jack, we *gotta* do something!" Napolie pleaded.

"No! Not until after the Republican Convention or Super Tuesday. If I don't win, then it won't matter and then we'll take care of business. And I'll take care of Parrissi myself," Cotti promised.

"I'll take care of the Parrissi problem. You gotta run the Family, Jack. I'll take care of Parrissi."

***

They had walked completely around two city blocks and were back at the club. Standing outside the front entrance, Cotti told Napolie something Napolie had never heard before. "Well, Johnny, if politics don't work out, maybe I'll retire and let you run the business and take control of the Family. Maybe, one day...who knows?"

Napolie looked deep into Cotti's face and for the first time saw an old and tired man. Something he thought he'd never see in his boss.

Cotti left to return home. Napolie stayed at the club and had a double scotch, while thinking about his boss's sudden "nice guy" routine. Cotti was never one to let a member of another Family take advantage of him or anyone in his Family. Was Cotti getting soft?

That was a no-no in Napolie's way of life. It used to be in Cotti's. Not seeking revenge on Parrissi was making him and the Family look weak. Napolie didn't like it. And to retire from the Family? That just didn't happen. Not in Napolie's eyes, anyway. Napolie wasn't happy the way things were going, but he had to do as ordered. For now, anyway. So he would ignore the slight that Parrissi had given to the Valoppi Family and put on hold any retaliation to certain parties.

***

Cotti was home entertaining his wife. His mentor Rove was also at home entertaining his friend, Rupert Murdoch. Murdoch had come to discuss the issue that Cotti had walked out of the debate hosted by his company, which he believed had made him look like a fool for backing Cotti. To say the least, Murdoch was pissed off and angry.

Rove tried to appease him. "Come on Rupert, calm down. It's not the end of the world. I mean, you know how Cotti talks. He sprinkles his punctuality with curse words. So what? You know he didn't do it on purpose. He's real, Rupert. He's no phony. And the reason Cotti walked out was because the producer scolded him as if he was a little child. He didn't deserve that. And I'm sure if he was here, he'd apologize to you for it."

"Carl, I just don't give a damn anymore. He made me look like a fool and I don't take kindly to that."

"So what do you suggest I do, Rupert?" Rove asked.

Murdoch thought for a minute. Scratching his head, he said, "Drop him. Fire him from the Republican Party...and take the funds you've gathered for him and give them to Jeb Bush. He's the man that will win the Republican nomination."

"Bush? Are you kidding? The voters don't want another Bush in office. At least not now. Maybe four years from now, when the voters have GW out of their system. Then they might want him. But Cotti's got more than a twenty point lead over Bush."

"I still say Bush is going to get the Republican nomination," Murdoch said.

"I beg to differ, Rupert. Before we decide which way to go, let's just see how he does in the next debate. Carol Crowley will be hosting for CNN and she's a pretty tough journalist. So let's just see what happens. Cotti's gone down seventeen points since the last straw poll. If he goes down any further, then all bets are off."

Rupert nodded in agreement.

Rove then opened an expensive bottle of red wine and poured drinks for his old and dear friend. They sat back and reminisced about past Presidential elections where both had been instrumental in producing a bona fide President.

***

The Feds had overheard the conversation between the two political muscle men and were delighted to hear that Murdoch wanted nothing more to do with Cotti, especially when it was Murdoch who'd gotten the ball rolling for Cotti. They were even more overjoyed when Murdoch ordered Rove to get rid of Cotti.

"Cotti's days are numbered," Agent Lundy said.

"That means he'll have to go back to stealing for a living," added Brunson.

All seven agents sitting in their surveillance room laughed at that comment.

***

Not only did the Feds overhear the conversation, but so did Rupert's bodyguard, who just happened to be working for a Cotti associate. He told that associate, who telephoned Napolie with the news.

"Jack, I got something to tell you," exclaimed Napolie over the phone. "I'll let you decide if it's important or not."

"What now, Johnny?"

"I heard something that has to do with Rove, Murdoch, and your political career. It comes from Rupert Murdoch's bodyguard, who works for one our associates' security company. He was with Murdoch at Rove's home. He says that Murdoch was pissed off at you for walking off the stage at the debate. Murdoch said you made him look like a fool and that he wants Rove to fire you."

"What did Rove say?" Cotti asked.

"He says he's gonna wait to see how you do at the next debate. I guess Rove did stand up for you."

"Yeah, Carl's all right."

Napolie continued. "The bodyguard said that Murdoch wants Rove to take the donations and move them to Jeb Bush's campaign. So it sounds like Murdoch wants Rove to jump ship and Rove is sitting on the fence, waiting to see what you're gonna do."

"Hmm. I guess I'll just have to win this week's debate then, and take it from there. Hell, I just may have to start my own Party," Cotti quipped.

"Are you kidding, Jack? You're gonna start your own Party? With what?" Napolie thought his boss was speaking crazy.

"What do you mean, with what? We got the organization and the people to get it going. But hey, I'm now a Republican, running on a Republican ticket."

"So what would you call this Party of yours?" Napolie asked, just for the hell of it, to amuse his wacky boss.

Cotti thought for a minute, then said: "I don't know. I'd have to think about that. Maybe the American Family Party. Or the Freedom Family Party. I don't know, but I'd want a Family in it somewhere. Like my slogan would be: *'Cotti's a Family man'.* Which I am."

"Geez, Jack. This political shit has really gotten to you. I wonder sometimes if somebody hit you on the head, because I think that you forget who you really are. You're a mobster, Jack…and regular folk will never forget that."

"You may be right about that, Johnny. But it hasn't hurt me so far."

"You've been lucky," Napolie replied.

"Luck's got nothing to do with it, Johnny boy. The People love me."

Napolie just closed his eyes and shook his head in disbelief at those last words. He hung up the phone and wondered when his Boss would come back to reality and return to his old self—the gangster that he'd wanted to be since childhood. It was like Cotti was bi-polar. One day, he was the gangster that everyone around him knew and loved and the next he would be some straight, business-like guy that thought he was a powerful politician. Napolie was beginning to question Cotti's sanity. His boss was now becoming more of a politician than a gangster; and that wasn't a good thing in Cotti's neck of the woods.

***

Cotti received his second phone call a few minutes after he'd hung up with Napolie. It was Rove on the other end.

"Jack," Rove said, "our second Primary debate will be held at the Convention Center in Los Angeles. AIG is loaning us one of their Boeing 707s to make the trip. We no longer have to use commercial aircraft to fly to our destinations. We have the use of this aircraft as long as we need it, pilots and flight attendants included."

"So, when do we leave?" asked Cotti.

"In two days. That'll give us a couple of days to rest up before the debate."

"Are we going to prep for this debate?"

"I don't know. You think you need to?"

Cotti thought for a minute. "Not really. We went over so many different questions and issues for the last debate, I don't think we overlooked anything. I am primed and ready to go."

"Ok, then. We'll fly in at Kennedy, Friday morning." Rove gave Cotti the time, gate number, and the name and address of the Charter Company.

Chapter 13

Cotti was waiting a half hour early at the gate where he was to meet the plane. About forty-five minutes later, the plane rolled in and airport personnel rolled a staircase to the door of the plane. Cotti grabbed his suitcase and climbed the stairs. The plane door opened, revealing Rove at the entrance. Rove grabbed Cotti's suitcase and shook his hand, to the roar of Cotti supporters inside the plane. The flight attendant shut and locked the exit door.

"I'm glad you could make it, Jack," said Rove jokingly,

"Yeah, me too," Cotti replied. Cotti was taken aback by all the applause. "Who the hell are all these people?" he asked Rove, pointing to the more than two dozen people aboard.

Rove introduced Cotti to the others riding with them. There were media personnel, writers, campaign workers, Reince Prebius, donors, and some just plain fans who were now volunteers working for the Jack Cotti Campaign.

"Jack, you know Reince Prebius," Rove said.

"Yes. How are you, Reince?" Cotti asked, as he shook hands.

Cotti also shook hands with donors, Sheldon Adelson, Harold and Annette Simmons, Robert Perry, and John Childs. They were all happy to be on Cotti's team and told him so.

"Let's keep up the good work," Perry said.

Cotti gave him a thumbs up.

A voice came over the intercom. "This is your Captain speaking. Please, take your seats and fasten your seatbelts. We'll be taking off in just a few minutes."

Seconds after an airport worker topped off the fuel tank, the plane began taxiing down the runway. It stopped, waiting for permission from the tower to prepare for takeoff. The pilot then revved the engines and a few seconds later, the plane took off down the runway like a bat out of hell.

Just a few feet from being airborne, the plane's engines suddenly seized up, forcing the plane to surge forward and giving nearly all the passengers whiplash.

The intercom sputtered again. "This is the Captain. We've had a shutdown of both engines. Please stay seated and wait for the flight attendant to check out any injuries."

Everyone on board was pretty shaken up. No one could understand what could have happened to cause such a meltdown. Luckily, nobody was hurt to the point of hospitalization. They took it in stride and were just happy to be alive. After all, had it happened after takeoff, at thirty-thousand feet in the air, the plane would have fallen like a brick, and most likely there would have been no survivors. Many thanked the Lord for their safety.

"Thank you, God. You are my savior," exclaimed Rove.

"Easy there, Carl. Let's not go overboard. We didn't get hurt," Cotti quipped.

"Damn, Jack, how can you be so calm? We could have been killed."

"Carl, you don't know what 'could have been killed' really means. I could have been killed a few times, but it wasn't from a plane."

The flight attendant's voice came over the intercom. "Please remain seated. Rescue personnel will be arriving shortly."

They did show up; it wasn't right away, but two hours later, even though the plane was blocking the main runway, which the airport had to shut down.

When the rescue workers were finally in place, the flight crew released the emergency chute. Within thirty minutes, everyone on board had slid down the chute and was safely on the ground, without incident. After being checked out by EMS technicians and given the A-OK, the passengers were then bused back to the terminal to await the arrival of another plane for the flight to Los Angeles.

Many of the passengers weren't sure if they wanted to resume the trip to LA. They were quite nervous and upset, to say the least. But to everyone's surprise, they refused to give in and stayed the course. Brave souls, all.

Most of the hurt came from waiting for hours in a small,

dim lit, empty terminal for its only carrier: AIG. Three hours had passed, four, then five; finally, seven hours after their rescue, a plane finally arrived to take them to their destination. Everyone, including Cotti, was tired, run down, and bored.

When the passengers finally boarded the plane, it was nearing midnight. Once they were seated, many just fell fast asleep, especially the old guys like Rove, Prebius, and Cotti.

***

About four hours into the trip, a flight attendant quietly awakened Rove and handed him a note. Rove read it, then shook Cotti awake. "Jack, the flight attendant just handed me a note about that engine trouble we had on that plane."

"So! What the hell does it have to do with me?"

"It seems the FBI is investigating the guy who topped off the plane with fuel."

"Yeah, and why would I give a fuck?" Cotti asked.

"Well, the note claims that the person they're investigating is Danny Angelo, the son of Lucchese Capo, Anthony Angelo. Do you know him, Jack?"

"Yeah, I know the kid's father. I don't know the kid, though. And yes, the kid's old man is with the Lucchese Family."

"The FBI think that the kid mixed water or acid in with the fuel," Rove said. "That's why the engines seized. But they won't know for sure until the fuel and plane are inspected." He added, "You know, Jack, if the engines would have shut down while we were airborne, we all would have died."

"You're probably right about that," Cotti replied.

Rove remained silent for a good minute or two before asking Cotti a perplexing question. "Jack, is somebody in the Mafia still trying to kill you? And would they kill everyone on the plane just to kill you?"

Cotti thought for a minute, then exclaimed, "I don't know. I hope not. That wouldn't be good for any of the Families. But you can bet your ass that I'm gonna find out. Forget about it!"

"Who wants you dead bad enough that they would try bringing down a plane full of passengers just to take you out?" Rove asked.

"Carl, that list is longer than my arm. But none of my enemies in the *life* would do that now. We have a truce. They wouldn't do anything to jeopardize that."

Rove just shrugged. He was satisfied with Cotti's answer. He shut off his overhead light and went back to sleep.

Cotti had a harder time trying to sleep. He kept thinking about what Rove had told him about the mishap with the plane. The thought that his enemies may have contributed to the engine failure and wanted him dead continued to dance in his head. He tossed and turned in his seat the rest of the flight, punching air while fighting his inner demons of times past.

***

They arrived at LAX at six in the morning. By eight, the entourage had moved on to their hotel in Simi Valley and checked into their rooms.

Soon after, Cotti and Rove met in the hotel's restaurant, to eat a late breakfast and "shoot the shit." Afterwards, Cotti returned to his room and Rove, along with a half dozen volunteers, went out to sign the papers with the State for Cotti's Presidential run and to scout different locations for a possible Cotti campaign Headquarters.

***

While Rove was out taking care of business, Cotti, too, was also taking care of business, phoning his Underboss to get some answers.

"Johnny, it's Jack," he said over the phone. "I need you to get in touch with the Detective and TSA Agent we got on our payroll. See if they can find out the cause of the engine problem of AIG's charter plane that was heading to Los Angeles yesterday morning."

"Why? What's up?"

"The fucking engines seized up just as we were about to get off the ground. If it had happened when we were in the air, I wouldn't be talking to you right now."

"Well, it seems everything turned out all right in the end. I mean, you're in LA, safe and sound, right?" Napolie replied, not really knowing what to say.

"Yeah, but the reason I'm calling is because the Feds thinks it was sabotage. They believe someone fucked with the plane's fuel. They're investigating Anthony Angelo's kid."

"Are you kidding? Angelo's a Capo in the Lucchese Family. You don't think Parrissi ordered Angelo to have his kid sabotage the plane, do you, Jack?"

"That's what I want you to find out. Don't do anything crazy until we know for sure just what happened. It just might be a coincidence and an accident that the engines seized up. Who in the fuck knows? But I want you to find out for me, Johnny. We'll either laugh about this or take serious action against those involved. Get me?"

"Forget about it, Jack. I got it under control. It's gonna take me some time, but I'll let you know something as soon as I know. I'll talk to you when you get back."

***

Napolie hung up the phone. If it turned out that Angelo's kid had sabotaged the AIG plane, Napolie would have good reason to have Parrissi whacked and not get any flack about it from Cotti. Strictly Family business.

***

Cotti walked downstairs to the restaurant and ordered a late lunch. The restaurant was fairly empty when he sat down but he noticed that quite a number of men, all dressed in black suits, had walked in behind him and were now seated at nearby tables. Cotti sensed danger all around. He thought maybe a hit, and had no bodyguards or gun to protect himself. He really wanted a smoke to calm his nerves, but he wasn't in Kansas anymore. He was in smoke-free California. Only the smoke from the smog was legal.

He stared cautiously at the many men surrounding his table and wondered just what the hell they wanted. His food arrived and one of the men in black arose from his table and began walking towards him. Cotti subconsciously grabbed for his gun under his suit jacket, but then remembered it wasn't there. Instinctively, he balled up his fists, ready to fight.

The man got closer.

Cotti stood up to challenge him.

The man flipped open a leather wallet, revealing a tiny gold badge. "Mr. Cotti, don't be alarmed. I'm FBI Agent Donald Preston, and I'm here to warn you."

Cotti let out a sigh of relief and sat back down. "Shit, for a minute there I thought you guys were here to whack me."

"It's not the FBI that you have to be worried about. We put people in prison; we don't kill them."

"Fuck you! So what do you want to warn me about?"

"Mr. Cotti, we believe people in the Lucchese Family may be trying to kill you. We overheard a conversation between Angelo Parrissi and one of his Capos. I'm not at liberty at this time to say which Capo, but orders were given and threats were made against your well-being. We just wanted to warn you and make sure that you were aware that your life may be in danger, if you didn't know that already."

"And so now you've warned me. Am I supposed to say 'thank you'? Forget about it! You guys I can live without. You are a pain in my ass!" Cotti exclaimed, to all the men around him dressed in black.

"Mr. Cotti, and you're a pain in our ass," retorted Agent Preston. "We came here with best intentions. We are under orders to keep a close watch out for your well-being while you're here in California."

"Yeah, right. I'm sure you could care less," Cotti replied, angrily.

"No, Mr. Cotti, you're wrong. We do care what happens to you…because we are going to put you behind bars, hopefully for the rest of your life, and we don't want anybody to spoil that for us by putting a bullet in the back of your head. So, you enjoy your stay here in sunny California, while you can. And I'm sure you'll be seeing a lot of us."

"Now, do you mind if I eat?" Cotti barked. "My food's getting cold."

Agent Preston returned to his table and watched Cotti as he ate his steak and cheese hoagies, before trailing him to his room.

***

The FBI presence in and around the hotel made Cotti

decide to phone Napolie concerning the news he had just received. But Napolie didn't answer the phone. Cotti decided to take a nap and wait for Rove to return. A few hours later, Cotti was awakened by a loud knock on the door.

"Yeah," he yelled from bed.

"Jack, it's Carl."

Cotti opened the door. "Come in, Carl."

"Jack, let's go to dinner. I need to speak with you concerning the campaign. We got quite a bit done today. So meet me in the restaurant. I'll see you there in ten minutes." Rove walked away, shutting the door behind him.

Cotti had slept in his clothes, so after relieving himself and washing his face, he met Rove at his table in the hotel restaurant. "Hey, Carl. Tomorrow night's the big night," he quipped, as he took his seat. Again, he noted the many FBI agents sitting nearby.

"Sure is. Bigger than you know," Rove replied.

"Why do you say that, Carl?"

"We can't have any slipups like we had last debate. We can't afford to have another drop in the polls. That wouldn't be good."

"You're not losing confidence in me, are you, Carl?"

"Of course not, Jack. But if we want the money to keep rolling in, let's hope we go up a few points in the polls. That would keep our momentum going for Super Tuesday." Rove hoped Cotti still had it in him to woo the audience.

"You're not thinking of jumping ship anytime soon, are you?" Cotti asked suspiciously, remembering what Napolie had told him.

"What gave you that idea, Jack? Of course not."

But Cotti knew Rove was lying. A liar always looks down or stares into his glass when trying to cover up his true feelings. Rove had stared into his glass while answering Cotti's question.

"Well, don't worry, Carl. I won't let you or the Party down. I'll be on my best behavior tomorrow night," Cotti promised.

Rove smiled. "Let's order some food. I'm famished."

They ate a meal of steak and truffles, then sat back to digest their food and finish their conversation.

"We scouted some excellent areas today for campaign headquarters," Rove said. "If we do well at the debate, we will begin opening Cotti campaign headquarters in every major city across the country. Then our volunteers will began gathering enough signatures to get you on the ballot in every state."

"Hey, I got nearly twelve thousand people across the country that will help in that endeavor. In fact, I contacted their bosses months ago," Cotti exclaimed.

"Are you talking about Family members, Jack?"

"They might be. Why?"

"We have to be careful. We don't want any fuckups."

Cotti nodded. "Me either."

Rove leaned in close and told Cotti in no uncertain

terms, "This is just the beginning, Jack. We still have a hell of a ways to go to the finish line. I hope you're up to it."

"Forget about it!" Cotti said, confidently.

It was getting late so they retired to their respective suites, to have a smoke before going to bed. Cotti was going to phone Napolie again but then remembered the three hour time difference. He put it off; he'd talk with Napolie when he returned home.

Cotti finally went to bed about two in the morning, dreaming about his Presidency.

***

Rove dreamed about raising money. And that's exactly what Rove did for the rest of the trip. He had meetings with his billionaire friends, hoping they would give money to help a charismatic man run for President of the United States. But Rove was not new to this game and knew he would have to make promises that he might not be able to keep in order to pry money out of their tight little grips.

After lunch on debate day, Rove prepped Cotti in a question-and-answer session for nearly two hours. Soon after, they went to the Reagan Presidential Library and signed in. Cotti and Rove then met with the competition and made no qualms about who would win the debate— again.

"You guys should hang it up," Cotti told his opponents. "The only one leaving here tonight with a *gold star* is yours truly. Forget about it!" He and Rove walked away.

The competition snickered at Cotti's remark and left it at that, not wanting to say anything to antagonize or anger him. They just watched in silence as he walked away.

Just before taking the stage, Cotti felt a little tired. "Damn, Carl, I'll be glad when these debates are over. They're wearing me out."

"Hey, it could be worse," Rove replied. "We used to have twenty-seven. This year it's only nine. So consider yourself lucky."

A few minutes later, all the candidates were on stage primed and ready to go. It was the same candidates as the last debate but Wisconsin Governor Scott Walker took the place of dropout candidate, former Governor Rick Perry. The others: Bush, Christie, Cruz, Paul, and Cotti were behind their respective podiums, just itching to answer that first question to get the ball rolling.

The first question, asked by Carol Crowley, was on Global Warming. "Do you believe in Global Warming? Let's start with you, Ted Cruz. You have one minute to give an answer and thirty seconds if a rebuttal is necessary."

"Do I believe in Global Warming? Of course not," Cruz replied, in his feminine voice. He smiled. "It's just another fraudulent claim made by the Liberal politicians and media. We have a change in weather, like we have with the four seasons. But that's it. Nothing more."

Carol Crowley asked the same question to the rest of the candidates; each gave a similar answer. Everyone but Cotti. He told it like he saw it.

"The way I see it, Carol, Global Warming is caused by the Greenhouse Gas effect. This is what supposedly causes climate change. A warming of the weather, which will have devastating effects on our planet if something isn't done...and *soon*. The CO_2 gases are suffocating the ozone layer. *Not for nuttin',* but I have to go with the scientists on this one. They're much smarter on this subject than me."

Rove cringed when he heard Cotti's answer. So did the audience. Rove figured Cotti would definitely fall in the polls again, but changed his mind when he heard Cotti's answer to the last question of the night.

"How would you stop ISIS if you were President?" Crowley asked the candidates. "Jeb Bush, I'll let you answer first, seeing it was your brother that got us into this mess."

"Now, now, Carol, be nice," Bush replied, in a condescending voice. "But seriously, I would use the resources necessary to get the job done."

"Does that mean ground troops?" Crowley asked him.

"Whatever is necessary! Everything is on the table."

All the others again gave a similar answer, but never gave an explicit answer; they always danced around the subject, like a typical politician answers a question for which he has no answer. Jack Cotti, however, was not the typical politician.

"Jack Cotti, I ask you the same question. How would you stop ISIS from creating havoc and a caliphate in the Middle East?"

Cotti had an answer that nobody expected, but one that they seemed to thoroughly enjoy. "Well, I see that ISIS loves to destroy the world's antiquities and people. I would make one bold threat to them. I would make them an offer that they couldn't refuse."

"And what would that be, Mr. Cotti?" asked Crowley.

"I would give them a choice. Either they stop their killing and destruction, or I would destroy their antiquities in the cities of Medina and Mecca in Saudi Arabia. I would bomb both cities to the ground. Decimate them back to the desert from which they came. This is where their Prophet Mohammad lived and died. And I would blow it up to where it would just be one very deep crater. There would be nothing left for them to fight over. If they're too stupid to know when they're licked, then I'd have our military kill every one of them, to the last man. Pure and simple. And if the rest of the Muslim world was upset over the bombing, then I guess we'd have another crusades. But not all Muslims are fanatics and aren't out to kill those who have different religious beliefs than them. But this senseless fighting has got to stop before the Middle East erupts into World War Three. And I'm the right guy to stop it."

At first, the crowd remained silent. They really didn't know how to react to Cotti's answer; that is, until one member of the audience began clapping very loudly. Then everyone got involved in the outburst of clapping and hooting, calling out Cotti's name. And his was the only name that audience members cried out: "Cotti for

President!"

Rove at first didn't know how to react, but after seeing the reaction of the crowd, he believed Cotti had really pulled it off and a big smile crossed his face.

Cotti wasn't as happy. He was upset over the answers his competitors had given. He was quite unhappy over their answers given in the first debate. But the answers that were given on this night made Cotti not just upset, but ready to beat some sense into some of these "gentlemen." However, Cotti controlled his anger and instead confronted them verbally in the hallway as they walked towards the front entrance. He ran ahead of them and corralled them to a stop.

Cotti gave it to them with both barrels. "You guys really kill me. You act like you give a fuck about the People, but you don't. None of you do."

Only Rand Paul had left the building. The others were trying to, but were too afraid to offend Cotti so they remained and patiently listened to his outburst on their moral behavior—especially on their views of same-sex marriage and gays.

Cotti continued. "You know, I know politicians like you that visit our whorehouses and drug dens...and gamble with Family bookies, but then, afterwards, they play politician again. Fooling everyone around them, with their *holier than thou* routine, like their *shit don't stink*. Well, I got news for you fuckers. You don't fool me! Not for a second. You'd sell your mothers, if need be. Forget about it!"

Cotti said what he had to say and stormed off.

Rove followed, but before leaving, apologized to those offended by Cotti's behavior. "He's tired." Rove left it at that and rode back to the hotel with Cotti in the limo.

Once there, Cotti went to his room to sleep, while Rove once again worked the phones, looking for large donations.

Chapter 14

An hour before taking off from LAX airport, Rove was notified by phone of the poll results. He had figured that even though the crowd had reacted favorably to Cotti at the previous night's debate, Cotti would definitely drop at least a few points in the polls. Surprisingly, Cotti had gained four points. Jeb Bush, again came in second with thirty-two percent, Rand Paul in third with six, Christie with two, and Cruz and Walker each with one percent: pretty much the same results as the first debate.

Rove was happy with the news. In fact, everyone on board was in a jovial mood after hearing the poll results. It was a five hour ride of celebrating to the max!

Rove sat back in his seat and wondered how Cotti had done it with the answers he gave. Rove turned to Cotti and said, "Those weren't Republican answers."

Cotti replied, "I know. They were the truth. Everyone wants to hear the truth every now and again."

Rove nodded. "Well, just keep doing what you've been doing, Jack...and we'll be in the White House in no time."

***

Rove dropped Cotti off in New York and then continued on to DC. Five minutes after entering his house, Rove heard the ring of his phone. Rupert Murdoch was on the other end.

"Carl, you've got to quit the Cotti campaign," Murdoch demanded.

"Rupert, I can't quit as long as he's winning," Rove replied. "Once he drops in the polls, I'll have an excuse to quit. But if I do it any sooner and leave him out in the cold, you just might find my body resting on a cold slab. Cotti will have me killed if he thinks I've double crossed him."

"Cotti's not a true Republican. He's a phony," Murdoch ranted.

"You're wrong, Rupert," Rove answered, angrily. "Cotti's no phony. And the Republican voters seem to like him enough that fifty-nine percent favored him over the others. I think Cotti's got a damn good chance to win the nomination and win the Presidency. I really believe that. Hell, Cotti's polls are even higher when it's taken across the spectrum."

Murdoch didn't respond to Rove's rant about his golden boy. He wanted Rove to throw all his weight behind the boy wonder of the Bush Dynasty, Jeb Bush. He no longer had confidence in Cotti's ability to lead the country even though he, himself, had at one time called Cotti a "political powerhouse."

***

While Rove and Murdoch continued their conversation, Cotti was at home speaking with Johnny Napolie concerning the sabotage of the plane. They sat in Cotti's den, smoking cigars, eating cannolis, and drinking coffee.

"So, Johnny, what did you find out?" Cotti asked.

"I spoke with Old Man Angelo. He says that his kid told him that some man in a black suit flashed a badge and handed him a gallon can with no label and ordered him to add it to the fuel, which he did...and then gave the empty can back to the man that gave it to him."

"Did you learn anything from the detective we got on our payroll? Or the guy from TSA?"

"Well, I talked with our security guy at the airport and he told me that's he's helping in the investigation. He said the Feds don't believe the kid's story and think he sabotaged the plane for Parrissi. They believe Parrissi was willing to bring down that plane when it was in the air and kill all on board...just to get to you."

"I can't believe it. They wouldn't break the fucking truce."

"Jack, Parrissi ordered the hit. Truce or not," Napolie said. "Look, Angelo's kid confessed to adding a can of something to the fuel. They don't yet know what that something is. But you can bet it was something strong enough to seize those engines. We gotta retaliate, Jack. We gotta hit Parrissi."

"Fuck no! No! Not until we know for sure. I'm not gonna break the truce as long as I'm running for President. We have to wait and see what the FBI says in their final report. So leave Parrissi alone. That is, until you hear differently."

"That makes us look weak, Jack. How many passes are we gonna give Parrissi?"

Cotti didn't answer.

***

Napolie left Cotti's home disgruntled and upset. His boss was acting weak when weakness in his line of work was a death sentence. It was eating Napolie up inside, wondering why his boss was acting this way. He knew Cotti as a "man of action," not some lightweight who played it safe.

Napolie knew that if he didn't act soon to take out Parrissi, then nobody in the Valoppi Family was safe. But he was stuck between a rock and a hard place. He again, reluctantly, did as ordered.

***

Napolie wasn't the only person angry and upset. Rove was also pissed off at Murdoch for "putting him on the spot." Rove knew he had a winner in his midst. He knew that Cotti had the best chance of winning the best prize in the US: the Presidency of the United States.

After a few days, Rove's dissatisfaction with Murdoch

was all but forgotten. Rove began spending some of the money the campaign had collected for the political essentials that were needed for a Presidential campaign. He had his people in every major city in the country renting buildings for Cotti campaign headquarters.

Rove wasn't going to wait until Super Tuesday. He knew he had a real winner in Jack Cotti and that the candidate appealed to a broad range of voters, from the very young to the very old. In the eighteen- to twenty-eight-year-old bracket, the polls showed Cotti getting sixty percent of the vote. The twenty-nine to forty-four age bracket he garnered seventy-two percent. The forty-five to sixty-four age bracket gave him sixty-six percent of the vote. The smallest percentage of votes he received was from the sixty-five to eighty age bracket, with thirty-eight percent of the vote.

Cotti, as far as Rove was concerned, was a very real contender and a true political powerhouse; something very rare in the political world and only came about every fifty years or so.

So, during the next few months, Rove concentrated on getting Cotti through the debates without any major outbursts or non-Republican answers that would take away from Cotti's message to the voters and allow him to slip in the polls. And it worked...for a time.

Debate three was held in Colorado and went like the two before it. So did four through eight.

But during those debates, the answers given by Cotti's

opponents to some of the questions infuriated Cotti. He believed many of them were bigots, racists, and hypocrites.

And because of it, Cotti became increasingly more agitated with and alienated from his opponents, and Republicans in general. Cotti's moral compass was very similar to that of many of his Republican candidates, but for many of the issues raised, his views were opposite to those of his peers. His were blue-collar views. They were views of the "street." And Cotti didn't mince words. He knew, from experience, how it was to grow up in the streets, poor, never getting new clothes, always getting hand-me-downs from his older brothers.

Fate had intervened and now he was encased in riches beyond his wildest dreams and headed the largest crime family in the country. So when debate nine, the final debate, came about, Cotti gave it to the viewing audience with both barrels.

The NBC host, Chuck Todd, asked a question about pot and drugs in general. Cotti's opponents pretty much gave the same answer, as if they had been given a memo from the Republican Party to parrot nearly word for word.

"What do you think about marijuana and drugs in general? Should pot be legalized for recreational and medical use or should it stay illegal, as the DEA and Federal Government insist?" Todd asked the candidates. "I ask you first, Ted Cruz."

"Rand Paul, and I believe—"

Paul interrupted Cruz. "Don't speak for me, Ted. I can

answer the question myself."

"Well, as I was saying: the states' voters should have the power to decide whether or not they want medical marijuana. And as far as legalization, I won't go that far."

"I'm not for recreational marijuana being legalized," responded Paul, "but like Mr. Cruz, I too, believe the states should have the only say on that subject. As you know, I'm sponsoring a bill to get marijuana reclassified to a Class Two narcotic."

Christie went even further. He revealed that he would ban legal pot in all states that legalized it against Federal law. "I would make recreational marijuana illegal. I will crack down on those states that voted for legalization. The Federal Government needs to send a strong message that we won't tolerate legal pot."

The others, especially Jeb Bush, wanted nothing to do with pot, whether it was for medical or recreational use. Bush, however, admitted to smoking the herb and some said he'd dealt it while in college and had, allegedly, used harder drugs. So he was not only a drug user but a drug dealer. In Cotti's eyes, Jeb Bush was definitely a hypocrite.

Cotti's answer to the question surprised Rove and made him queasy and upset. Cotti seemed to have the debate won until he gave *his* answer to the question.

"Let me first say that I don't do drugs and I've never smoked pot." The audience roared with approval. Cotti continued. "I'm for medical marijuana and for legalization if the People see fit. If America were truly a Democracy, then the Federal Government shouldn't be violating non-violent drug users' civil rights. They should have the right to use drugs, drink alcohol, and smoke cancer-causing cigarettes without being punished for it—as long as they are responsible citizens when using the product. I mean, Jeb Bush's father was able to get the Federal Government to issue legal pot to a half-dozen needy citizens before the Drug Czar had the program stopped dead in the water. And most of the politicians that made these draconian laws had used drugs themselves at one time or another. And I could name a few that are here tonight. I mean, the Declaration of Independence states that we have the right to Life, Liberty, and the Pursuit of Happiness. And for some, doing drugs is in Pursuit of Happiness."

"Drugs make people into rapists," yelled an audience member.

Cotti replied: "No, rapists make rapists. And a rapist will rape without drugs. But, as I was saying, there are millions of recreational drug users out there that aren't criminals. They have high paying, and extremely important jobs. I mean, I know about three hundred high profile professionals, stock brokers, CEOs, COOs, VPs, assistant VPs, and the list goes on. Are these people criminals? I say, No!"

"Then what would you candidates do about the War on Drugs?" Todd asked the men. "I ask you, Jeb Bush."

"I would make the drug laws much harsher," he replied.

Many of the others agreed with Bush. Rand Paul,

however, was a little apprehensive about the answers given by his peers. He made a point that the Justice system was broken and needed revamping due to the fact that mandatory-minimums hadn't worked as planned.

Cotti gave another reasonable answer to the problem. "The War on Drugs is a complete failure," he said. "The government allows the drugs to flood into the country and then arrest its own citizens: kids, teens, even their own kids. And for one reason: To keep the economy going."

"Are you saying our government is complicit in the dealing of drugs, Mr. Cotti?"

"If you'd let me explain," Cotti retorted.

"By all means, do," Todd replied.

"I'll give an example: Customs allows one ton of cocaine to enter the country. The cops let the dealers sell three-quarters of it, then bust them. The cops get to keep any drug money found and then can show the public the drugs that were confiscated, proving that they're doing a great job by keeping drugs off the street and throwing the drug dealers in jail. It's one big con job, a scam. I could go on and on. For instance, the prison system is the largest manufacturing company in the country. It employs nearly two million inmates at slave wages—ten to twenty-five cents an hour. Those could be good paying jobs for our citizens that have no criminal record. Ask the gentlemen standing next to me, Mr. Todd, what they are going to do about that?"

"If we get to it, Mr. Cotti. That question wasn't on my

Bobby Legend

list of questions," replied Todd. "But I do have another to ask you candidates. How would you stop the US from getting into another war before it started? I'll ask you, Governor Walker."

Walker stated he would try diplomacy first and if that didn't work he'd warn the country with military destruction. And go to war if necessary.

All the other candidates except Cotti stated similar answers, parroting the words: "I wouldn't leave anything off the table."

Cotti, on the other hand, had a completely different answer, one that stupefied the audience and totally surprised Chuck Todd. "What would I do to try and stop the US from getting into a war?" answered Cotti. "I would call the country's leader by phone and make him an offer he couldn't refuse. If George W. Bush and Saddam Hussein had used my idea, the Middle East might not be in chaos right now."

"And what idea might that be, Mr. Cotti?" asked Todd.

"I'd have a rap-off. And let the audience decide the winner. Then the winner could declare victory and the loser could return home with his tail between his legs. All without firing a shot or putting troops on the ground. My rap would go something like this: I'm the top guy from the US of A. Don't step on my toes or get in my way. I'll hit you so hard you'll go to sleep. And when you wake up, I'll have you kiss my feet. Forget about it!" When he was finished, Cotti smiled to the crowd, hoping for accolades.

He received only silence. The audience didn't know what to think, let alone the TV viewers. But Todd got a kick out of Cotti's answer.

"Mr. Cotti, it might sound crazy, but I actually like the rap-off idea," quipped Todd. "If all country leaders did that, instead of creating wars, then we'd have peace on earth and wouldn't have to spend a half-trillion dollars on our military budget each year."

The other candidates scoffed at Cotti's answer and especially at Todd's response. They all just shook their heads in disbelief and dissatisfaction. Todd didn't want to hear any blowback, so he started to ask another question.

Jeb Bush jumped in and asked Cotti, "What if the leader refuses?" All the other candidates nodded in response to the question.

Cotti thought for a minute, then answered: "Then we'd annihilate him and his whole frigging country."

Todd didn't want to hear any rebuttals, so he immediately asked another question. He was immediately interrupted by audience applause. This was the Jack Cotti that they knew and loved.

Rove was also happy with Cotti's last answer. It brought Cotti back from the abyss, from the grave he had nearly dug himself into with that crazy answer about the rap-off. Now if Cotti could just keep his answers low key, without making waves or shocking the audience and viewers, then he could stay atop the polls. Rove kept his fingers crossed. There was only time for one or two more questions.

The next question asked was about taxes. "If you were President and there was a need to raise taxes, would you raise them? And if so, would you raise the taxes on the rich instead of the middle-class?" Todd asked.

All but Cotti refused to raise taxes for any reason. And they also mentioned the "pledge" they had taken with Grover Norquist.

When it was Cotti's turn to answer, he didn't mince words with the other candidates and gave it to them with both barrels...again. Cotti spoke directly to the viewing audience. "You know, these guys take a tax pledge with their Messiah, Grover Norquist, and refuse to raise taxes on the people who can afford it...or raise taxes at all. And because of it, our cities and towns are crumbling to the ground. Schools have closed because cities can't afford to pay the utilities to keep them open. It's asinine. It's utterly ridiculous. I mean, I don't like paying taxes any more than the next person. But ***not for nuttin',*** if we want to continue to have our bridges and roads—our infrastructure— repaired, then the rich and billion dollar corporations need to pay their fair share. I mean, it would be nice to send in what you want to the IRS, but everyone wants a strong military and it takes tax money to pay for it. These guys next to me are blind if they don't see it. And their trickle down economy hasn't worked at all. But do they try something different? Hell, no. Well, I say, if a CEO can earn forty million dollars, then he can afford to give back half of it to the country in which he made it. Then he would be called a Patriot instead of a Wall Street crook. And it's not the CEO that makes the money for these corporations but the low paid workers that work there for thirty years and then lose their pensions because some crook on Wall Street was too interested in earning his fees than looking out for his clients. I'm sick of it and the voters should be fed up with it too."

Cotti paused and took a breath. "I'll tell you what. If I'm elected President, I'll guarantee that members of Congress will take a pledge with me to help make this country strong again. And if they don't, they do so at their own risk."

"That was some rant, Mr. Cotti," interjected Ted Cruz. "Have you gotten it off your chest?" A half-hearted smile crossed his face.

"I have," Cotti replied, levelling an angry stare at Cruz. "And I'd like to come over there and tear the hair off your chest," he muttered under his breath.

"Excuse me. I didn't hear your last remark, Mr. Cotti," Cruz retorted.

But before Cotti could answer, possibly with more crude remarks, Todd asked the last question of the night.

"Well, folks, this is the last question of the night and it's on immigration reform. What should be done with the over eleven million illegal immigrants that are now in the country?"

Before Todd could ask a particular candidate, Cruz jumped in with his answer. "They need to be deported and immigration reform needs to be a top priority."

"I second the motion," quipped Rand Paul. "We definitely need immigration reform."

Jeb Bush refused to give a concrete answer concerning immigration reform and how it should be executed. The others gave definitive answers that the illegal immigrants shouldn't be made legal citizens and should be deported. Cotti was the only one who was man enough to stand up to ridicule over his answer. But he didn't care. He was going to tell the People how he felt about it. And let the chips fall where they may. He hadn't lied to the People before and he wasn't about to lie to them now, polls be damned.

Cotti looked to his opponents with disdain and barked, "I don't believe you guys. We're all from a family of immigrants. Because families are coming from our neighboring countries for a better life, you want to send them back to where they came from. There's room for hard-working immigrants in this great country of ours. And not to belittle the point, I'm appalled. My parents came from Italy and immigrated to this country with sixty cents in their pockets. And now I stand here, running for President of the United States." He looked at Cruz. "Ted Cruz, you're an immigrant from Canada, your father, an immigrant from Cuba—and you have the audacity to ridicule these people. And you, Jeb Bush, are married to a Mexican woman. I wonder how her family feels knowing you view immigrants as criminals and inferior human beings. All of you make me sick. How many people are here with an outdated visa, which would make them illegal immigrants? You seem to pick on the ones that have a brown skin tone instead of white. Only illegal immigrants that are violent criminals should be jailed and then returned to their country of origin. What ever happened to the 'Compassionate Conservatives'? Even Ronald Reagan made legal citizens of over six million illegal immigrants. If it was good enough for him, then it should be good enough for us now. That's just how I feel."

With that answer, the debate ended.

Rove nearly fainted when he heard Cotti's answer on immigration. He thought earlier in the debate that Cotti had sailed through it without making any waves. But now, he wasn't so sure how Cotti would do in the polls. Republican voters were adamant at not wanting illegal immigrants to become legal citizens, no matter what the circumstance.

Rove was sure Cotti would sink in the polls, enough, in fact, that he could probably make his exit from the campaign without any grief from Cotti, thereby fulfilling Rupert Murdoch's wishes. But Rove had to be careful. He didn't want to become Cotti's enemy. He knew that many of Cotti's enemies either disappeared as "*food for the fishes*" or were murdered...or tortured and then murdered. And Rove wanted none of that. So he would wait for the poll results before deciding.

There was only Super Tuesday left on their docket before the Republican Convention.

Cotti would have to make appearances in many of the

states before voting occurred. First to Iowa for the Caucus, then to New Hampshire, South Carolina, Florida, and many others, before taking a little respite to recharge his batteries for the Convention.

Chapter 15

While flying home to New York City in the Charter jet, Rove, again, was given a written message from the flight attendant. This time it showed the poll results. Rove was definitely surprised by the results. Cotti had only slid two points, to fifty-seven percent. Jeb Bush, again, came in second with thirty-two percent of the vote. He seemed to have plateaued. Rand Paul received eight percent, while the others each walked away with one percent of the vote.

Rove couldn't believe what he had read. They evidently liked his frankness. He gave Cotti the good news and a pat on the shoulder. "Good work," Rove quipped.

"The Ronald Reagan reference must have made the difference on the immigration thing," Cotti replied.

With this news, however, Rove couldn't leave the campaign under these circumstances. He would have to ride it out and wait until after Super Tuesday.

Cotti, though, had a few choice words for Rove concerning the Republican Party's message to the People. That message focused only on a small portion of the American People, and not on everyone. Unless someone conformed to their way of thinking, that person was not wanted or needed.

"You know, **not for nuttin'**, Carl. But those guys I'm running against are a bunch of idiots and bigots. I can't believe they run our government. And they have no conscience. Not a compassionate one, anyway."

"You may be right about that, Jack. It's not what you say, but how you say it. If you're in this business for any length of time, you'll learn."

"Ya know. Over these many months, I've learned that Republicans are only concerned with conformity; to be morally sound. Or that's what they want you to believe. But that can't happen, Carl. That's why people are called individuals."

"There's some truth in what you say. But that's politics, Jack. Let me tell you a little story. Do you know how a preacher gets the people to come to his church?"

Cotti shrugged.

"Well, I'll tell you. He tells them what they want to hear. That's the same in politics. You're the preacher, Jack, preaching to your flock the words that are dear to their hearts. That's politics!"

"I'll tell you one thing. Preacher or no, if I ever see any of my opponents on the street on a dark night, I'll give them a free ride," Cotti quipped.

"A free ride? What the hell you mean by that?" Rove asked.

"A free ride in an ambulance. They wouldn't be able to

walk after I got through with them. Forget about it!"

"Whatever you say, Jack. But now we have to get you ready for Super Tuesday. You'll have to visit twelve to seventeen states within a very short period of time. I mean, are you ready for that?"

"Forget about it! I was born ready," Cotti answered confidently.

***

When the rest of the passengers learned of Cotti's win, they were overjoyed. Champagne was served and cigars were smoked.

However, two of the passengers were dumbfounded by the results. They were two FBI Agents paid to watch over Jack Cotti and to insure his safety. Had Cotti fallen in the polls, it was a good bet that Rove would have quit the campaign and Cotti would more than likely have dropped out of the race. But to their chagrin, it didn't work out that way.

"Are you fucking kidding me?" griped Agent Mark Press. "How can people vote for this guy? What the fuck do they see in him?"

"Come on, Mark. Don't get so upset. He's going to screw up sooner or later. And when he does, we'll be there to take him in," replied Agent Alan Firby.

"You hope!" Press retorted, adding, "I wish Parrissi had taken him out. Another missed opportunity."

The two Feds were still griping about Cotti's win when

the plane finally landed at Kennedy. They disembarked the aircraft with Cotti, to make sure he made it home safely, while Rove and entourage continued on to DC.

As Cotti and the two agents walked towards the agents' car, a shot rang out. The bullet missed Cotti's head by inches, plunging into the parking lot's asphalt.

The agents pulled their weapons to return fire. Another shot rang out. Agent Firby shoved Cotti to the ground and crouched over him, protecting him from harm—something he did out of instinct, not out of loyalty. Again, the bullet just missed Cotti as he fell, but hit Firby, leaving a superficial shoulder wound. The bullet actually did more damage to the agent's suit coat than to his body. The bullet wound, when checked, was only burned skin from the heat of the bullet as it passed through the suit coat and shirt.

No other shots were fired. Other agents were called to the scene to investigate. An hour later, Cotti was driven to his home by Agent Press, while Firby was taken to the hospital for observation.

During the short ride to Cotti's home, Agent Press asked, "Jack, who do you think's trying to kill you?"

"You tell me," Cotti replied. "How do you know the shooter wasn't firing at you guys?"

"The bullets weren't aimed at me, Cotti," Press retorted. "They were aimed at your head, not mine."

"You sure about that? Your buddy was hit, not me."

"Yeah, and I think because of you. And we have to protect you. I don't like it and I don't like you, Jack. But I

256

have a job to do and I do as ordered."

"Just like a good soldier." Cotti gave a smug little laugh.

"Fuck you!"

"Hey, I don't ask you to protect me, or watch over me. I'd rather you didn't. You guys have been following me damn near my whole life. Forget about it!"

The car pulled into Cotti's driveway. Before Cotti could open the door, three carloads of FBI Agents pulled up and jumped out to check the area for any threat. Finally, after a good five minutes, Cotti was ushered into his home.

Many of the Agents reluctantly remained nearby in different vehicles, doing surveillance on any suspicious activity, preferably illegal activity.

***

The minute Cotti entered his home, he went directly to his den and phoned his Underboss, ordering him to his home for an important meeting.

***

An hour after the phone call, Johnny Napolie arrived. A smile spread across his face when he saw his boss, but the smile quickly dissipated when Cotti told him about the hit.

"What?" screamed Napolie. "Are you shitting me, Jack? Was it Parrissi's guys?"

"I don't know. They shot from a good ways away. So

they had to have used rifles with scopes, like our soldiers use."

"Yeah, but Jack, we're not the only Family that uses snipers."

"The Feds seem to think it was Parrissi again," Cotti acknowledged.

"So what do you want to do? Do you want me to take care of it?"

"Not until we know for sure. We still haven't seen the final report on why the engines failed. So let's see what the Feds dig up on the hit before we get mad."

Napolie just shook his head in disgust and disbelief. Cotti had first refused to seek vengeance on Parrissi over his deceit concerning the making of his kid. Then he'd given the benefit of the doubt to Parrissi over the engine mishap. Now he was letting slide this latest incident.

Napolie was beside himself. He wanted Parrissi. And he wanted him dead…yesterday. He had to somehow get Cotti to ok the hit. Soon. Or he, Napolie, might have to do something that he might regret later.

***

Napolie wasn't the only one beside himself. When Rove heard about this most recent attempt on Cotti's life, he put the pedal to the metal and came up with a plan to get his "golden boy" away from his enemies. He set up town hall meetings all across the country to get Cotti away from New York City: the mobs' dumping ground for dismembered bodies. Or was that New Jersey? Yeah, New Jersey.

Rove phoned Cotti and told him to travel with a good number of bodyguards: "Get your soldiers to protect you, Jack."

"Why?" retorted Cotti. "I have the Feds to protect me."

"Well, that's up to you. I just don't want anything happening to you. We're so close to putting you in the White House, we sure don't need any complications now. So your tour begins in two days and your itinerary and some written speeches will be given to you on the plane. My assistant, Janet, will be coming along with you for moral support. She'll be taking my place. So if you have any questions during the tour, just ask her."

"What plane, Carl?"

"The charter plane is yours, Jack. And we have an RV at the airport of each state, with driver included, to take you where you need to go. I'm staying behind to make sure that we have the correct number of signatures to get you on the ballot in every state. And I have to oversee the opening of Cotti Headquarters. Super Tuesday is coming up in ten days, so we have to get you ready. These meetings are very important, so it's essential that you do a great job. I have faith in you, Jack."

"Thanks, Carl."

Carl gave him the departure time and wished him good luck.

***

Those two days couldn't go by fast enough for Cotti. The large presence of police near his home and in the neighborhood made him remain inside his home, cooped up with his wife.

She did nothing but argue with him the whole time. She insisted her husband was being unfaithful on the road. That was not true, of course. And Cotti denied it, but the more he denied it, the more she yelled and cursed at him. So, when that time came, he wouldn't be able to get out of the house fast enough. He just figured it was that time of the month.

Then she threw some photos onto the kitchen table and told him to look at them: "They prove you are a liar," she snapped.

Cotti picked them up and shuffled through them but showed no reaction. "What the hell are these?" he shouted. He shoved the pictures close to her face. "Where did you get them?"

"I've been spying on you for a long time, Jack. I know you're screwing another woman. Even the Feds came here and brought me adulterous photos of you and some blond bimbo. They had pictures of others that showed you in compromising positions. I didn't want to believe it. How could you, Jack?" she whined.

"Why did the Feds come? Just to show you these pictures? I don't think so!"

"You're right, Jack. They wanted me to *rat you out*. But

I'm Sicilian, mister. And I would never do that. I threw them out of the house."

"Babe, we'll talk about this when I return. This is between me and you, honey. We don't need anyone else's nose meddling in our business. Especially our business that takes place in our bedroom."

Cotti's conversation was cut short by the loud blast of a car horn. The Company limo had arrived just in time. He quickly gave his wife a kiss on the cheek and turned to leave. His wife threw a large glass vase at him as he headed out the door. It crashed into the wall a foot from Cotti's head and broke into a thousand pieces.

"You son of a bitch!" she yelled.

Cotti continued out the door, shaking his head at the reaction he had gotten from his wife over his infidelity. But he couldn't think about that now.

Outside, Cotti was met by two of his most loyal soldiers, who would join him for the trip as his personal bodyguards. The three sat in the limo, but Cotti didn't speak. He was deep in thought about what he had done to his wife and he felt guilty to a point. That feeling lasted as far as the airport, then he thought about it no more.

Cotti and Company entered the plane and were met by Janet Goldberg for the very first time. She had always stayed behind to coordinate the campaign and do what was necessary to take care of any problems that came up. Now she was Cotti's "right hand man." After introductions, she and Cotti sat next to each other and got acquainted.

"You know, my girlfriend's a Jewish broad," Cotti said.

"Your girlfriend's a Jewish broad, huh?" Goldberg retorted. "So you're not married, I take it."

"No! I'm married with four kids. But my wife and I have an open marriage," Cotti lied.

He and Janet hit it off right from the start. She was a pretty little thing: Five feet, two inches tall, not more than a hundred pounds, with an hourglass figure, long, flowing dark brown hair, and a beautiful smile.

After some small talk, Goldberg got down to business. She gave Cotti his itinerary, which showed every minute of every day for the next seven days filled with town hall meetings and visits to out of the way places to meet with "regular" folk. When Cotti heard that word "regular," he became incensed.

"What the hell do you mean by that, Janet?" he snapped. "I'm regular folk. You act as if I'm something special."

"Sorry, Jack. Geez, don't take it personal. But you are a Republican candidate for President of the United States. And that takes a special person and special personality to get where you are in such a short time. I mean, a year ago, nobody had heard of you as a politician. Only as a mobster."

"I got news for you, Janet. Many people I know still think of me as only a mobster."

Janet gave out a nervous laugh, but really didn't know how to react to Cotti's answer. When he looked into her eyes, it sent chills down her spine. But not in an evil way—in a sensuous way. Half of her said, **Don't trust him**, while her other half said, **He's a heartbreaker and I'd really like to get to know him.** She was a little afraid of him, at first. Over time, though, she warmed up to his charismatic personality.

That was the last time they'd speak until landing at Phoenix Airport.

"Where to now?" Cotti asked Janet, as the plane taxied to its designated area and allowed the passengers to disembark.

"The RV should be ready and waiting for us...to take us to Phoenix's Chamber of Commerce meeting. These are important people, Jack, so make a good impression," she replied.

"No problem. Forget about it!"

Janet was right. As soon as they exited the aircraft, they eyed the RV, which was nearby, waiting for their presence.

Five people traveled in the RV: Cotti, Janet, Cotti's two bodyguards and the driver, an elderly black man named Samuel. The rest of the passengers followed in SUVs, while the FBI Agents followed in their unmarked police cars.

The meeting went off without a hitch. The audience of twelve hundred listened intently to Cotti's plans for the future and evidently liked what they had heard, because the overall majority gave him a standing ovation. They waded through the audience, shaking hands; some folks wanted

Cotti's autograph, while others just gave him a "well-done" pat on the back. Then, the group was back in the RV, heading for their next destination: Denver, Colorado at a VFW Hall, to talk with the veterans.

A few hours later, Cotti was standing on the stage, giving his speech to nearly nine hundred vets. Every now and then, he was interrupted by a question from one of them.

"Mr. Cotti, what would you do about ISIS?" asked a Viet Nam vet.

"Just let me say this about ISIS. You know, *not for nuttin'*, but if ISIS had been a little more inconspicuous, had kept a low profile, they could have taken over the Middle East without anyone being the wiser. I mean, I know plenty of guys that cut the heads of their enemies, but then buried them and never bragged about it. It was business. So ISIS brought this retribution onto themselves. They only have themselves to blame when they are annihilated. And they will be. Either by me…or someone else. I just hope, if it has to be done, that I can set the deed in motion as President of these great United States." With that, the meeting came to an end. Again, his audience gave him a rousing ovation, very satisfied with what they had heard.

That was how most of Cotti's town hall meetings went. That is, until the last destination of the tour before Super Tuesday. It was held in Miami at the Convention Center. It was not only Jeb Bush territory, but also territory held by associates of the Lucchese Family, who now were asking Cotti for special concessions into his Family businesses in return for votes from the sixteen Florida county districts and twenty cities under their control. They promised to order polling officials in those districts to look the other way when their voting machines were rigged with new software that would send nearly every vote Cotti's way.

Cotti turned them down cold, without discussion, and threatened repercussions if they interfered with his political campaign. They were not happy with Cotti's decision and threatened hard times for him and his Family.

Cotti phoned his Underboss to take care of the situation.

"Will do, Jack," Napolie said.

"But don't go overboard. We don't need another war. I'm too close to victory. So put this one to bed, Johnny."

"What kind of message do I send Parrissi?"

"Talk with him. Make him see the light. Just don't go overboard. Get me?"

"Oh, yeah. I'll make him see the light all right. He'll be seeing stars by the time I'm through talking with him. Leave it to me, Jack."

When the conversation ended, Cotti went back to what he did best. And that was to "wow" the crowds and pull them in to his campaign. So far, so good. Now his speech at the Convention Center would be the *coup de grace* to this never ending story: "*Poor boy makes good*!"

***

Cotti did his best to convince everyone in attendance to vote for him. But there were some instigators in the crowd that tried to get under Cotti's skin.

"Hey, Cotti. How can you be President? You don't even have a college education," yelled a male audience member and Jeb Bush lackey.

Cotti tried to ignore the remark. So when the guy yelled out again about his college education, Cotti struck back.

"Would that help?" Cotti asked the crowd. "So what if I don't have a college education. I got my education from growing up in a tough neighborhood and tougher streets. And right now, this country needs a tough President to deal with this crazy world and more importantly, these crazy politicians in Congress. I've dealt with these kinds of people all my life and the professional politicians in DC are sissies compared to the hard asses I'm used to. So let me conclude this speech with a heartfelt *Thank You* and please, help me get into the White House to help you! God bless you and God bless the United States of America."

The audience went wild as Cotti left the stage. Three thousand people chanted: "*Cotti for President. Cotti for President.*"

Fox News and other media outlets covering the town hall meeting were surprised at the outcome and flowing support for Jack Cotti as President, especially Fox News political analyst and commentator, Chris Wallace.

"I can't believe what I'm seeing," shouted Wallace to

his viewers, over the celebratory cry of *Cotti for President*. "Just over twelve months ago, Jack Cotti was just a glorified gangster. Now, with Carl Rove's help, Jack Cotti is a true Presidential contender for the Republican Party. If he can win Super Tuesday next week...and Las Vegas bookmakers are making Cotti a two to one favorite, the convention is all but sewn up."

***

Wallace's words were prophetic. Cotti won all twenty-four states on Super Tuesday, including states that were supposed to go to Jeb Bush. Because these states allowed Democratic voters to participate in the Republican Primaries, their votes put Cotti over the top. However, Jeb Bush did come away with quite a few delegates.

Anyone betting with Vegas bookmakers on a Cotti win would have doubled their money. The bookmakers were now making Cotti a three to five favorite for the Convention. And for President, a five to two long shot against Democratic Powerhouse, Hillary Clinton.

***

Rove, hearing the news of Cotti's win, was ecstatic. He knew they were one step closer to the Presidency and the next step was to meet with other candidates, possibly to make concessions with them in a deal to certify a Cotti win for the Republican Presidential Nomination.

***

When Napolie heard of a Cotti victory, he called his boss to congratulate him. "Good work, Jack," he said. "Can you believe it? Everyone says you're a snap to win the Republican nomination for President. Congrats!"

"Thanks, Johnny. It's working out just like we hoped it would. Thanks for calling. I appreciate it."

"Oh, by the way," Napolie added, "I fixed our Parrissi problem. We won't have any more trouble from him."

"I hope you didn't do what I'm thinking."

"Don't worry, Jack. Parrissi took a long vacation. If you know what I mean." Napolie snickered.

"Oh, shit, Johnny. I hope there's no blowback from the other Families."

"Don't worry about it. I got it totally under control. You just worry about the Convention. I'm happy for you, Jack."

***

The Feds, though, who were listening in on the conversation, weren't as happy. They were again dissatisfied with the outcome. And even more dissatisfied with the voters.

"Fuck! What is wrong with these voters? How can they elect a gangster for President? I just don't understand it. But I'll tell you one thing. I'll never vote Republican again," promised Agent Press.

"Mark, it ain't over till it's over," quipped Press's partner, Agent Firby.

268

"Man, I'm getting tired of this. I'd rather they stick me behind a desk," whined Press.

But these two agents had been handpicked to stick to Cotti and protect him from his enemies, and they did just that for the next few months. Cotti again went out on the road with Goldberg to do more Town Hall meetings, to try to wean votes away from his main competitor, Jeb Bush. The fewer delegates Bush had at the Convention, the less power he could wield.

So, after all Cotti's hard work giving speeches to his followers, he was primed and ready to go when Convention night finally rolled around in Cleveland, Ohio, at the Quicken Loans Arena. Cotti waited in his dressing room to hear from Rove concerning the delegate count.

***

Rove was in the smoke-filled VIP back rooms trying to make a deal with Jeb Bush and Company so Cotti could win on the first round of voting. The deal the vested parties came up with was one that was questionable. The *powers that be* wanted Cotti to select Jeb Bush as his running mate. This would give Cotti enough delegate votes to win the nomination in the first round.

Now Rove would have to convince Cotti to agree with the deal. But that wouldn't be so easy, as he found out when he confronted Cotti with the news.

As Rove and Cotti were talking it over, the voting was already taking place. In between their conversation, the

Captain of each state's delegates shouted out as the majority of delegates went to Cotti.

"Alaska gives all its votes to Jack Cotti," the Captain shouted happily.

"Arizona gives all but twenty to Cotti. The rest go to Jeb Bush," shouted another.

While the states were shouting their numbers, Rove was begging Cotti to make Bush his Vice President.

"Are you kidding me?" barked Cotti.

"Jack, be sensible. If we choose Bush, the nomination's in the bag," Rove promised.

"Carl, I want someone I can trust. And I don't trust Jeb Bush. Hell, his people would have me whacked a week after being elected. Forget about it!"

They quarreled and argued over the situation. The voting was at a lull. States were still adding up their votes, so Rove tried his best to convince Cotti to adhere to his demands.

"Jack," Rove begged, "if you want the nomination and the Presidency, then do this for me."

But Cotti stood his ground and refused to be swayed. "Carl, the person I'd pick to be my Vice President would be the guy I've trusted the most, whom I've known all my life. And that is my Underboss, Johnny Napolie."

"Jack, you can't be serious. I don't know if the voters would go for two mobsters on the ticket."

"If I tell the People that I want Napolie as my running mate, then they'll agree with me...and see that we're a winning team," Cotti said, with an air of confidence.

Rove shook his head with disgust. "Jack, you're not thinking rationally. Think about it!"

"I'll tell you what, Carl. Let me toss it around in my head. We have all night before the voting's finally counted, so let me see if I can swallow this without throwing up. I still think the guy's a loser."

"For Christ's sake, Jack. You're not making him a member of your Family. You're only making him your running mate. And with Bush and his money, that will give us the best shot at winning this whole thing."

After a few hours of thinking it over, Cotti relinquished and decided to give Bush his shot. But to say the least, he wasn't at all happy with his decision...because the Bush Family was Political Royalty and a dynasty, whereas Cotti was just Mafia Royalty. He had no dynasty. Not yet, anyway.

Cotti and Rove walked to the VIP room and confronted Bush about the decision Cotti had made.

"Well, Jeb," Rove said. "I think we've got a deal. In another hour or so, with your help, Jack should have enough delegate votes to win the nomination. And he would be happy to have you as his running mate. Congratulations!"

"Thanks, Carl. And thank you, Mr. Cotti. Or should I say, Mr. President?" Bush said happily, and with a big smile, as the three shook hands.

"Well, let's not get too far ahead of ourselves, Bush,"

Cotti told him, in no uncertain terms. "You're gonna do things my way. Get me!"

"No, no problem, Mr. Cotti," Bush replied, not expecting Cotti's indignation. "You're the boss."

"You got that right. But let's not play games. I don't like you, or your brother. I know who you are and you know who I am. You don't give me problems. I won't give you any. *Capisce*?"

Bush nodded, as did his bigwig backers, and the room full of cigar smoking Fat Cats shook hands with Cotti and Rove. The deal was now set. Jeb Bush would be Jack Cotti's running mate.

Cotti saw how Bush's people were kissing his ass and falling all over him, as though Bush was the Presidential nominee. Cotti had seen enough and told Rove his true feelings.

They had a big argument about that subject back in their dressing room, while waiting for Texas's Captain to shout out their votes that, with luck, would put Cotti over the top for the nomination.

"Damn it, Carl," Cotti snapped, "the more I think about this Bush deal, the less I like it. I'd never forgive myself if I went through with it. I'm sorry."

"What are you saying, Jack? You can't back out now! We gave them our word."

"No, Carl. You gave them your word. I just went along with it."

Rove was shocked and dumbfounded, to say the least.

He couldn't believe what Cotti had just told him. All he could say was, "Jack—"

"Enough, Carl. Right now I need to be alone. I just want to think."

Rove left the room to give Cotti space and time alone, to think about his future.

The Bush thing kept festering in Cotti's head. The more he thought about it, the angrier he became. He really didn't want to go through with it. He saw Jeb Bush as a phony who had gotten to where he was by his family's money and political organization. He wanted none of it. The more he thought about it, the more he wanted nothing more to do with the Republican Party. He had had enough.

Cotti saw that the Republican Party was nothing but one big scam. Their donors laundered their money through their political contacts to get government contracts. As far as Cotti was concerned, the US Attorney General should be charging both political parties with the RICO act for running a continuous criminal enterprise to enrich themselves. Their organizations were no different than how the Mafia Families ran their organizations. And that's just how Cotti saw it.

So Cotti came to the conclusion that he would be better off leaving the Republican Party to form his own party. Then he would be beholden to no one.

***

Rove came back into the room after nearly an hour.

"Carl, you better sit down," said Cotti. "I have something to tell you."

"Sure, Jack." Rove sat down and waited to hear what Cotti had to say.

"Carl, I'm quitting the Republican Party."

At that moment, a voice rang out over the loudspeaker. Jack Cotti had just won the Republican nomination for President of the United States.

"Jack, listen. The nomination is yours. How can you quit now? This is ludicrous. You can't do it!"

"I'm sorry, Carl. I've made up my mind. I'm gonna start my own party."

"Are you serious? You're throwing away the Presidency. For what?"

"For peace of mind, Carl. For peace of mind."

"What can I say to change your mind? I mean, you just heard it. You are the Republican Presidential Candidate. Don't throw it away."

Rove was beside himself. In all his years, he had never had to deal with this type of problem. Rove's "golden boy" had the nomination sewn up and now it was slipping through his fingers, like the grains of sand sifting through an hourglass and Rove couldn't stop it.

A Convention head knocked on their door. "Mr. Cotti, you're needed on stage. The audience is waiting."

Rove answered, "We'll be there soon. Give us some time to get a speech ready."

"Don't take longer than fifteen minutes," replied the

Convention head. "The delegates want to see their candidate."

Rove nodded and shut the door. He confronted Cotti. "Well, Jack. What are you going to do?"

Cotti didn't answer. He was in deep thought.

"So what are you going to do?" Rove repeated himself a number of times, before Cotti acknowledged him.

"What, Carl? What did you say?" Cotti mumbled.

Before Rove could answer, there was another knock on the door. It was a Bush assistant wanting to know when Cotti would announce Jeb Bush as his running mate.

"When Jack calls out his name, Jeb can come on stage. And not before," Rove replied, somewhat angrily, not knowing what to expect from Cotti.

Rove slammed the door and tried again to change Cotti's mind.

But Cotti didn't want to hear what Rove had to say. His mind was set.

Rove tried a different approach on the subject. "Jack, it's not easy to start your own political party. How are you going to do it? You don't have the organization or the money." Rove then thought about it for a second and blurted out, "Or do you?"

Cotti smiled. "I just might have both. You forget, I have Cosa Nostra. And with your help, I know we could do it. The funds that were collected will stay with me and I want you to continue running my campaign."

"But Jack, that's not possible. I work for the Republican

Party," Rove countered.

"No, Carl. You will continue to work for me. And only me! And I want your friends to continue donating to my campaign," Cotti told him, in no uncertain terms.

"Why would they do that? They only back Republicans."

Cotti looked deep into Rove's eyes, gave him an evil smile, and said: "Just tell them it would be good for their health."

"Is that a threat?"

"Come on, Carl. You know I don't make threats. I don't have to."

Rove turned white as a ghost.

"Just tell them it would be wise to continue funding my campaign." Cotti continued to smile. "Right now, they are still friends of mine. And if I win the Presidency, they surely don't want to be my enemies. You tell them that, Carl. 'Cause I'm finished with the Republican Party. Let the others fight for the nomination. I'm running on my own Party ticket. And you're gonna help!"

With that, Cotti walked out of the room towards the stage. Rove followed, along with Jeb Bush and entourage, and stood in the wings as Cotti walked out on stage to thunderous applause.

Once the audience quieted down, Cotti told them what they didn't want to hear. "Thank you! Thank you!" he shouted. Then he went into a long diatribe about how he had come so far in such a short time to win the nomination.

He thanked a number of people, including the donors, delegates, and voters. "And a special thanks to Carl Rove and Janet Goldberg and all the Cotti volunteers who really made things happen. If it wasn't for their help, I wouldn't be here tonight."

The crowd was going wild on just about every word that came out of Cotti's mouth. But the words that came out of his mouth next stopped the crowd in their tracks.

"We've had some good times, but now all that must end. Because I cannot accept the Republican nomination for President of the United States. I just can't run on a Republican ticket. The Party is too commercialized. They want conformity. Well, I can't conform. I am my own person and I will continue to speak my mind and tell the truth as I see it. I relinquish my throne to Jeb Bush and the others. Let them fight for the nomination." Cotti then turned and walked off the stage.

The crowd had been jovial and upbeat when Cotti began his speech, but now they were confused, dumbfounded, and bewildered. To say the least, everyone was in shock, including Carl Rove and Jeb Bush.

Even the media couldn't believe what was happening. Just an hour earlier, they had heard the rumor that Cotti had selected Jeb Bush as his running mate and reported that to their viewers. Now, everything had changed.

While the media was in a flurry to get this breaking news on the air, Bush and his entourage returned to the back room to talk over strategy for their next moves, as did the other candidates.

Rove, on the other hand, went back to his dressing room and sulked, while Cotti sought out Chris Wallace of Fox News to explain in more detail the reason behind his unexpected decision.

As Cotti fought through the crowd, he unexpectedly ran into Ted Nugent. When their eyes met, Cotti instinctively popped Nugent square in the mouth with his fist, knocking Nugent to the ground like a sack of potatoes. The man was then stepped on by people in the crowd. Cotti continued on his quest to seek out Chris Wallace.

Wallace was very surprised when a sweating Cotti came to his anchor desk, demanding an interview.

"I'm here with Jack Cotti, who just refused the Republican Nomination for President. Can you tell us, Mr. Cotti, why the change of heart? You had it made in the shade with lemonade."

"And you're a poet and didn't even know it," Cotti retorted.

"But let's get serious. What could possibly have turned you away? You stated that not only could you not accept the nomination but you're also leaving the Party? Is that right, Mr. Cotti?"

"Yes, that's true. It was a hard decision, but I had to do it."

"But why? That's what all our viewers want to know."

"Well, for one, the power brokers wanted me to select Jeb Bush as my running mate, which I reluctantly did. But

278

after I thought about it and learned exactly what the Republican Party was all about, I decided to quit the Party and start my own political party. I want to run on my own ticket."

"So what will you call this new party?" Wallace asked.

"I don't know yet. Maybe I'll ask your viewers to contact our campaign website, to help us decide on a name. They can go to *Cotti for President dot com* and give their suggestions. We'll be deleting anything that has to do with any Party but my own."

With that, Cotti turned and walked away to his dressing room.

***

Rove was sitting and holding his head in his hands when Cotti walked in.

"You okay, Carl?" Cotti asked him.

Rove looked up, with tears in his eyes. "Yeah, I'm alright," he answered. "I just can't believe it. You had the nomination in the palm of your hand and you let it slip away. You gave it away!"

"Forget about it! Let's get out of here. We got lots of work to do before election time."

"Jack, you've left the Convention in chaos. This has never happened before in the history of politics. I have to stay here in case they need me."

"Carl, you work for me now, not the Republican Party. We're starting our own party, remember?"

***

And that's how the American Family Freedom Party began. That's the name Cotti's fans and voters suggested when they were given a number of choices to choose from, like the Italian Stallion Party, Blue Collar Boys' Party, The Family Party, the Cosa Nostra Boys' Party, and the one that was picked, the American Family Freedom Party. The reason those names came about was because Cotti had picked his old friend and Underboss, Johnny Napolie, as his running mate. And Napolie accepted, as ordered. The VP pick resulted in an even larger voting block wanting Cotti and Company as President than the polls had showed when he was running as a Republican. He was now beholden to no one, and the voters responded with donations of all denominations.

Chapter 16

Rove and Goldberg were still running Cotti's campaign and were surprised at the support he was getting from people across the aisles and in every age bracket. His poll ratings were higher now than before and by more than ten points. It seemed many of the voters from the Party he had deserted had stayed loyal to him.

Even more surprised were the media outlets. Jack Cotti was on their minds and the minds of their viewers. They couldn't get enough of Jack Cotti. The McLaughlin Group was one of them.

McLaughlin, held up the front page headline of the New York Times, which read: *COTTI LEAVES REPUBLICAN PARTY. STARTS OWN.* "Can you believe it?" McLaughlin quipped. "Cotti wins the Republican nomination for President but before he accepts, he quits the Party. Unbelievable. Never in the history of politics has that happened before, and I doubt that it will ever happen again. I ask you, Pat Buchanan. Can you make sense of it?"

"Well, John. Cotti said it himself. Neither the Republican nor Democratic Party, or for that matter, any other political Party, is deserving of a Jack Cotti candidacy. He said to be President you had to be tough and none of those Parties were tough enough. He made a mistake, John. He'll never have a chance for the White House now. He just doesn't have a chance."

"John," quipped Eleanor Clift, "when he quit the Republican Party, he really quit politics. He was a powerhouse. Now, he's in the dog house,"

"But what about the recent polls?" interjected McLaughlin. "His poll results are even higher now than when he ran on a Republican Ticket. How do you account for that? I ask you, Mort Zuckerman."

"John, I can't account for it. In reality, Cotti shouldn't be running at all. This is all like one big nightmare. Why would anyone think a mobster can become President? I have no idea, but it won't last."

"Yeah, but that's what we said over a year ago," quipped Tom Rogan.

All the guests nodded to that reality. Cotti had been written off as a viable candidate for dog catcher, let alone President. But Cotti had fooled them all.

"And why would Carl Rove stay with the Cotti campaign?" McLaughlin asked his guests. "You'd have thought that he would have latched on to another Republican, like Presidential candidate Jeb Bush. But instead he stayed with Cotti."

Zuckerman rang in. "I don't really have an answer for that one, John. Evidently, he sees something in Cotti that the rest of us don't see."

"You can say that again, Mort," interjected Rogan.

"And the fact that Cotti is starting his campaign all over again sure doesn't help his cause," quipped Clift.

"Yeah, but evidently it hasn't hurt his chances either. I mean, he's shot up in the polls by ten points. He has staying power, John," said Buchanan.

"Well, it looks like we'll be talking about the Cotti candidacy in the near future," acknowledged McLaughlin. "Bye, Bye."

***

Clift was right though. Cotti's campaign did have to start over. They had to replace their old signs with new. And everything else that had a Republican trademark, from hats and buttons to pencils, cups, and any and all political trinkets. They also had to redecorate their campaign headquarters in every city and state across the country.

There were some hiccups in the Cotti campaign. Some of the Fat Cat donors were complaining to Rove that Cotti's people were putting the squeeze on them.

"Jack, some of our big donors are complaining that your guys are threatening them with beatings and even death if they give to your opponents. We can't have that, Jack."

"Don't worry, Carl," Cotti replied. "I'll take care of it."

And he did, with one phone call to his right hand man, Johnny Napolie.

***

The only other problem that came up was that a few Cotti headquarters, especially in New York State, were bombed and destroyed. No one was hurt, as the bombings took place very early in the morning. Investigations were ongoing.

And just to be on the safe side, Cotti volunteers went out again and gathered new signatures in all fifty states. They did so with very little trouble, except for a few instances where some volunteers threatened, accosted, and slapped some registered voters when they refused to sign the petitions. It was found out later that the suspects turned out to be associates or soldiers of the Valoppi Family and were quickly dismissed from the campaign and chastised by Cotti himself. Cotti then ordered all of his soldiers across the country to cease and desist from those types of tactics. And they quickly obliged.

***

They weren't the only ones that had listened to Cotti: So had the Feds, when Cotti had mentioned Cosa Nostra. They figured they could arrest him on conspiracy charges, but they knew the charges wouldn't stick and would just give him more publicity.

But almost a week after the Convention, they were much closer to dampening Cotti's political dreams. They learned of Angelo Parrissi's disappearance after his wife telephoned the police and reported him missing. The police department then informed the FBI and now *they* were investigating the disappearance. The FBI believed Cotti had something to do with it and went to his home to confront him with their evidence. They really had none, but went with "gut instinct." The government sent two of their finest agents: Agent Dennis Arms and Agent Ken Lundy, who had visited Cotti's home more than once.

Cotti invited the two G-men into his den to see what was on their minds. "What's up, guys?"

"We're investigating the disappearance of Angelo Parrissi, Godfather to the Lucchese Family," Arms said. "And we believe you are involved."

Cotti smiled and shook his head in disbelief. "Sorry to bust your bubble, guys, but this is the first I've heard about Parrissi's disappearance. When did it happen?"

Lundy became quite upset with Cotti's answer, and barked, "Quit fucking with us, Cotti. We know you ordered the hit...and when we find his body you'll be heading to jail instead of the White House! You piece of shit!"

Cotti remained calm and smiled at the men who were disrespecting him in his own home. "When you get the evidence come back and arrest me. But until then, get the FUCK out of my house," Cotti snapped. He then escorted the two G-men to the front door and out of his home.

Cotti contacted his Underboss to find out exactly what had gone down. They met at their club and walked around the block to talk so the Feds couldn't listen in to their conversation.

"Johnny, what the fuck did you do? You whacked Parrissi!" Cotti bellowed.

"Jack, I took care of the problem as you ordered," Napolie answered.

"But I told you to speak with him and not to go overboard. I think whacking the guy was going overboard."

"Jack, don't worry about it. They'll never find Parrissi's body. He's *food for the fishes*!"

Cotti was disgusted by Napolie's reaction to the problem, but Napolie was right. Cotti had ordered him to take care of the problem. So Cotti cut Napolie some slack. "Forget about it!" Cotti barked.

They then went their separate ways.

***

Cotti wasn't about to stick around and wait to be arrested. He was busy doing what Jack Cotti did best. And that was "wooing the crowds." They would come from hundreds of miles away just to get a glimpse of him, hoping to shake his hand. He was charismatic, confident, and an infamous gangster and criminal: all qualities that made for a great politician. And the polls proved it. Gallop had Cotti beating Hillary Clinton by five points and Jeb Bush by seven. Las Vegas bookmakers had Cotti by twelve over both candidates.

After Cotti threw the Republican Convention into a

tailspin, the voting began anew. And after a long drawn-out fight, Jeb Bush had become the nominee for President, while Marco Rubio was picked as his running mate.

Hillary Clinton won hands down, without anyone challenging her for the Democratic nomination. Joe Biden was her running mate.

So the Presidential race began in earnest. Three debates were set between the Democratic and Republican Presidential candidates, but none had Cotti participating and that wasn't kosher with his voters. The two Parties disingenuous reactions to a Jack Cotti appearance made his followers very unhappy. So they used social media and texted, tweeted, blogged, phoned, and sent letters, anything to get their point across. They wanted Cotti's participation in those debates and wouldn't stop the harassment until he was added.

But two of the debates had already taken place, without the front runner participating. But the third and final debate was hosted by Fox News Station and Rupert Murdoch caved to the voters and allowed Cotti to participate in that debate.

Even after taking heat from Party heads concerning Murdoch's decision, Murdoch refused to bow down to them and stuck by his guns. He set them straight, saying, "You guys don't make the rules. The sponsor makes them. And I'm sponsoring this final debate. Cotti's participating. If you people don't like it, then don't bother showing up for the debate. It's as easy as that."

According to the ratings on debate night, Murdoch had decided the correct course of action. By allowing Cotti to participate, the ratings went through the roof, with over one hundred million people watching the outcome.

The candidates were introduced, and told of the rules. The host, Roger Ailes, asked his first question. "What are your views on Gun Control? First, we'll go to Mrs. Clinton, then to Mr. Bush, and last but not least, Mr. Cotti. Mrs. Clinton?"

"Yes, we need more control over the gun explosion in this country. We have more guns on the street than people living here. I would like to see rational gun laws. I mean, who needs a rifle or gun that can shoot a hundred rounds a minute? I believe only the military needs those types of weapons. I'm all for guns. But I strongly suggest we work on gun safety," Clinton answered.

"Thank you, Mrs. Clinton. Mr. Bush, it's your turn to answer," acknowledged Ailes.

"I believe in the second amendment wholeheartedly," Bush retorted. "A rational gun owner will use his gun safely and without putting anyone at risk. I have no problem with the type of weapon they want to own, as long as they are responsible gun owners."

"Thank you for your answer, Mr. Bush," said Ailes. "And now, Mr. Cotti, you're up. Please, give us your take on gun control."

"Thank you, Mr. Ailes. Yes, I believe in gun control. I think everybody that owns a gun should have control of it.

But seriously, of course I'm in favor of rational gun control. But not to rid the country or people of them. A gun is just an extension of one's hand."

"What about machine guns, Mr. Cotti? Are you in favor of people owning machine guns?" Ailes asked.

"Hey, if you got twenty guys shooting at you, looking to kill you, and your gun only holds six or fifteen shots, hell yes, a machine gun that spits out a hundred or two hundred rounds a minute would be very handy at that time. So yes, I'm for a gun owner to own a machine gun."

But both Clinton and Bush thought differently.

Bush interjected, "I'm all for guns, but there is a limit to what the average person is allowed to own. And a machine gun, unless you apply for the proper permits, is not allowed under Federal law."

"I agree with my colleague Mr. Bush," Clinton said. "There are limits to what type of firearm a person can own. And I agree with those limits."

The debate lasted more than two hours. The questions asked were about immigration, the war on drugs, medical and recreational marijuana, same-sex marriage, gays, ISIS, the military, and Obamacare. That was the last question asked by host, Roger Ailes.

"What do you think needs to be done with Obamacare? I ask you, Mr. Bush."

"I think it needs to be repealed. The government is giving away too much in entitlements. Let the healthcare system put a plan in place that can help the people with no insurance."

"Mrs. Clinton, what are your thoughts on Obamacare?" Ailes asked.

"There have been some bumps in the road but more than ten million of the uninsured are now insured and not bankrupting hospitals anymore. Now these hospitals know that they will get paid by the Federal Government for providing the care necessary to help and protect their patients. And at a reasonable cost."

"Mr. Cotti, I ask you the same question. What is your opinion on Obamacare?" asked Ailes.

"Well, I don't care to say anything bad about Obama. He has done some great things as our President. He's also done some stupid things too. But we won't go there. But what's so wrong with trying to get our healthcare system in order? I remember when Mrs. Clinton's husband tried and failed back in the nineties to get national healthcare. I believe the Affordable Healthcare Act is good for the people and the country. And Congress passed it. If anyone else had a better idea other than doing nothing, then they should have spoken up. But ten million Americans who now have healthcare that didn't, that's a good thing. I can't fault President Obama for that. Forget about it!"

And with that statement the debate ended.

After shaking hands with his competitors, Cotti and Rove headed to their dressing room to talk over their strategy for the upcoming election.

While waiting for the polling results, they turned on

their portable TV and listened to the commentators' thoughts. All had similar opinions.

First, they turned to NBC's Lester Holt and Chuck Todd. With audience members watching nearby, Holt and Todd began telling their viewers their opinions on the night's debate.

"How do you think the debate went tonight?" Holt asked Todd.

"It went well," Todd replied. "I just wish Cotti had participated in the two previous debates. It wasn't right that he wasn't allowed, especially when he led all candidates in the polls. We could have learned much more about him. But I thought Cotti did a good job. His answers I'm sure satisfied his voters. I think Cotti is what this country needs: a tough, down-to-earth President."

"But Chuck, aren't you forgetting? Cotti's a mobster," quipped Holt.

"Lester, if you believe in the Bible, then you must forgive his past sins and pray for his redemption and that he changed his ways, which I'm sure he has."

"Cotti's a Hottie," shouted a female member of the audience.

"Cotti for President," yelled another.

"Cotti all the way," shouted a male audience member.

"Well, there you have it, ladies and gentlemen. In just a few weeks, you can decide for yourselves and vote who you think suits your needs best. For NBC, I'm Lester Holt, saying Good Night from the Quicken Loans Arena here in

Cleveland, Ohio."

***

Rove and Cotti left the Arena feeling good about Cotti's performance. By the next morning, they felt even better when they learned that Cotti had won the vote. He won fifty-two percent of the vote, with Bush and Clinton evenly dividing the rest, each receiving twenty-four percent.

And as Election Day approached, Cotti was back on the road with Rove, making stops in family restaurants and malls, just out meeting potential Cotti voters. Cotti was truly enjoying himself. But ten days before the election, the FBI came to a McDonald's where Cotti was kissing babies and charming the others, especially the women. Cotti found himself suddenly surrounded by a dozen G-men.

"Jack Cotti?" one Fed asked him.

"Yeah. What's up?" he asked, somewhat bewildered that they'd make an arrest in a place with dozens of kids milling about. Had something gone awry, those kids could have been seriously injured.

"Jack Cotti, you are under arrest for conspiracy to commit murder. You'll have to come with us." The G-men were in a state of ecstasy, finally getting their man after playing babysitter for him for the last few months.

Cotti remained calm and took the arrest like a man. He just smiled and called out to Rove: "Carl, call my lawyer and have him get me out of this mess. I'm innocent!"

***

Rove seemed to be more shocked over Cotti's arrest than Cotti was himself. He couldn't believe what had just happened. For the second time, he'd been beaten down, losing once again the real possibility of putting his candidate into the White House. He was so close. Less than ten days before the election, and his golden boy was now sitting in jail, not knowing if he'd ever get released. But that wasn't Rove's only trouble.

An hour before Cotti's arrest, the G-men also arrested the American Family Freedom Party's Vice Presidential Candidate, Johnny Napolie, on the same charge: conspiracy to commit murder.

Napolie was already sitting at FBI Headquarters in New York City, while Cotti was being taken by car to FBI headquarters in Baltimore, Maryland.

***

The driver of the agents' car, Agent Rex Zoumbaris, really rubbed in deep the fact that Cotti was now in *their* back yard. "Now you can kiss your political career goodbye, asshole. Ain't nobody going to vote for you now, Mr. President." The two Agents laughed at that one.

"Fuck you. You guys ain't got *nuttin'* on me. And you know it," Cotti shot back.

"You think so, uh, Cotti? Well, we got the body. And we got a witness. And he's going to sing like a canary at your trial. It seems your killer forgot to puncture the

293

stomach of old man Parrissi and he finally floated to the top. He's no longer *food for the fishes*," declared Zoumbaris, laughing.

"You think that's funny? I don't," Cotti barked. "You guys are supposed to be above that stuff."

"But we're happy," quipped Agent Jack Tarry.

"Oh, and by the way," interjected Zoumbaris, "we got your Underboss locked up too."

"You got Johnny, too?"

"You got it, Mr. President," joked Tarry.

The two Agents were really sticking it to Cotti. Their time had finally come. They finally had the evidence needed to put Cotti away for life. They were so happy they were giddy.

And so was the current President, when he heard the news of Cotti's arrest. He immediately phoned the Director of the FBI to congratulate him on a "job well done."

But the political pundits thought the sky was falling. The Media Moguls smelled a good story and ran with it. They all wrote Cotti off as Presidential material, figuring he wasn't ever going to be released from jail and right away he began falling in the polls. He had dropped below fifty percent for the first time ever, although he was still many points above his other competitors and all the while sitting in jail.

Cotti's followers thought it was a setup job—that the *powers that be* didn't want Cotti to run the government and this was one way to get him completely out of the picture.

They never faltered or lost hope and demanded the release of their Presidential hopeful. They demanded that both he and Napolie be released before the election. But their demands were met with arrogance and indifference.

Even the McLaughlin Group was questioning the timing of the Cotti arrest. McLaughlin held up the front page headline of the New York Times, which read: *COTTI BUSTED! PRESIDENT ELECT?* "Can you believe it?" McLaughlin told his pundits and viewers. "Less than ten days before the election and Cotti is arrested: for murder, no less. The timing of his arrest *stinks*! Had this not happened, I believe Cotti would have become the forty-fifth President of the United States. Now it looks like it's *Sayonara* for Presidential hopeful Jack Cotti. What do you think of the mess Cotti has gotten himself into? Was he set up? I ask you, Pat Buchanan."

"I don't know, John. We all know Jack Cotti is a mobster. And we all know how one becomes a member of the Mafia. Is it possible that he is guilty of the murder the FBI says he is? I don't know. We'll have to wait and see."

"Do you think he was set up, Pat?" interjected McLaughlin.

"The timing is pretty suspect," said Buchanan. "And we all know that the Justice Department is none too fond of Jack Cotti, let alone the prospect of having him as their boss."

"I agree with Pat, John," crooned Clift. "But guilty or not, his political career is finished. C'est la vie."

"Yeah, John," interjected Mort Zuckerman, "Cotti's political career is definitely finished. I'm just wondering why the Feds didn't arrest him fourteen months ago, before he started his illustrious political career."

"Probably for the same reason we thought," said Tom Rogan. "That Cotti's political career would have sputtered before it got started. But like us, they were wrong."

McLaughlin asked another Cotti question. "Can anyone tell me why Cotti's poll results haven't suffered? I know they're down below fifty percent, but my God, he's still fifteen points above Bush and Clinton. What gives? I ask you, Mort Zuckerman."

"John, I have no idea. It's beyond logic. Maybe the People haven't heard about Cotti's arrest yet. But I'm sure, the longer he's in jail, the more his poll results will fall."

"I agree with Mort," said Pat Buchanan. "His poll results will take a nosedive real fast, especially, when the voters know he'll never leave jail again."

"John, the American Family Freedom Party is no more," quipped Eleanor Clift. "Or will soon be defunct. Jack Cotti, himself, murdered any chance now of a Cotti victory next week."

"Hey, let me just add one comment," interjected Rogan. "You know, it might not sound logical, but Cotti could win the Presidency sitting in jail. I think, by the most recent polls—and this is after Cotti's been sitting in jail for the last three days—Cotti still has a chance to pull this thing off. I mean, the voters still want him as their President. The polls prove it. By all rights, Cotti should be dead in the water. But he's still afloat."

"Yeah, but what good will it do if he's in jail? Even if he wins the election, it will be a moot point. And it would put this country in a big quagmire," said Buchanan.

"Who would then become President?" McLaughlin asked his pundits. "With both Cotti and Napolie behind bars, would they take the second place winner of the election? I ask you, Tom Rogan."

"I wouldn't know, John. Maybe the Speaker of the House? Maybe John Boehner?"

"Tom could be right," acknowledged Clift. "But who really cares. Like Pat said, this subject could be moot. Cotti's poll numbers could fall faster than you could blink an eye."

Chapter 17

Everyone, except for Cotti's followers, thought Cotti's chance at political greatness was over. But that kind of thinking would prove terribly wrong.

Everyone who owned a badge thought bringing down Cotti as a Mafia thug was a good thing. But bringing down a Mafia thug who was about to win the Presidential election was even better. Unfortunately, their happiness would be short-lived. Three days before the Presidential election, the FBI had to drop all charges and release both Jack Cotti and Johnny Napolie.

Their only witness to the murder was killed in an unfortunate car accident. As the witness being transported from the jail to a safe house, another car plowed into the one he was traveling in and killed him instantly. Now the Feds were back to square one regarding their investigation of the Parrissi murder.

***

Carl Rove was waiting as Cotti left FBI headquarters in Baltimore. They needed to get back into the thick of things and try and bring up Cotti's poll ratings. Since his unfortunate incident, Cotti had dropped to thirty-eight percent. Fortunately for him, Bush and Clinton were still tied at thirty-one percent.

The media was all over the Cotti story. The New York headline read: *Cotti: CASE DISMISSED!* The Chicago Tribune headline read: *COTTI: 4 GOVT: 0!* The LA Times headline read: *COTTI CAN WIN IT ALL!* To the media, Cotti was the story. Bush and Clinton were old news. Cotti was something no one had ever seen before. A rarity. Like John Dillinger—Bigger than Life.

While the media people were writing their next stories about Jack Cotti, Rove was thinking about their next step. Cotti couldn't chance falling any lower in the polls. It would be a very close race. And even being in jail, he was still ahead of the other candidates. Cotti was still in the running, to nearly everyone's surprise, and to others' dismay.

Rove came up with a great idea. He had an advertisement made that ran the last three days before the election on every channel on every TV network and radio station, every hour on the hour. It showed Candidate Jack Cotti making a simple statement to the voters: "If you want a President that is tough, but fair, knows when to listen and not speak; if you want change and not the same ole, same ole, then I ask you to choose me as your next President of these great United States."

And it was those few words that seemed to hit home with the voters. The day before the election, the polls showed Cotti still leading by six points. Gallop had it much closer, with Clinton winning by two points: thirty-five to thirty-three percent. Bush lagged in third place, with twenty-six percent.

Cotti, Napolie, and Rove, on the night of the election, bided their time at their headquarters in Queens, along with three hundred of their closest friends and volunteers. The two political powerhouses watched the voting unfold, sitting nervously in a back room in front of a television, drinking brandy, and smoking their Gurka cigars. And, of course, they were watching the Fox News channel.

At close to nine pm the results started to come in. The Fox News pundits—Chris Wallace and his TV partner, Roger Ailes—were telling the audience that voting in the East was too close to call. Only one state so far was given to Jack Cotti, and that was Cotti's home state of New York.

Rove was so nervous that he would constantly rise and sit or pace back and forth, while waiting impatiently to hear more results. He even changed the channels, hoping that they might have more results. But all news stations were being very cautious, all stating "too close to call." So Rove turned to the Fox News channel once again.

As the clocked ticked almost to twelve, Chris Wallace began calling out states that had gone to Cotti. "We're getting some results from some Eastern states," acknowledged Wallace. "As we said earlier, New York went to Cotti. It looks like New Jersey, Connecticut, New Hampshire, Rhode Island, and Maryland have also voted for Cotti, who now has a total of sixty-eight electoral votes. Clinton and Bush have not as yet won a single electoral vote. But, ladies and gentlemen, it's still very early. And according to our straw polls, it's going to be a long night. So stay tuned and keep watching. It's going to be an intense and interesting night. But once again, six states have gone to Cotti. We're going to take a little advertisement break for a few minutes, so while our viewers are watching that, we'll try and get you some more results."

Before the station could go to break, Wallace came back on. "We are now calling California for Cotti. Although it was close, Cotti pulled it off. So California goes to Cotti, who now has a total of one hundred and twenty-three electoral votes. And remember, he only needs a total of two hundred and seventy to win the election."

Fox finally went to break.

***

Napolie and Rove were ecstatic. Cotti wasn't fazed, as though he knew the outcome. And, so far, it was all one-sided, with Cotti taking all the electoral votes.

"Hell, Jack. If the night continues like this, we should be able to wrap this up in no time. Maybe another hour, tops!" bantered Rove.

"Jack, can you believe this shit?" remarked Napolie. "Me and you as President and Vice President of the United States. Am I dreaming or what? Pinch me! I must be dreaming."

"Easy does it, Johnny. It ain't over till the fat lady sings," Cotti reminded him. "We still have a long night ahead of us, so let's not get too cocky. Not yet anyway."

Just then, Chris Wallace's voice caught their attention.

"We have more results coming in. Yes. Yes. It looks like Texas and its thirty-eight electoral votes go to Jeb Bush. South Carolina and their nine votes also go to Jeb Bush, who now has a total of forty-seven electoral votes, with Hillary Clinton yet to win any. Wait, it looks like I spoke a little too soon. Clinton has just won Arkansas and their six electoral votes. So, right at this moment, Cotti has one hundred and twenty-three electoral votes. Bush has forty-seven, and Clinton has six. Wait a minute. Clinton has taken Oregon, Washington, and Colorado. Yes, we're calling Colorado for Clinton, which now gives her a total of thirty-four electoral votes."

For nearly an hour, Cotti didn't receive any more electoral votes. But around one-thirty in the morning, Cotti's ears picked up when Wallace began calling additional states for Cotti. "We're giving Cotti Maine and Nevada. The Cotti camp now has a total of one hundred and thirty-three electoral votes."

But that was it for Cotti for a while. Bush was holding steady with forty-seven electoral votes, while Clinton was racking up nearly as many as Cotti had.

Wallace began calling out state after state and giving them to the Clinton camp, for nearly ten minutes:

"We've got some more results coming in," said

302

Wallace. "It looks like Hillary Clinton has won quite a few more states. The District of Columbia goes to the Clinton camp, along with Wyoming, Vermont, North Dakota, Alaska, Delaware, Montana, West Virginia, Hawaii, and New Mexico. That's a total of thirty-eight additional electoral votes, which now gives her a total of seventy-two electoral votes."

"What's happened to Jeb Bush? He hasn't won a state in nearly two hours. Is he out of the race, Chris?" Ailes asked his partner.

"Yes, I believe he is. Cotti has won many of the states that should have gone to Jeb Bush. I believe the race is now between Clinton and Cotti. But if Bush wins a few more states, we might not have a candidate to reach the two hundred and seventy electoral votes needed to win the Presidency. And what happens if that occurs, Rog?"

"Boy, that would be quite the predicament," said Ailes. "I pray that doesn't happen. That would be a bigger debacle than the turmoil Cotti left the Republican Convention in."

The conversation was suddenly interrupted when Wallace began spewing out more news on the election.

"We have more results coming in for Clinton. Yes. Clinton has won Oklahoma," Wallace acknowledged.

"That was supposed to be Bush territory," quipped Ailes.

Wallace continued. "Clinton has also won Kentucky, Louisiana, and Alabama. That's another four states for Clinton, who now has one hundred and four electoral votes, with more than a dozen states yet to chime in with their results."

"There's only about two hundred and sixty electoral votes still out there," Ailes noted. "If Jeb Bush can win a few more states, we may have a three-way runoff. Or, at best, a two-way runoff between Cotti and Clinton, as you said before, Chris. The Clinton camp got knocked backward when California went to Cotti instead of her. That really hurt her chances. This is getting down to the nitty-gritty. And that's how I see it's going to end. Clinton, I'm sure, will win Pennsylvania, Illinois, and possibly Florida. That's nearly seventy votes right there. All I can say is it's going to be close."

"But Bush should win Florida," Wallace said. He leaned to listen to his earphone and watched as the monitor began spewing results. "Okay, here we go again," he interjected. "We have more results coming in for Clinton. We're calling Minnesota, Wisconsin, and Missouri for Hillary Clinton. That's another thirty electoral votes added to her already one hundred and four votes, which gives her a total of one hundred and thirty-four votes. One more than Cotti's total."

The station went to break. Within those few minutes, more polling results came in.

"We're seeing more states going to Clinton. Massachusetts, Indiana, Arizona, and Tennessee are now in the Clinton camp. That's another forty-four electoral votes, which now gives her a total of one hundred and seventy-eight," Wallace told his viewers.

"She is definitely on a roll," interjected Ailes. "She's even won southern states slated for Bush. This election is upside-down and right side up. To say the least, it is definitely a roller coaster ride."

Wallace again relayed the news. "We have more results, but this time for all three candidates. Clinton has won South Dakota and its three electoral votes, which now gives Clinton one hundred and eighty-one total. Jeb Bush has won Nebraska, which adds five electoral votes to his forty-seven, for a total of fifty-two. Bush has lost his way. And we don't really know why."

"Evidently, the voters didn't agree with his message that he tried to convey," said Ailes. "Cotti, on the other hand, has taken the *gold ring* from both Clinton and Bush. But I still say this year's election will end in a runoff. I'm certain of it."

"Let's hope not, Rog," replied Wallace. "But let's get back to business. We have some news for the Cotti camp. Illinois, Pennsylvania, Ohio, and Michigan have gone to Cotti, along with the seventy-four electoral votes, which gives him a total now of two hundred and seven. He has just taken more states away from Clinton, proving the polling experts all wrong. This is history in the making. Jack Cotti only needs sixty-three more electoral votes to win the election. But will he get them?" He looked to his partner for the answer.

"I still say Florida will go to Bush," quipped Ailes.

"And that's twenty-nine electoral votes right there. If that happens, Cotti would need to win nearly every state in play. And I don't think he can do that."

Wallace again gave more results. "Cotti has just picked up another sixteen electoral votes by winning Georgia. That's a total of two hundred and twenty-three electoral votes. Clinton has also picked up twenty-two electoral votes by winning Mississippi, Kansas, Utah, and Idaho. She now has two hundred and three. We know that there are not enough electoral votes for a Clinton win—or, for that matter, a Cotti victory. It is going to come down to Florida, North Carolina, Virginia, and Iowa. Cotti still needs to win the three big ones. If he loses any of those races, it's a runoff between Clinton and Cotti. I don't think Cotti can win the number of votes needed for his Presidential bid."

"It looks that way, Chris," replied Ailes.

The two commentators continued "talking shop," but the monitor showed that Cotti had picked up North Carolina and Virginia, for another twenty-eight electoral votes and a total of two hundred and fifty-one electoral votes. "We have just been notified that Cotti has won North Carolina and Virginia," Wallace acknowledged. Thirty seconds later, he added Iowa to the list of Cotti states. "Cotti now has a total of two hundred and fifty-five electoral votes. And only Florida is left in the running. Nearly all the polling pundits have picked Florida to go to Bush. This is a nail biter, ladies and gentlemen. I'm told it is a very close race. They haven't said between who, yet. I can't take this much longer, Rog."

"I know what you mean, Chris," Ailes agreed. "Will we have a President elect tonight or a runoff? That is the question we're hoping to answer for our viewers in the next few minutes."

It was nearing three in the morning, and votes were still being counted and recounted in Florida. The counters were sure to do everything in their power to give the win to anyone other than Cotti. But that was yet to be seen.

Nearly everyone in the Cotti camp was on pins and needles awaiting the results. Cotti, however, was confident as ever. He said to Rove and Napolie, "Not to worry. I got it in the bag. Forget about it!"

"Fuck you, Jack!" exclaimed Napolie. "I don't know how you can be so fucking calm. If we win Florida, we're in. If not, we gotta go through this shit all over again. I don't know if I can take that."

"Sure you can, John. If it goes another round, we'll do even better," Rove predicted.

***

The Cotti camp members weren't the only ones waiting nervously for an answer. The Clinton camp was also on edge. They wanted to go another round. Another shot at the title. And the Bush camp, they just wanted the win to keep Cotti away from the White House.

Nearly ten minutes had passed before the news came

over the TV. It was three forty-five in the morning when Wallace gave the final results. "Jack Cotti will be the forty-fifth President of the United States!" shouted Chris Wallace. "He has won Florida and the Presidency, with a total of two hundred and eighty-four electoral votes. He took States away from both parties. I guess the voters have spoken. They voted for change and they sure got it. The American Family Freedom Party has won the first time out. And Carl Rove has as much to do with winning the Presidency as does Jack Cotti. I guess you could say that soon we'll have true Family members running our country."

"Yeah, if they don't get killed first," joked Ailes.

Wallace shot back, "I'm glad you said that and not me. I want to stay on Cotti's good side. I'm hoping he'll give me another interview."

"That's right," remembered Ailes. "You got the exclusive after Cotti scuttled the Republican Convention."

Wallace nodded. "Well, that's all for now from here. We'll go now to Cotti headquarters where Jack Cotti is about to give his victory speech."

The Cotti people were in the celebration mode, drinking champagne and smoking those expensive Jack Cotti cigars. Before the final result was called, those same people were dead to the world, many falling asleep while waiting for the outcome. But now they'd come alive again and there couldn't have been a happier crowd of people.

But the celebration at the Cotti camp was ill-timed.

They soon learned that the people running the Bush campaign had filed a complaint with the state voting commission to have the vote recounted, as had been done after the Bush-Gore debacle.

Luckily, the threat only lasted about an hour. After speaking with Jeb Bush about the decision, it was decided that the complaint would be withdrawn. Shortly thereafter, Jeb Bush gave his concession speech. The camera suddenly switched from Cotti to Bush headquarters, just in time to show a tired and dejected Jeb Bush wish the winner "good luck."

"It's been a long night for all of us, so I'm gonna make this short," Bush told his dejected audience and the viewers. "I just want to thank everyone here and all the volunteers and especially my wife and kids. And I just want to say to President Elect Cotti that he proved to be a worthy opponent and I know that he will make a great President. I wish you the best!" Bush then walked off stage, so the camera switched back to Wallace.

"Okay. We just got word that Hillary Clinton is ready to make her concession speech, so we'll switch locations to the Clinton headquarters," Wallace told his viewers.

Clinton was already on stage, thanking her people. "Be proud," she told them, "for a job well done." Then she spoke directly to the voters. "You spoke out loud and clear about who you wanted as President. I just want to say to the President Elect Jack Cotti that I wish you the best. And if I can be of any service to your administration, don't hesitate to call me. So, again, I congratulate you, Mr. Cotti. And people, be patient. He's got a tough job ahead of him. Thank you and good night."

As she walked off stage, the camera switched back to Wallace and Ailes.

"There you go, ladies and gentlemen," Wallace told his viewers, at nearly five in the morning. "Hillary Clinton just gave a heartfelt speech with a heavy heart. We know she's hurting, as I'm sure Jeb Bush is hurting." Wallace listened to the words coming from his earphone, and announced: "Right now, we're going to Cotti headquarters. President Elect Jack Cotti is about to give his victory speech."

The camera switched locations to Cotti headquarters. Cotti was on stage, listening to thunderous applause. He pumped up his chest and bobbed his head as he strutted across the stage like a young Mick Jagger or the top rooster in a chicken coop. The crowd again went wild, clapping, whistling, and stomping their feet as they watched their newly elected President strut his stuff. This went on for nearly ten minutes before he calmed the crowd.

Once they had quieted down, Cotti shouted: "I told you we'd do it!" He pumped his fists in the air, while the crowd roared their approval. "You had the faith, baby! It's great to be an American!" The crowd continued to give their *guy* a rousing ovation.

Again he quieted them to begin his speech. "Thank you for that wonderful greeting. I just want to say that you should follow your dream. I'm proof of that. I grew up on the streets and came from a very poor and large family, but a very loving one. But I didn't know that we were poor. Everyone around me basically had what I had. But I worked hard and started climbing the ladder. Then I grew and was taken into a much larger Family." He gave a wink to the audience. "Again I worked hard, was a good earner, and climbed that ladder even higher. Now look at me. I'm gonna be the next President of these great United States."

Napolie came onto stage.

"And here is the next Vice President, Johnny Napolie," shouted Cotti, as he introduced his Underboss. Again the people went crazy and nearly shook the roof off the building. Cotti could no longer handle the noise, so he yelled: "God bless its people and God bless America. Goodnight." And off he went with Napolie, his biological family members, and his close Family members.

***

Cotti and friends might have been happy, but Clinton and Bush were far from happy. They each had fought a long, drawn out battle, but in the end they just didn't have it. They were angry with themselves. And some others were angry over the situation. Those others were the G-men who had to protect and serve Cotti's every wish.

"Fuck. I can't fucking believe it," bellowed a pissed off Agent Firby. "This motherfucker is going to be our next President. Mobster Jack Cotti, President of the United States. That's sick."

"That's only half of it, Alan," quipped Agent Press. "Johnny Napolie will be our Vice President. How do you like them apples? Pretty soon the Halls of Congress will be filled with Mafia. Trying to buy the politicians."

Once the bitching stopped, the Feds escorted Cotti and Company home. It was past seven in the morning before Cotti's head hit the pillow for a quick nap.

***

While Cotti was dead to the world, the media was alive and kicking over their "story of the year," President Elect, Jack Cotti. They figured he would make "good copy," whatever predicament he got himself into. They were even counting the days to his Inauguration.

The McLaughlin Group, for one, had much to say about the "bad boy makes good" story. John McLaughlin held up the New York Times headline to show his pundits and viewers: The GODFATHER PRESIDENT! He held up the Detroit News, which read: COTTI WINS ELECTION! He then held up the LA Times: MOBSTER WINS WHITE HOUSE! McLaughlin then asked his guests, "Can you believe it? We now have a mobster for our next President. But that's not the worst of it. We also have a mobster, allegedly, Jack Cotti's Underboss as our Vice President. What do you make of it? I ask you, Pat Buchanan."

"What can I say, John?" answered Buchanan. "The People have spoken. They were sick of the status quo. We thought of him as a big joke in the political world. But now,

John, the joke is on us. He fooled us all. He truly is, as reporter Bobby Legend anointed him, the Godfather President."

"He's right, John." Tom Rogan jumped into the fray. "We've made fun of Jack Cotti for nearly a year and didn't take him seriously. But I guess he showed us."

"That's right, John," interjected Eleanor Clift. "We did think of Jack Cotti as one big joke. The voters, I guess, didn't. But to me, he's still nothing but a no good gangster and—"

"Watch what you say, Eleanor," retorted Mort Zuckerman. "Jack Cotti, or should I say the President Elect Cotti, may come back to haunt you...Or have you whacked! But seriously, you have to give *kudos* to Jack Cotti and Carl Rove. As far as I'm concerned, Rove made a mountain out of a mole hill. He conquered Mount Everest with a cripple by his side. They did an amazing job."

"Enough with the metaphors already. We get your point, Mort," quipped McLaughlin. They all laughed.

"To change the subject a bit," said McLaughlin. "What happened to the Bush campaign? Winning only two states? What the heck happened to the Bush Machine? I ask you, Eleanor Clift."

"I haven't figured that one out yet," she replied. "Evidently, Jack Cotti took the states that the polling people thought Bush had wrapped up. But, as we see, that wasn't the case. His campaign got off to a slow start and continued getting slower until it sputtered to a stop. I mean, after South Carolina, he was out of the running. A pitiful showing!"

"Tell me this, Pat Buchanan," McLaughlin asked. "How did Cotti win the election when he lost the popular vote to Hillary Clinton by over five million votes, and she won over half of the states? It just doesn't make sense."

"Come on, John. He won the states with the most electoral votes," Buchanan stated matter-of-factly. "I will say there, for a while, the election was a nail biter. I thought Hillary Clinton was going to run away with it. I mean, for almost an hour, she had won a total of like twenty states and Cotti hadn't gotten any. But then Cotti came back in the end and won the whole darn thing. Incredible race!"

"Yes, Pat, it was an incredible political race," interjected Zuckerman, "but I'm wondering what the heck went wrong with our political system. I mean, a mobster starts a new political party five months before the election and now has as many followers as the Democrats and much more than the Republicans. It just doesn't make sense. What the hell is happening to this country? I just don't understand it."

"Mort's right!" Rogan replied. "Cotti has changed the whole dynamics of our political system as we know it. It will never be the same, especially if Cotti can get the other Parties in Congress to work together."

"Oh, I'm sure they'll do as he says," retorted Mort Zuckerman. "Because he'll make them an offer they can't refuse. What was the quote Al Capone once said? 'You can get more done with a kind word and a gun, than with a kind word alone.' I think that's the kind of philosophy Cotti's going to have to use in order to get things done his way: by making threats and then taking the initiative. 'Have gun will travel!'" They all laughed at that one.

"That's a good one, Mort," said McLaughlin.

When the laughing stopped, McLaughlin asked, "Who will Cotti choose to work in his administration? Will he want other mobsters to take important positions within government? I ask you, Pat Buchanan."

"Well, John. Cotti's Party is called the American Family Freedom Party. It does have the word *Family* in it. But, I imagine that he will ask the people he knows he can trust. But the Mafia has always said: 'Beware of the person standing behind you'."

"They also say something similar about whacking a boss, Pat," retorted Rogan. "'It's your best friend who does it.' So, if he does hire Mafia members within the White House, he better have eyes in the back of his head."

McLaughlin jumped in, as time was short. "Well, I'm sure we'll have more to talk about the Cotti situation in the weeks and months to come. Bye, Bye!"

***

Journalists and reporters were clamoring to get an interview with President Elect Jack Cotti, but the only one Cotti wanted to speak with was his Underboss and now the next Vice President.

Napolie wove his way through the reporters, Feds, and Cotti bodyguards and finally entered Cotti's home. He was met at the door by Jack Cotti himself.

"Hello, Mr. President!" Napolie gave his boss a congratulatory salute.

"Fuck you!" answered Cotti, as the two dear friends walked into the den to talk business.

"What do you need, Jack?" Napolie asked, as the two took their seats.

"We gotta go over some important things that I want done before we get into the White House. I have major responsibilities. It's not just the *Borgata* anymore, but the whole country. I gotta do something to get Congress to start working for the country and not for their respective political parties."

"How you gonna do that, Jack?"

"How do you think, Johnny? We'll make 'em an offer they can't refuse."

"And if they refuse?" Napolie asked, as he lit up a Cuban cigar.

"Let's just say: It would be very bad if they did." Cotti smiled as he too lit up a cigar. "That's why I want you to buy a large trunk, big enough to hold a body."

"Who we gonna kill, Jack?"

"Naw! Not now. I mean, when I get into the Oval Office."

"What do we need it for?"

"I'm gonna call every Senator and Congressman into

my office and have them take a pledge," Cotti explained.

"What kind of pledge?" asked Napolie, now curious.

"They are gonna pledge their loyalty to me and the country."

"And if they refuse?"

"I'll give them an ultimatum. They can either leave the room walking on their own power...Or they can be carried out in the trunk and be buried in it. It's as simple as that. It's their choice."

Cotti continued. "Then I want our most trusted and loyal soldiers to take over the Secret Service. With all the trouble they're having lately, I don't want to take any chances. 'Cause I hear they're a bunch of drunks. And that could get me killed."

"Can you do that, Jack? I mean, I think it's in the Constitution. It's their job to protect the President."

"I'll write what they call an executor order. I mean, for Christ's sake, I'm President. I can do anything. Within reason, that is," quipped Cotti, puffing on his cigar.

"I think you mean an executive order, Jack."

"Forget about it! And I want you to get me the names of those two Generals that owe Joe the Bookie big time on those gambling debts. What are their names?" he asked Napolie.

"I don't know off the top of my head, Jack," admitted Napolie. "I'll have to ask Joe. But I know they sit on the Joint Chiefs of Staff. I mean, in the military, there is no higher rank. Forget about it!"

"Well good. Maybe we can hold the *Vig* over their heads if they don't cooperate with my administration. You make sure they get the message. And I want our soldiers roaming the halls of the Capital Building to make sure everything goes smooth so we can keep peace and harmony between us and those mindless politicians in DC. Get me?"

"Loud and clear, Mr. President," replied Napolie. They both laughed at that one.

Cotti added: "I want no stalemates. We will get something done for the country or *heads will roll*. And I mean that literally. We'll roll them into watery graves. *Food for the fishes*. We'll have Congress in ship shape to help nurse this country back to health. Like it used to be, back in the fifties and sixties. Those were *heydays* for us. Hey, Johnny."

Johnny nodded and said: "*Not for nuttin',* Jack. But can we talk about this stuff another time. I'd like to get back with the family. You know, we were on the road for so long, I didn't get to see much of the wife and kids."

"Sure, Johnny. No hurry. Let's recharge the batteries for the next few days and maybe then we'll get together for another sit down. I gotta talk to Benny, too. I want to make him my Secretary of State. I know I would make a better one, but I can't be both President and Secretary of State. There's not enough time in a day. And there are a few guys from the Family that I want to take to DC. So keep all this in mind. And we better get a trustworthy Capo to take over the Family while we're away. I have a few guys in mind.

So think about it. *Capisce?"*

"*Capisce."*

"Oh, and one last thing. I want you to find that kid reporter. I think his name is Legend. I want to make him my Press Secretary."

Napolie nodded. "Will do, Jack."

The two wiseguys walked out the front door to the throng of media correspondents, but they were met by G-men trying to get Cotti back into the house for safety's sake.

"Please, Mr. Cotti. Go back in the house. It's not safe right now. We're waiting for the Secret Service to take over our duties. They should be here shortly. So please, go back inside," warned Agent Firby.

"Forget about it! People have been trying to kill me for years," retorted Cotti, as they hurried down the steps.

Cotti followed Napolie to his ride and was very surprised. "You came in that?" Cotti asked him, when he noticed it was an agents' car.

"What can I say, Jack? They're my shadow. They go where I go. Ain't no getting away from it," Napolie admitted.

Cotti watched as his Underboss drove away with two Agents and then another four cars full of Feds followed in front and behind them. Cotti just turned and headed back to his home. As he passed Firby, Firby suggested he stay in the house until told otherwise. "Please stay inside, Mr. Cotti," he said.

"That's Mr. President to you, G-man," Cotti answered angrily.

"Please, Mr. President. When the Secret Service gets here, they'll be responsible for your protection. But until then, please do as we say."

"Great! You guys have been tailing me long enough. I'm looking forward to having new G-men following my every move," he replied sarcastically.

Cotti gave the agent a mean look and then continued through the crowd, dodging questions as he went.

The agent didn't like Cotti's attitude or the words he had spoken to him and lagged behind as Cotti stood at the top of the porch. Just before Cotti entered his home, shots rang out. The crowd scattered and the Feds pulled their weapons and looked to see if they could find the shooter.

As they looked, Agent Firby noticed Cotti was lying on the porch, blood pouring out of his body. "Shots fired! Shots fired!" Firby yelled into his radio. "We need an ambulance NOW! The President Elect is down. I say again, President Elect Jack Cotti is down! Get that ambulance here...Pronto!"

But Cotti was bleeding so badly that the Agents decided to whisk him off to the hospital in one of their cars. Even though they cared not if Jack Cotti died, it was their job to try and save him if at all possible.

When they reached the Emergency Room, Cotti was taken into the examination room, where the doctors tried to stop the bleeding, take X-Rays, and get the bullet out of his body.

***

The Cotti family members waited nervously for word concerning their loved one, but the news wasn't very promising. The doctor came out and gave Cotti's wife an update on her husband's condition. The FBI Agents stood in the wings.

"I'm sorry, Mrs. Cotti, it doesn't look too good for your husband. We don't know if we can save him. The bullet is a millimeter away from his heart. Surgery is going to be very tricky. You might want to make funeral arrangements."

But Mrs. Cotti and family waited and waited, long into the night and early morning, before returning to their homes, feeling beaten and downtrodden by circumstance.

The Feds, however, were gleefully happy concerning the health of the guy they were supposed to protect.

"Well, Cotti will never be President now!" quipped Agent Firby.

"I'll bet he'll be dead by this afternoon, if not sooner," said Agent Press.

"Let's hope you're right," retorted Firby, as they left the hospital.

The End...Or is it?

CPSIA information can be obtained
at www.ICGtesting.com
Printed in the USA
BVOW08s2149230617

487713BV00002B/151/P